The
MATCHMAKER
and the
COWBOY

The
MATCHMAKER
and the
COWBOY

ROBIN
USA TODAY BESTSELLING AUTHOR
BIELMAN

Entangled Publishing, LLC
644 Shrewsbury Commons Ave., STE 181
Shrewsbury, PA 17361
Visit our website at www.entangledpublishing.com.

Amara is an imprint of Entangled Publishing, LLC.

Edited by Stacy Abrams
Cover design by Elizabeth Turner Stokes
Cover art by Stepanenko Lera/Shutterstock, Anton
Violin/Shutterstock, Oleksandr Kavun
Interior design by Toni Kerr

Print ISBN 978-1-64937-278-9
ebook ISBN 978-1-64937-296-3

Manufactured in the United States of America

First Edition November 2022

AMARA

ALSO BY ROBIN BIELMAN

WINDSONG SERIES

The Wedding Crasher and the Cowboy
The Matchmaker and the Cowboy

SECRET WISHES SERIES

Kissing the Maid of Honor
Her Accidental Boyfriend
Wild About Her Wingman

WHEREVER YOU GO SERIES

Talk British to Me
Lips Close to Mine
Too Hard to Resist

KISSES IN THE SAND SERIES

Keeping Mr. Right Now
Blame it on the Kiss
The Best Friend Bargain

To my hubby, my perfect match even when life is anything but perfect. Love you forever.

CHAPTER ONE

"Ready or not, here I come!" Hunter opened his eyes and immediately spotted his adorable target's small rainboots sticking out from behind a stack of hay bales. "Hmm…where could Princess Pipsqueak be?" he asked, really playing it up.

His niece, Jenna, chose the same spot inside the barn nine times out of ten, and his heart gave a little kick every time. At eight years old, she knew the names of every horse breed, could recite all fifty states, and had an appreciation for burgers with a fried egg on top. But when it came to hide and seek, she hid about as well as a giraffe in a sandbox.

They played this game after every riding lesson he gave her, the time together the most important of his week.

"Is she in here?" he asked, making exaggerated banging noises as he searched the tack room.

Out of the corner of his eye, he noticed one yellow rainboot tapping anxiously from the side of the haystack, like she was considering making a run for another hiding spot if he got too close. She wore the boots rain or shine, the footwear her favorite for the past couple of years. She did that a lot—stuck to one special thing. And lately, he was happy and proud to say she'd been glued to her uncle Hunter when she got home from school.

He loved her something fierce right back.

Also, he was a total sucker for her big brown eyes.

The smell of this morning's drizzle hung in the air as he walked past the stalls, making eye contact with each animal. "Or maybe in here…" He pretended to look inside George's stall. George, their whip-smart mule who loved to play chase with Jenna, stuck his face through the gate for some ear scratches. Hunter obliged, using both his hands to give George a good scratch. "You hiding our girl in here?" he asked.

Jenna giggled. At the sweet sound, George nodded in her direction. No lie. The animal had impressive intelligence that visitors to the ranch found remarkable—and entertaining. Hunter considered himself the most sociable person in the family and among their staff, but George took top honor when it came to bringing smiles to their guests' faces.

"Uh-oh, did you hear that, George? Princess Pipsqueak is that-a-way."

George nibbled his arm in affection before stepping back to allow Hunter to continue his search. Total genius-mule move right there.

And as expected, Jenna tried to make a run for it just as he caught sight of her in the middle of the center corridor. Their eyes locked for a split second before she spun around to take off through the open barn door. In their game, he had to physically catch her.

He gave chase at a cool jog, prolonging her lead. They wove through the dozen or so pumpkins they'd picked up from the patch yesterday. Passed the chicken coop. Ran toward the pond and small, white-painted wood bridge. As she finished crossing the bridge to the other side, her yellow boots landing in the soft, bright green grass, he lifted her off her feet and swung her around in a circle.

"Got you!"

"No, I got you!" she said, turning to wrap her arms tightly around his neck.

She had him more than any other female ever had. Well, except for one. But Callie Carmichael barely registered his existence. Which was why he'd finally decided to move on from his longtime crush.

In theory, anyway.

"How about we sneak into the kitchen for a cookie?" he asked, already knowing her answer.

"Follow my lead," she said, letting go of him and putting her feet on the ground.

They made like bandits, skulking toward the main house and entering the kitchen through the back door. There atop the counter, like they always were, sat a plate of homemade chocolate chip cookies. He'd never tell Jenna her grandmother left them there specifically for her to pilfer from.

Jenna raised her eyebrows at him. *Can I take two?* her expression said.

Like he ever said "no" to her. He nodded, took one for himself, and they hightailed it out of there. They landed at their favorite tree by the rose bushes and took a seat, leaning against the sizable trunk and shaded by the immense canopy of branches and leaves.

The Owens House Inn & Guest Ranch had been in his family for over one hundred years. Four generations of blood, sweat, and hard work to make it a multi–award winning inn in the heart of the "happiest seaside and mountain town in California."

The people who came to stay on the Northern California property appreciated the rural setting like they'd found a piece of heaven. Hunter loved the ranch and his hometown of Windsong. So much so, he'd applied to be their small town's first ambassador. He wanted the position badly.

Once he had it, he'd be taken more seriously. He'd be regarded as more than Cole and Maverick's little brother or the town's friendliest (and, as many said, most eligible) bachelor. He had it on good authority that the mayor thought his video application outstanding, which meant he had to be her top choice.

"Did you know Baby Gia is the size of a head of lettuce?" Jenna asked after she'd swallowed a bite of cookie. "Rebel could eat her in two bites."

Hunter choked on his late afternoon snack. Rebel was his horse and Gia was his unborn niece. His oldest brother Cole and sister-in-law, Bethany, were blessedly having the second child they'd struggled for years to have.

He looked at his favorite tiny human to try and assess where her head was at today. She bit into her second cookie, appearing not at all sorry or worried about what she'd said.

Two things were happening here: The first was his niece had expressed her distaste for a sibling many times over and thus the idea of Hunter's horse eating her baby sister was appealing to her eight-year-old mind. The second was she felt this way because Bethany's pregnancy hadn't been an easy one.

Which meant a lot of focus and doting had been placed on Bethany, and his energetic and spirited niece felt a little left out. And scared.

"It's a good thing horses don't eat humans, then." He tried his damnedest to let her have her feelings and not undervalue her emotions.

She shrugged.

"How about you and me ride Rebel again tomorrow?"

Her face lit up. "Yes, please."

"It's a date," he said, giving her ponytail a gentle tug and pushing aside the sorry state of his dating life. Between his newly opened Owens Boot Camp, ranch obligations, the ambassador opportunity, and spending time with family, he hadn't been out with the fairer sex in months. He didn't miss the drama that tended to follow him when he dated and ran (in a very nice way), but he did miss the intimacy.

Jenna crawled over to the empty pots and gardening equipment Nova had left out. Not a single person matched his sister's talent with flowers. She spent hours each day keeping the ranch's colorful blooms healthy and vibrant. It looked like she'd be back to clean up, but in the meantime, something caught Jenna's eye.

"There's a spider!" she said, reaching her hand into one of the pots. She held zero fear when it came to the creatures on their property.

"Hang on." He quickly made his way over to be sure the arachnid was harmless. Black widow spiders were a frequent guest to the ranch.

"It's okay, Uncle Hunt, I know what I'm doing."

He loved her confidence, but it was his job to keep her safe, and she tended to look at things hastily. He also knew, now that he was closer, that the spider's shiny, globe-shaped abdomen belonged to the poisonous black widow even without seeing its red underbelly.

A second before Jenna touched it, he pushed her hand out of the way with his own. The spider, mad at the disturbance, bit him in the fleshy part of the skin between his thumb and pointer finger. He yanked his arm back and pressed his lips together to keep from cursing. Damn, that stung. A second later, Cole came flying out the kitchen door of the inn.

When his older brother saw him and Jenna, he came to an abrupt stop. "Bethany's water just broke!"

Jenna frowned at her dad. "Is Mommy okay?"

Hunter's hand burned with pain, but he ignored it. He lifted Jenna up with him as he got to his feet. Looked like his new niece planned to make an entrance three weeks early.

"She's fine, sweet pea. It just means it's time to take her to the hospital to have your baby sister." Cole bent down to his daughter's eye level. "You remember our plan?"

"Yes."

Being the awesome parents they were, Cole and Bethany had worked everything out for when this day came.

Jenna stepped closer, took Hunter's hand—the one the spider had sank her fangs into—and squeezed tightly. The pain intensified, but again, he had no choice but to ignore it. Because this was the plan: stay with Uncle Hunter. Jenna needed him.

"Anything I can do before you guys go?" Hunter asked, gritting his teeth to stave off the sharp sting from the spider bite. He'd been bitten by different animals over the years, and none had been this uncomfortable.

"Cole!"

They turned to see Nova, jogging in place outside the kitchen door, her face flushed and one arm waving furiously for their brother to return inside the inn. "You need to get back here. The baby is coming!"

"What do you mean the baby is coming?" Cole called back.

"I mean like, right now!" Panic turned his younger sister's normally soft voice to a pitch high enough for dogs in the next town to hear.

Jenna squeezed his hand harder. Glancing down at her, he recognized her worry. Lifting his head to gauge his brother, he recognized his, too. Normally calm and cool, Cole now looked like a deer in headlights, and that was the very last thing his daughter needed to see.

"Your beautiful wife is going to be just fine," Hunter said, "And so is your baby daughter." Hunter pulled his phone from his back pocket. "I'll call Kennedy and tell her what's happening while you go inside and remind Bethany how amazing she is."

Hunter managed the phone with one hand so he didn't have to let go of Jenna's. Kennedy was his future sister-in-law and the town doctor. She could deliver the baby if need be.

Cole stood there, frozen.

"Bro, you need to walk back into the house like you've got this." Hunter's heart pounded inside his chest, but babies were born at home all the time, so everything would be fine. He shook off the thought that poison from the black widow was circling the vital organ and that's why his heart beat faster than normal.

"Daddy?"

Jenna's sweet voice shook Cole out of his trance. He brought her in for a hug, kissed the top of her head. "You stay with Uncle Hunt and I'll let you know as soon as your baby sister is here. Don't forget how much Mommy and I love you." He cut Hunter a meaningful glance, then jogged back inside the house.

Everything after that happened at warp speed...

Kennedy arrived within minutes.

His brother Maverick, too. Maverick and Kennedy were head over heels in love and planning a Christmas Eve wedding here on the ranch.

Mary Rose Owens—his, Cole, Nova, and Maverick's awesome mom—had been by Bethany's side the whole time. No surprise there. She had a sixth sense for surprises, among other things. Their dad, unfortunately, was out of town for a couple of days and would no doubt be disappointed he'd missed all the excitement.

Then an ambulance and paramedics showed up, siren blaring and lights swirling. *It's just a precaution*, he assured Jenna.

While they waited for news on the baby, the two of them moved to the porch on the main level of the inn. Jenna lay on her stomach on the planked white wood coloring a picture for her mom and dad. She had earbuds in her ears and listened to a playlist of Disney music he'd created on his phone just for her. While watching her make the drawing, he googled "black widow spider bite" on his phone, tracking the basics since his discomfort made it difficult to concentrate on a deep dive. Biggest takeaway: bites could be fatal to young children. Thank God he'd pushed Jenna's hand out of the way.

He wasn't sure how much time passed, maybe thirty minutes, when he excused himself for a quick minute to go puke in the bathroom. He tended to do that when worried. The million-dollar question was what had him worried more — Bethany or spider bites.

He returned to the cushioned bench on the porch and nonchalantly examined his hand. He now knew that in most cases black widow spider bites weren't life-threatening to adults, but they did cause pain along with some swelling and redness. Check, check, and check. And look at that: two small fang marks.

If not for the commotion inside the inn, he'd probably be more focused on the other symptoms from Google making an appearance: a muscle cramp in his hand that made it difficult to move his thumb, a killer headache, stomach pain, and chills.

He grabbed a blanket off the nearby rocking chair and covered himself just as Bethany let out a blood-curdling scream that sounded like an alien had invaded her body. She followed that with curse words for her husband, which was a riot because she never cussed.

He watched Jenna to be sure she wasn't hearing

any of it. This was the only occasion when he would not ask her to turn down the volume to protect her hearing. He should probably offer all the guests on the property a pair of headphones, but strangely, he couldn't muster up the strength to even sit up taller. Very inconvenient given the feeling of nausea telling his brain to find a toilet again.

Jenna smiled up at him, and he remembered his duty, his *love* for her and his family. He straightened his back, willed the queasiness to go away, and smiled at her. At least he hoped it was a smile. In all honesty, he wasn't sure he had control over any muscles in his body. He tried to take a deep breath. That didn't work so well, either.

Sweat trickled down the side of his face. He managed to wipe it away with his good hand.

He wiggled his toes inside his boots. They still worked, but his legs felt heavy. Being poisoned was worse than the time Brett Porter punched him in the face and broke his nose. (Hunter *had* kissed Brett's on-again/off-again girlfriend, Janey, so he deserved the blow, even though the kiss had been orchestrated by her to make Brett jealous.) What a blood bath that was, not to mention mind-numbingly painful. Brett had become a good friend since then and helped him run the bootcamp now, so things ended well there, and they'd end well here, too.

One tiny little spider had nothing on Hunter's six-foot frame.

·A baby's cries pierced the air, pulling his thoughts back to his family. Joy overwhelmed him, thankfully interrupting the uncomfortable feeling of poison circulating through his bloodstream.

A minute later, Maverick stepped out the front door. At seeing her second-favorite uncle, Jenna pulled her earbuds out and jumped to her feet. "Gia is here and everyone is doing great," Maverick said.

Jenna flew into Maverick's arms for a hug.

Hunter watched his niece move with ease and wished he could do the same.

"Let's have you meet your sister and see your mom." He kissed the top of Jenna's head, then looked down at him, eyebrows raised. *You coming?*

"I'll be right there." No way was Hunter ruining Jenna's first moment with her baby sister or causing anyone undue worry by walking inside like a drunken sailor who'd also eaten bad sushi.

"You okay?" Maverick asked.

"Fine."

Maverick didn't look convinced, but he and Jenna disappeared inside the inn anyway, leaving him alone to figure out what the hell to do. He should probably wash the bite area more thoroughly with soap and water. Take a couple of pain relievers. Text Kennedy to come outside and check him out. Flag down one of the EMTs.

And he would. Just as soon as the joy and excitement of Gia's arrival calmed down. He hated to think of his sickly state taking precedence over the miracle and happiness of bringing a human being into the world.

A few minutes later, the paramedics came out with Bethany on a stretcher, Gia snuggled against her chest. Cole had his hand on Bethany's shoulder and Jenna tucked at his side.

"What's going on?" Hunter asked.

"We're going to the hospital to get Mom and Baby properly checked out," Cole said with a mix of relief and joy.

"They're both doing great," Kennedy assured from the head of the stretcher. She winked at Jenna. "But they'll get a thorough examination at the hospital."

Everyone followed Bethany and Gia down the stairs toward the ambulance to see them off. Halfway down the steps, Kennedy stopped and looked over her shoulder at him. It was unlike him to keep his distance, and someone finally noticed.

Having the keen eyesight of a doctor—not to mention being a great friend—she must have also suspected there was something not quite right, because she jogged back up the steps to sit beside him. "What's wrong?" she asked.

"I think I'm dying," he said, right before everything went black.

CHAPTER TWO

Callie Carmichael stood outside her childhood home with a far-too-familiar knot of disappointment in her stomach. The knot could take a flying leap. She knew better, and she'd told herself as much on the drive from the airport, but it hurt all the same. She allowed herself five more seconds of letdown and then squared her shoulders and shook off her family's absentmindedness.

There was a small chance she didn't know what she'd find inside the house, but with no sign of life, she felt confident it wouldn't be her parents and sister with a *Welcome Home! We Missed You!* banner.

She supposed that after being away for six months, it was easier to forget about her than when she was here in the flesh. Not that they forgot about her on purpose or didn't love her. They did in their own way. But since Callie was eleven years old and had decided she'd rather sew things than hammer them, she hadn't fit in with the Carmichael Construction family. And after her serious horseback-riding accident, and her parents' divorce-remarriage-divorce-conscious-uncoupling—or whatever they were calling it now—it only got worse.

Both sides were to blame. Her, for being extra cautious and wary, and them for not even trying to inch her beyond her comfort zone. Mostly because dear old Mom and Dad were too busy trying to figure out their own lives.

In the last group text they'd shared, she told them she'd be home on October tenth. They'd responded they couldn't wait and even included happy face emojis. Maybe they were trying to fake her out and *think* they weren't at home, when in reality they were combining her return home with her birthday last week and waiting inside to yell, "Surprise!"

She rolled her ginormous suitcase behind her and walked toward the front door. She'd missed the smell of pine and damp grass, the tree-lined street, and the cottage-style homes. With daylight giving way to night, she hurried her steps.

She used her key to open the front door.

Silence and darkness greeted her.

So did a house in the middle of obvious construction. Plastic covered the furniture in the living room. The wall that had once separated the kitchen from the family room had disappeared, and the kitchen looked completely gutted. Tools and small machinery were pushed into the corners. Loose nails littered the floor.

"Hello?" she called out, the one word echoing around the room as she made her way further inside the house.

The bathrooms and upstairs rooms were similar works-in-progress, the carpeting completely ripped out and everything off the walls. After a moment of panic in her bedroom, she found her sewing machine and fabric bolts tucked safely inside her closet. Her dad had mentioned wanting to remodel, but he hadn't indicated it happening now. No one had. Once again, keeping her updated had slipped their minds.

Or perhaps it was a not-so-subtle reminder she

didn't live at home anymore. She'd let go of her apartment before her trip and moved her belongings back home for safekeeping, the plan being she'd find a new place upon her return.

Looked like she needed to do that sooner than later now.

Because no way could she stay in the house like this. It wasn't safe. She breathed slowly in and out. Being displaced for who knew how long wouldn't impede on her plans for growing her company with an actual storefront and becoming the first Ambassador of Windsong.

She and her suitcase strode back outside—and almost bumped right into their next-door neighbor, Birdy, holding a meat tenderizer raised above her head.

"Oh! It's you," Birdy said at the same time Callie lifted her arm in defense and said, "Wait! It's me!"

Birdy dropped her arm to her side. "I see that now. I thought you might be one of those scotters."

"I think you mean squatter."

"That's it."

"And since when do you carry a weapon?" Windsong had the designation as one of the safest cities in America, but beyond that, she didn't want Birdy to hurt *herself*.

"Since I started watching true crime shows. Now get in here for a hug."

Callie obliged, comfort settling over her as they embraced.

Pulling back, Birdy studied her with affection. "Darling girl, what are you doing home?" Birdy looked the same as she had the day Callie left for her trip—not a day over her eighty-two years and in a pink tracksuit. Her hair, a glorious shade of gray, was pulled back into its usual chignon, and her dark skin remained almost wrinkle-free. The tiny lines around her eyes and mouth spoke only of a lifetime of smiles.

"My program ended, so here I am. I told Mom and Dad I'd be home today."

Birdy got that sympathetic look on her face, the one that said she understood miscommunications happened way too often in the Carmichael family. "Come over for something to drink and we'll get this sorted out."

Something to drink meant a Death in the Afternoon. (Supposedly Ernest Hemingway created it, not Birdy.) She served a signature cocktail every month—one of the many reasons she was everyone's favorite neighbor and octogenarian. There were only two ingredients in this one: absinthe and Champagne. The eerie green hue made it the perfect spooky cocktail.

Callie settled in at the kitchen table, relieved things looked the same here. The colorful room with its terracotta floor and whitewashed cabinets felt like home, given how much time she spent here. Not just for cocktails, but for conversation and their secret Instagram account, @BirdCall.

"Your parents thought you were coming home on November tenth," Birdy said from across the table.

At least they hadn't completely forgotten about her return. "Where are they?"

"Louisiana. They stopped everything here and took off to help with hurricane relief."

"Brooke, too?" She didn't know why she asked. Brooke worked side-by-side with their parents in their construction business, and they often traveled to help communities clean up and rebuild after natural disasters. She loved and admired them for it. They volunteered for at least a month out of every year with Habitat for Humanity.

"Yes."

Callie nodded and took a sip of her drink. "How are you?"

"I don't want to talk about me. I want to hear about your trip!"

"It was amazing." She pulled out her phone, tapped the photos icon, and turned the screen to Birdy. "These are some of the women we helped."

"Oh, Callie, that is a gorgeous picture. I assume you made or helped them make the dresses they're wearing?"

She nodded, suddenly too choked up to reply. The photo of herself and her volunteer leader with a group of women, all of them in handmade clothing, filled her with pride and happiness.

She'd spent the last six months in Africa as a Women's Empowerment volunteer, designing and making dresses, but more importantly, empowering women by teaching them how to sew and make clothing for themselves and their children. The work had also empowered *her* to make some final decisions for herself.

"I'm so proud of you." Birdy's grandmotherly face and soft smile were such a welcome sight that Callie's stomach tightened. This was the homecoming she'd hoped for.

"Thanks. I have about a million pictures to show you, but first…" She searched through her oversize shoulder bag. "I brought you a gift."

"You didn't need to do that, but I'm glad you did." Birdy moved to the edge of her chair. "By the way, your magic worked while you were gone."

Callie stopped rifling in her bag and looked up.

"The Kormondy sisters both got engaged."

"*Both* of them?" Twin sisters, they'd been maids of honor for their older sister the weekend before Callie left for Africa. Neither of them had been seeing anyone at the time.

Birdy nodded. "They met twin brothers passing through on a road trip." At Callie's wide eyes, Birdy added, "I think that makes an even six women to get engaged after wearing one of your dresses."

"Holy shit." Before Callie had left for Africa, talk of her "magical" maid-of-honor dresses had happened a few times.

Creating the special MOH dress had been by design. Thanks to her late grandmother, Callie believed in magic. Believed her grandma had passed on her power of influence when she'd given Callie a butterfly charm for her sixteenth birthday. When she started designing MOH dresses, she decided to add something special and designed an applique with two small butterflies to hide inside the skirt. Callie felt sure that if the wearer sought true love after wearing the dress, they'd find it.

When the first maid of honor to wear her dress design got engaged a few months later, Callie quietly celebrated. When it happened a second and third time, she knew her own brand of pixie dust was at least partly responsible.

"You mean holy matrimony!" Birdy delighted in saying. "Word is your dress is luckier than catching the bouquet."

Excitement wove through Callie's body. She might be unlucky in love herself, but she loved that she brought good love karma to others.

She pulled the Pink Lady Gin glass bottle with a short neck out of her bag and slid it across the table. "This is for you. It's the local favorite made in Cape Town. It's infused with hibiscus flowers and rose petals."

"It's pink!" Birdy took the bottle in her hands to admire it. "And the bottling is gorgeous. Thank you."

"You're welcome." Callie rubbed her fingers over her Africa-shaped pendant. The colorful necklace, made from recycled flattened protea flowers, was her favorite souvenir. She brought one for her sister and best friend Nova, too. "I'm glad you like it."

"I love it. It's definitely going on Insta."

"I had a feeling you'd say that." Callie covered a yawn with her palm, exhaustion quickly settling in from the long flight and time difference. "Photo shoot this weekend?"

"You betcha."

"Did my parents say when they'd be back?"

"No, but they only left two days ago."

"Oh." Safe to assume they'd be gone for at least two weeks, then. Callie wanted to be mad at them, but how could she when they were helping others? Despite the impact her parents' relationship had on her own feelings about love and commitment, she respected how much they were committed to their career.

"I'm sorry you can't stay here," Birdy said, and right on cue, her cat, Sunshine, strolled into the room and Callie sneezed. One look at the giant furball after being away for six months and her body reminded her of her allergy. There were two more like Sunshine elsewhere in the house.

"I know. I'm sure I can stay with Nova. I'll give her a call now." Just as Callie scrolled up on the home screen of her phone, it rang. She chuckled. "Speak of the devil." She pressed the answer icon. "Hi!"

"Hey! Are you home?"

"I am."

"Yay! Welcome back," Nova said excitedly, then more somberly added, "I need you."

Grateful and always happy to be there for her best friend, she said, "What's up?" She couldn't wait to see Nova in person for a proper catchup—messaging and FaceTime weren't enough—and to help with whatever she needed. They'd been like sisters since their freshman year of high school when Nova had been the volunteer to bring Callie her schoolwork while she continued to recover at home from her horseback-riding accident.

"Bethany had her baby."

"Congratulations! Is everything okay?" Callie knew she wasn't due for a few more weeks.

"Yes, she and Gia are great. Kennedy delivered her. It's a long story, and I'll tell you all about it. Right now, though, it's Hunter we're worried about."

"Hunter?" At mention of Nova's older brother, Callie immediately pictured him wearing his well-worn, buttery-soft jeans, scuffed boots, and the dangerously attractive smile that made more than a few women in Windsong fall all over themselves for him. She didn't understand the appeal or know for a fact his jeans were buttery soft, but they looked like it.

She'd known Hunter for as long as she'd known Nova. Longer actually. He'd been there the day she was thrown from a horse and suffered multiple injuries. She'd tried to block that day from her memory, but the one thing she couldn't forget was seeing the scared, pitying look on his face right before everything went dark.

Right or wrong, she hated him for that look. Or, according to her therapist, she hated that he'd witnessed the most painful and humiliating day of her life.

He was also reckless, too free and easy for her liking, *and* she'd caught him kissing not one, but two women at the annual Halloween Bash last year. Windsong's most eligible bachelor had a lot of fans.

Hunter might be nice to look at and friendly, but he rubbed her the wrong way. If not for Nova, they'd have absolutely nothing in common, not to mention she hated that he didn't seem to know how to act around her. He acted normal around everyone else, and it put her slightly on the defensive.

"Callie, are you still there?" Nova asked through the phone.

"Yes, sorry." She blinked away thoughts of Hunter. "What happened?"

"Can I come pick you up and then I'll explain?"

"Absolutely." Callie didn't like the sound of urgency in her best friend's voice. "I'm at Birdy's and free for whatever you need." Fingers crossed it didn't interfere with the favor Callie needed to ask, too.

CHAPTER THREE

"It's a win-win," Nova said an hour later as the two of them walked toward the bunkhouse on Nova's family's property. Actually, it wasn't a bunkhouse anymore. Hunter had finally finished remodeling the building into his own "bachelor pad," according to Nova.

Callie rolled her suitcase behind her, thinking "win-win" didn't come close to describing the situation, but sometimes a person had to do the unthinkable.

"Hunt needs someone to keep an eye on him for the next couple of weeks and you need a place to stay. I'm sorry it's not with me, but we appreciate your help so much."

Nova lived in her brother and sister-in-law's guesthouse, but Bethany's mom and sister were arriving tomorrow to spend a few weeks to help with the new baby and they were staying in the guesthouse. Nova was temporarily moving into the spare bedroom inside Cole and Bethany's house. The last thing they needed was another person invading their space during this special time.

They no doubt would have been fine with it because they always welcomed Callie with open arms, but Hunter needed someone to keep watch over him after his severe reaction to being bitten by a black widow spider. He'd been rushed to the hospital along with Bethany and injected with antivenin.

The remedy had worked to help alleviate his reaction, but it came with its own set of side effects, too, and thus the doctor recommended he be monitored at home for the next two weeks, just in case.

"I'm not sure Hunter is going to appreciate it."

"He's going to love having you stay with him."

"Ha! Is the poison affecting his brain, too?"

Nova darted a deprecatory look at her. "Trust me, you're just what he needs."

Callie had no idea what to make of that. "I doubt it, but I am happy to help out and thankful for the place to stay." She tucked a wayward lock of hair behind her ear, ready to get out of her travel clothes and curl up in bed with a book. Given the late hour, and his sickness, Hunter would hopefully be asleep for the rest of the night.

"Knock, knock!" Nova called out as she opened the door to the bunkhouse without an actual knock.

Callie followed her inside. They walked through the dimly lit narrow building that included a well-appointed, functional kitchen, a living area with a deep leather couch and coffee table, and lastly a bedroom with a gunmetal-gray down comforter on a large platform bed. Each room flowed into the next, apart from a sliding barn door that gave partial privacy to the bedroom. The lump underneath the comforter with a shock of light brown hair belonged to their small town's heartbreaker.

Kennedy rose from a sheepskin-upholstered armchair in the corner. "Hi, girls. You just missed Mom." She motioned for them to step away from the bed. "Callie, it's good to see you. Welcome home." Kennedy wrapped her in a hug.

"Good to see you, too."

"How's the patient?" Nova asked.

"He's grumpy, which is to be expected, and bummed about not meeting his new niece yet, but otherwise okay. Thanks so much for being here, Callie. He should sleep through the night with all the meds we've got in him, and for the next two days he should stay in bed, especially if he's still got a fever. After that, we'll need to watch for breathing problems, skin lesions, a rash or hives, joint pain, and any swelling to his face."

"That's a lot," she said with concern and worry. She knew poisonous spiders could be harmful, but his breathing? She shuddered at the thought of him unable to take a deep breath. She had no medical background. At least half the Band-Aids she applied were crooked or fell off immediately. And she only knew how to do CPR from watching *Grey's Anatomy*, which meant she'd be of no proper help there.

Maybe she wasn't the right person for this job. "I thought he was bitten on the hand."

"He was, but the poison spread through his body." Kennedy squeezed Callie's forearm in comfort. "I can see you're worried, so if anything looks upsetting, or you feel something is wrong, text me and I'll be right over."

"If we didn't have a wedding this weekend, and a brand-new baby to boot, I'd be here with you," Nova said.

"I'll check in on him in the morning before I go to the office." Kennedy glanced over her shoulder toward his bed. "And again on my way home.

Maverick will stop in when he has a spare minute. I'm sure Mary Rose will, too."

The Owens family was close-knit, and everyone would no doubt be by to check on Hunter when available. Callie nodded. She could do this.

Kennedy said goodbye, and then Nova took a minute to point out where everything was in the bunkhouse.

"There's only one bed," Callie said, the realization finally hitting her. Jet lag had set in, so it wasn't entirely her fault she hadn't noticed sooner.

Nova scrunched up her nose. "True, but the couch is super comfy." She grabbed some blankets and a pillow and placed them on the couch. "You're the best for doing this, Cal."

"I'm glad I could help." Truly. Nova and her family had been there for her countless times over the years, Mary Rose like a second mom. And it wasn't as if Hunter was a stranger. They didn't know each other beyond the typical stuff, but if she had an emergency and no one else was around, he'd help without question. It was part of the sisters-best-friend code of conduct.

She and Nova said goodbye, and then Callie wheeled her suitcase to an empty spot along the wall and did a little unpacking. She'd mastered traveling and sleeping in small, minimalist surroundings while away, so this felt like being in a four-star hotel room.

With the couch all set for sleeping, her book near the pillow, and her pajamas on, she grabbed her toiletries bag and walked toward the one and only bathroom on the other side of the bedroom.

She'd taken all of two steps when Hunter entered

her line of sight—buck-ass naked.

Ass being the key word because her eyes were immediately drawn to his firm, round gluteus maximus, paler than the rest of him. She gasped…or something. The sound was brand spanking new, so she didn't know what to call it.

Hunter stopped, glanced over his shoulder. She quickly forced her gaze up, lest he think she was checking him out. She was fairly certain her tongue hadn't gotten stuck hanging out of her mouth, but just in case, she bit down.

He stared at her for one second. Two. Then, like his being naked was the most natural thing in the world, the corners of his mouth lifted into a come-to-bed-with-me smile. She stood stock still and glared at him.

He gave a tiny shrug and resumed walking to the bathroom. She stared at his backside as he did so, unable to look away. Broad shoulders, trim waist, perfect ass, long muscular legs. A body born from hard work on the ranch, not a gym. Only when he disappeared inside the bathroom did her wits come back.

Irritation followed immediately afterward. If he thought he could prance around in his birthday suit while they were under the same roof, he had another think coming. There were rules to this arrangement, and they would be discussed right away.

A tinkling sound met her ears—he was peeing with the door open? Ew. She was a closed-door peeer and liked others to do the same.

The toilet flushed. A sink turned on. She held her ground, ready to set some rules, dammit, when the image of his nakedness hit her upside the head with embarrassing clarity. When he stepped out of the bathroom to walk back to bed, she'd get a whole *different* eyeful.

She spun around so fast, she tripped over her own feet, then dove for the couch like the floor had suddenly disappeared. She covered herself with the blanket and pretended to be asleep. She'd seen enough of his naked body for one night, thank you very much. He'd given her his flirty smile, and when she hadn't responded, he'd moved on. Right?

At least for tonight.

Faint footsteps, followed by the rustling of covers, eased her mind. He'd crawled back into bed. *Thank you, cowboy fairies*. She remained still, just in case, until his heavy breathing hinted that he'd fallen back asleep.

Relieved, but extra cautious, she mentally altered the new dress pattern she'd been working on for a few minutes before standing and tiptoeing to the bathroom. She didn't so much as peek at the bed, cursing Hunter for the new image she now had of him.

Ugh. The next two weeks were going to be the longest of her life…

CHAPTER FOUR

Hunter woke with a start. He hated the recurring dream where he was falling off the roof of the barn, only this time he was falling into the wide mouth of a giant spider with a Gene Simmons KISS tongue.

He was pretty sure spiders didn't have tongues, but his head hurt too much to dwell on it.

Swallowing thickly, his eyes landed on someone sitting in the corner chair. He wasn't too surprised to have company; his family worried about him. However, there was nothing familial about the beautiful redhead watching him. He'd dreamed about her last night, or rather pictured her here with him when he'd gotten up to use the bathroom.

Obviously, his mind was still playing tricks on him, a damn shame considering the best cure he could think of was Callie Carmichael in his bunkhouse.

"Are you okay?" Dream Callie asked. She had a soft voice that soothed all his aching muscles. "You squealed in your sleep."

Definitely still dreaming, since he'd never *squealed* in his life. "I'd be better if you climbed in here with me," he drawled lazily. He'd kicked off his pajama bottoms during the night so he had nothing on underneath the sheets, and a certain part of him loved the idea of her joining him. She, on the other hand, wore long-sleeve navy pajamas with white polka dots on them. Not what he would've picked, but he couldn't control every dream.

"I'm going to pretend you didn't say that and assume your fever is making you delirious."

He put his palm on his forehead. Yep, a definite heat wave was happening.

Wait. He didn't normally feel himself while dreaming. Was Callie actually sitting in his bedroom? Or had he died and gone to heaven?

"You're not a figment of my imagination?"

Rather than answer him, she got to her feet, came closer, and put out her hand.

For him to touch.

Hot damn. He still wasn't clear on why she was here, but he didn't care. She'd never offered any part of herself to him before, so he'd take it. Her light green eyes were softer than he'd ever seen them and her curly hair wild, like she'd been here all night, sleeping on his couch.

As far as gifts went, this took the top spot. He could tell himself all day he'd moved on from his crush, but this close to her, he forgot about the promise he'd made to himself.

The bed covers slipped slightly as he lifted an arm free to touch the top of her delicate hand. Soft, warm skin met his, just like he'd imagined.

She pulled her arm back and returned to the chair, too far away for his liking. "Now that we've got that settled, how are you feeling this morning?"

He pushed himself all the way up to a sitting position, exposing his bare chest as the sheet slid to his waist. She maintained perfect eye contact like she couldn't care less about checking him out. Holy cow, she *was* here. He knew this because she never gave him the once-over. Never paid him much attention beyond politeness.

Which meant...

Last night when he'd gotten up to relieve himself buck naked, she *had* been standing a mere five feet away. *And* a minute ago he'd asked her to join him in bed...

No wonder she was staring at him like she wished she were anywhere else.

"Umm..."

A little crease appeared between her pretty eyes. "You don't know how you're feeling this morning?"

"What are you doing here?" he asked, feeling totally tongue-tied. "Aren't you supposed to be in Africa?"

"I got back last night. No one told you I'd be here?"

He shook his head. Or if they did, he didn't remember.

"You need someone to keep an eye on you for the next couple of weeks, and I coincidentally needed somewhere to stay."

He gave himself a minute to let those words sink in. It was a lot to process given his weakened state. On the one hand, after years of pining away for Callie, she was here in his home—and apparently staying a while. On the other hand, though, she wasn't here because she wanted to be.

"I don't need a babysitter," he said kindly. He knew his body and what side effects to watch out for. Or at least they were written on the discharge instructions the ER nurse had printed out and given to him. He picked them up to show Callie. "I've got the instructions right here."

Plus, even though he felt awful, he had an invincible image to uphold.

She studied him, seeming to weigh what to say next, and in those few seconds he wondered what the hell he was doing. She'd said she needed somewhere to stay, and it was a dick move to refuse her because of his pride.

"Actually," he said, "forget I said that."

"Maybe I should go. I'm sure someone else—"

"No. I want you stay. Let's start over. Hi, Callie. Thanks for being here."

She waited a beat, then said, "Hi, Hunter."

He basked in those two little words. Hearing his name on her full lips made him warm for entirely different reasons than a fever.

"How are you feeling this morning?" she asked again.

His parents had always taught him that honesty is the best policy. "Like the spider won."

The corners of her mouth lifted slightly. "Maybe the first round, but I think you'll win the battle."

He wanted to say, "*With you as my nurse, I've already won*," but instead he said, "Thanks for the vote of confidence."

"Kennedy was here earlier and gave me some instructions."

"She instructed you to talk nice to me?" Damn. Most of the time when he talked to Callie, he screwed up somehow, but she always had nice things to say to people. He'd overheard her countless times with his sister and with people around town. His shoulders slumped and he slid back down into bed.

"No! I meant instructions on helping to take care of you."

"Ah, that makes more sense." He closed his eyes. "Should I be worried I don't remember her being here?"

"Honestly, I don't know. You're my first spider-bite patient."

He slowly raised his eyelids. He liked being her first anything. "You're my first, too." Oh, jeez. Could he be any more moony? "My first, uh, caretaker." That sounded more normal. "What's on this list of instructions?"

"Oh, right." She stood. "You need to take your antibiotic and Tylenol for your fever." She walked to the other bedside table, poured some pills into her hand, and presented them to him with a glass of water. He sat taller and accepted the meds with his injured hand. Her breath caught and her eyes widened at the swelling and redness.

"I imagine this is how the Pillsbury Dough Boy feels." He tossed back the meds and swallowed down some water.

"Does it hurt?"

"Only when I breathe."

"Your chest hurts?" Worry coated her words.

"No, my hand." He chuckled. Could they be any more out of tune with each other? This was how it always was when he was around her, and he hated it.

Hated how for some reason, he never acted like himself in front of Callie. He'd always admired her strength. Her kindness. Felt his knees go weak when he caught her smiling uninhibited. And when she was with his family, her warmth filled the room. Yet,

somehow, they'd never gotten beyond cursory greet-
ings.

"Itches, too," he added.

She gave a small shake of her head, as if she recognized their incompatibility, too. "It looks like it
would hurt all the time. Here, take this, too."

"What is it?" With his palm up, she dropped another small pill onto his hand.

"An antihistamine. It will help with the itching.
We can also put some prescription cream on it." She
lifted a small tube off the nightstand.

He liked the sound of "we" so he gave her his
hand to do the honors. He planned to take full advantage of her helpfulness, and if that made him
slightly despicable, then so be it.

A smart man knew not to waste a golden opportunity when it presented itself.

"You can't do it yourself?"

"Do you mind?" He gave her the best miserable
look he could muster, hoping it was enough to get
her agreement. His face didn't naturally grimace, so
it took some effort.

She sat down on the edge of the bed and un-
screwed the cap on the cream. It should not have
looked sexy, but somehow it did. "So, how long are
we shacking up together?" he asked.

"Please don't say it like that," she informed him
with a roll of her eyes.

"Like what?"

"Like there's more going on than there is." She
took his hand gently in hers and applied the cream.

To say he liked that her mind went *there* would
be an understatement, even if she did sound a little

disgusted by the idea.

"You worried people will talk?" He was pretty sure word of his spider bite—and Bethany's delivery—had made its way around town by now, so it would follow that Callie's return from Africa and their…*situation* would reach people's ears, too.

She delicately smoothed the cream on his hand, and her touch felt so nice that his eyes fell shut for a second.

"It's not that. We both know they will. I, uh…"

"You…?"

"Don't want *you* getting the wrong idea."

He'd had his own ideas going around in his head for more than a dozen years now, and none of them felt wrong to him. But still, he understood her concern. He had a ridiculous reputation as Windsong's most eligible bachelor now that Maverick was getting hitched, and he'd admit he did have an easy time with the ladies. Not to mention she'd caught him kissing more than one girl over the years, and her expressions always gave away her disapproval.

He took a silent, deep breath. Once again, he needed to move on from his crush and stick to it.

"So, you won't be climbing into bed with me?" The words were out before he could think better of them. He should just stop talking.

"Hunter!" She released his hand with an irritated huff, capped the medicated cream, and stood. Even annoyed, she was beautiful. "We need to establish some rules if this is going to work."

"Okay." He probably shouldn't tell her he'd never met a rule he couldn't break. Not any that were legal, anyway.

"Rule number one. No flirting."

In his defense, he genuinely didn't try to flirt—it just sometimes came out that way. It was in his nature. "I'll do my best."

She raised her eyebrows at him. If the expression meant to scold him, it didn't work. Her fathomless green eyes and long lashes flatlined any reprimand.

"Sometimes, I can't help it," he added.

"Well, help it while I'm here, please." She crossed her arms over her chest. "You also need to be clothed at all times." Her gaze dipped to his chest and abs before she blinked and resumed eye contact.

He thought about bringing up last night but decided to spare her any embarrassment. He seemed to recall her glaring at him, so he'd best let it go. "Fair enough. Same goes for you."

"Like I would walk around naked."

"You've never walked around in your birthday suit? Speaking of which, happy belated birthday."

All the tension left her body, and her arms fell to her sides. "You know when my birthday is?"

"I overheard Nova on the phone with you." He scratched the back of his neck, because of course he knew. His mom and sister had celebrated it plenty of times over the years. "But back to my original question…"

She tilted her head to the side. "I meant I'd never walk around *here* naked. I'm very comfortable in my own skin."

Her confidence was another thing he admired about her. She'd been through hell as a teenager and fought her way back to a strong body. She believed in herself and those she cared about, always sharing an encouraging word.

"Well, for the record, I wouldn't mind if you—"

"Hunter."

"Right. Sorry. No flirting. Any other rules on your mind?" He rubbed his shoulder, then reached around under the covers for his pajama pants and started to pull them on.

"What are you doing?" she asked with alarm.

"Putting some clothes on, Miss No Naked Here. I kicked them off during the night."

"Oh, okay. Thank you. And no other rules at the moment."

"I've got a rule. It only seems fair that I get at least one to your two."

"Sure. What is it?" She stepped away from the bed to look out the window, pushing aside the sheer curtains Nova had helped him pick out.

Another cloudy morning greeted them. Shit! What time was it? He had work to do on the ranch and a bootcamp class to lead at seven. He jumped out of bed.

Callie spun around in the nick of time to catch his arm before he lost his balance and fell over. The disorienting sensation had him closing his eyes to rid the dizzying range of hues.

"Whoa," Callie said. "You need to stay in bed."

"I can't. I've got work to do."

"Not today, you don't. Or tomorrow. Those are doctor's rules, not mine." She helped him lay down on the bed. "I'm pretty sure you're covered for whatever work you had."

"What time is it?"

"Around nine."

He groaned. "I hope you're right. This really sucks." He hated relying on others to do his job. He looked up at her sympathetic faces. Make that *face* after he took a second to blink her back into focus.

"It does. But some forced time off isn't always a bad thing."

She had him there. If only he could tell her *she* made it not a bad thing. He let out a deep breath. *Ouch, that hurt.* Note to self: take shallow breaths for the next few days.

"Are you okay now?" she asked.

"Yeah."

"Let's hear this rule of yours." She moved back to the corner chair and took a seat.

Hands on his stomach and eyes on the ceiling, he said, "You have to treat the bunkhouse like your own. I don't want you tiptoeing around. My home is your home."

He'd say the same to anyone staying with him, but it meant even more when said to Callie. Maybe something good would come out of this: a true friendship with her. It wasn't what his heart wanted, but he knew he couldn't keep pining away for her forever.

"Thank you. That's nice of you to say."

Their gazes connected. "Think you can do it?"

"As long as you follow the other two rules, yes." She pulled one knee up and wrapped her arms around her leg. A slim ray of sunshine shone through the window, the beam of light bringing one side of her face into a heavenly glow.

The memory of the first time he'd laid eyes on her filled his head: she'd come to the ranch with her older sister, Brooke, for a horseback ride. Her soft features and red curly hair had grabbed his attention, not to mention her enthusiasm for riding.

To the best of his knowledge, Callie hadn't been near a horse since. Whenever she was on the ranch with Nova, they steered clear of the barn and horses.

"Hunter?" Callie waved her hand at him.

"Sorry. Zoned out there for a minute. Sounds like we've got ourselves a solid plan for living together."

"We're not living together," she argued, without an eye roll this time. "I'm just staying with you for a little while."

"That's called living together," he quipped, teasing her. "But don't worry, I won't make it so fun you'll never want to leave." Or would he? Again, his brain could only handle so much in his compromised state. Plus, he had to tread lightly so as not to scare her away.

The joke was on him, though, when she fired back, "Don't *you* worry, I'm prepared for your level of fun."

CHAPTER FIVE

Hunter stared at the twinkle in her eyes, delighted to get a glimpse of a more playful Callie. He took her preparedness as a challenge, not that he'd tell her that. She exuded a different kind of confidence than he remembered, and he could no longer rely on what he thought he knew about her. He was impressed. Intrigued. Six months in Africa, he guessed, hadn't necessarily changed her so much as it emboldened her. "By the way, why can't you stay at your house? Not that I'm not grateful you're here."

"It's under construction." She went on to tell him about the state of the house and her parents and sister being out of town.

"Didn't they forget about you the time you and Nova got back from college orientation?"

"Good memory." Her tone, a mix between being impressed and sad, was one he'd never personally heard from her before. He knew from Nova and his mom that she often had a tenuous relationship with her mom and dad. Their two divorces had something to do with it, as well as Callie feeling abandoned when they constantly jetted off without her.

This was the longest conversation they'd ever had, and his pulse sped up at the thought of finally getting to know each other better. Or his rapid heart rate had to do with the antivenin. He couldn't be sure of anything this morning.

"I'm not just a handsome face," he teased.

"You're not?"

"So, you think I'm handsome?" She'd walked right into that one.

"I think *you* think that." She stood. "How about some breakfast? You hungry? We need to keep your strength up."

"You think I'm strong," he stated with zero modesty.

"Oh my God. I think you're *annoying*." She walked out of the bedroom and out of eyesight. The bunkhouse wasn't big, though, so he easily heard her continue to talk. "How about eggs and toast?"

"Sounds good, thanks."

He listened to her work in his kitchen with a smile on his face. Funny how certain events set in motion other events that only last week seemed impossible. Hands behind his head, he marveled at how a poisonous spider bite had turned into one of the best mornings he'd had in a long time. And this new situation with Callie was just getting started. He gave a silent one-arm cheer.

"You only had one egg left and your bread was moldy," she said, coming around the sliding barn door and almost catching him in celebration. He quickly tucked his elbow into his side. "But you did have Pop-Tarts." She handed him a plate with the frosted brown sugar cinnamon pastry on top. He could tell by the delicious scent that she'd warmed it up.

No one else he knew liked to eat them warm. Was it luck or coincidence that she must, too? "Thanks."

His phone rang before she stepped away, and she

looked down at the screen at the same time he said, "Whoever it is, they can wait."

She frowned. "It's the mayor."

"Oh, in that case." He hurriedly grabbed the phone and brought it to his ear. "Hiya, Mayor."

"Hello, Hunter. How are you feeling? I heard what happened."

"I'm okay." He made eye contact with Callie, her frown deepening but doing little to detract from her beauty. "Thanks for checking on me. Do you call everyone who's been bitten by a deadly spider, or am I special?"

She chuckled. "Considering I've known you since you were in diapers, let's go with the latter."

"Thought so," he said smugly.

Callie sat down on the bed beside him and took a bite of her Pop-Tart, seemingly very interested in his conversation. No sense in her straining herself when he was happy to put the call on speaker.

"I'm putting you on speaker. Callie Carmichael is here with me."

"I heard that, too," the mayor said. "Hello, Callie."

"Hi, Mayor Garnett." She sat taller like the mayor could see her, and he held back a chuckle. Then a groan because the move made her chest more pronounced.

"This phone call is actually two-fold," the mayor said. "I'm happy to hear you're feeling better, Hunter, but I'm also calling with an update on the ambassador position."

Hunter put his breakfast food down mid-bite. An update did not sound like a lead up to *"Congratulations, you're Windsong's first ambassador, Hunter."*

"Should I call you back on my phone, Mayor?" Callie asked.

Why would she do that?

"No, this is much better. I can speak to both of you at the same time."

Speak to both of them? Had Callie applied for the ambassador position? Her teeth sank into her bottom lip and her gaze darted to the floor.

"I had an overwhelming number of people apply to be ambassador. So many, in fact, that it's made choosing one person to represent Windsong on the Must-See Small Towns platform much more difficult. The good news, however, is that I'd like to congratulate you both on being finalists for the position." There was his unwelcome answer. They were in competition. *Friendly competition*. He didn't like the thought of beating her.

"Thank you," they said in unison.

"There are four other finalists vying for the position, and to make this as diplomatic as possible, my staff and I have come up with a list of activities that showcase the town and its history. We're asking each of you to participate in a bi-weekly event. For the next eight weeks, you'll write a one-pager about your experience, striving to wow us by sharing why our town is unique and interesting."

"So four different activities and four different summaries?" Hunter confirmed. This gig had to be his, and he'd outdo anyone who got in his way.

"Correct."

"What are the activities?" Callie asked.

"In order to keep things as fair as possible, we'll be randomly selecting activities for each finalist and emailing them the specifics on Saturday mornings, then you'll have two weeks to turn in your piece. The winner will be announced at a special dinner party in December."

"Can there be more than one winner?" Callie glanced at him from under long lashes. "I don't recall the details."

"Unfortunately, no. The purpose of the platform is to draw attention to the best small towns and encourage tourists to visit. The platform has always endorsed keeping things equitable regardless of population, so for now each town is only allowed one ambassador.

"Both of your applications were wonderful, by the way."

Hunter grumbled under his breath. Not wonderful enough, apparently.

"Any other questions? An email will go out tomorrow with all the finalists' names and the rules for the competition. On Saturday morning, you'll receive your first activity."

"No questions at this time," Callie said.

"Hunter?" The mayor rustled some papers on her end, the sound loud and clear over the phone.

"All good," he told her.

"Congratulations again, and may the best Windsonger win." With that, the mayor disconnected, leaving the bunk house too quiet and too still.

"Looks like we're in competition for the next couple of months." Hunter took a bite of his Pop-Tart. What this meant for their budding friendship, he didn't know. His gut, though, twisted in worry.

"I guess we are." She got to her feet, the bed

immediately colder. "Good luck. You're going to need it."

He cocked an eyebrow.

"What?" she said.

"I like this cheeky side of you. However…" He'd take that sassy tone and kindly show her. He needed this more than anyone else did. Being ambassador meant he'd be taken more seriously. He would be held responsible for showing off his hometown and bringing in more tourists. And he'd be known for something besides Windsong's most eligible bachelor.

"I can't speak for everyone else," he said, "but there is no way you're beating me."

CHAPTER SIX

Callie stepped outside onto the small porch for some fresh air. And if she were honest with herself, for a break from Hunter's bare chest and abs. His messy hair. His blue eyes and slightly crooked nose that somehow made his face even nicer to look at.

She'd noticed his good looks before, everyone did, but she didn't like being exposed to them any longer than necessary.

Ugh.

She preferred awkward over awareness, given that appearances could be deceiving. Trevor flashed through her mind. The unwelcome image had her reaffirming her promise to herself and thinking about the ambassador position instead. She *was* going to beat Hunter.

It had never occurred to her that she'd have competition. She'd sent her video application from Africa with a message about how much Windsong meant to her and how she'd work tirelessly to bring attention to all the wonderful things about their town. Being ambassador meant coming out from under her sister's shadow and finally being seen as someone other than the girl who'd survived being thrown from a horse.

Brooke had always been the more popular sister—homecoming queen, class president, head cheerleader, voted most likely to succeed. For once, Callie wanted to be recognized for something uniquely hers, something meaningful. Yes, she had her dressmaking business, but even though it wasn't true, Brooke had taken credit for suggesting Callie follow that passion.

She sat down in one of two cushioned wood armchairs and shivered at the chill in the air. A few shards of sunlight splintered the fog, but not enough to warm the earth yet.

"Here," Hunter said, handing her a large denim jacket lined with fleece. "It will keep you warm."

The sweet gesture caught her off guard and triggered a memory. Her parents fighting over the fact that her mom, cold on a job site, had been hurt and angry that her dad hadn't offered his coat. That he never offered her comfort or warmth when she needed it. Only when it suited him. Callie remembered that argument happening more than once. She remembered the knot in her stomach every time her mom felt slighted by something as simple as sharing a jacket.

Blinking away thoughts of her parents, she slid her arms inside the coat, immediately liking the cozy feeling and the smell of freshly laundered clothing with a hint of aftershave, like Hunter had put on the coat only to take it right off. "Thank you." She thought he'd turn around and go back inside the bunkhouse, but instead he took the chair next to her.

He'd covered up with a faded, black, long-sleeve thermal shirt. It fit him perfectly, not too slim, not too relaxed. His cheeks were flushed, and she guessed the cold air might be just what he needed for a few minutes.

"I haven't sat out here yet," he said. "My mom

insisted I needed some seating and bought these for me. I guess she was right."

"Moms usually are." She noticed him fold into the chair like it had taken a lot of effort to walk out here. "I never said how sorry I am that you were bitten by a black widow."

"Thank you, but let's agree never to bring up the BW again."

"Done." She fought a smile at his cute abbreviation. She'd forever think of black widow spiders that way now. Which meant the less they talked, the better. Hunter's vulnerable state confused her. The larger-than-life cowboy normally functioned with enough energy to spare. And she wasn't usually so aware of his appeal.

Around the side of the bunkhouse, the sound of a horse neighing met her ears. She shivered for reasons that had nothing to do with the cold.

"It's okay," Hunter said softly. "That was Magnolia, Maverick's horse. He's probably taking her out for a ride." Hunter's notice of her discomfort, and his subsequent explanation, took her by surprise. That awful day flashed through her mind for the millionth time.

Her first and last horseback ride.

It had been Brooke's birthday, and the two of them had come to the ranch for a ride. They'd been so excited that they were getting to do something without their parents, and Callie hadn't hesitated to get on a horse. They'd barely started the ride when her horse was frightened by someone setting off fireworks. She was thrown off into a tree, breaking her back and suffering a serious concussion.

Hunter had been riding by when the accident happened. He'd jumped off his horse, as did their guide, to help her. Hunter's worried face was the last thing she saw for three weeks, the head trauma causing temporary blindness.

That day changed her life.

A twelve-month recovery had included two surgeries, a back brace, and intense physical therapy. She'd missed walking onto the high school campus beside her friends for the first time. She'd endured her first breakup via text because her boyfriend couldn't handle her injuries. And mentally, she never regained her sense of adventure, instead playing it safe and handing over the spotlight to her sister.

Designing and sewing dresses, reading, and time with friends, particularly Nova, became her lifeline.

"I know who Magnolia is," she said, unease weaving through her shoulder blades. She hoped Hunter wasn't remembering that day, too.

He leaned his head back and closed his eyes, legs stretched out in front of him, arms crossed over his chest. "I wasn't sure."

"Nova keeps me up to date on everyone and everything."

"I guess that's why you landed here with me."

"That and the Spider Who Shall Not Be Named."

A small smile lifted the corners of his mouth. He opened his eyes, looked off in the distance. She followed his line of sight. With the fog lifting, the side of the inn came into view. "I'm trying to decide if I can make it to the house. There's always eggs and toast there. Probably bacon, too."

"The Pop-Tart didn't cut it?"

"Ludicrous, I know, but no."

"I'll go round you up some breakfast and you stay put." She got to her feet, grateful for the chance to leave his company and her embarrassment over the accident.

"I could get used to this." His smug (and annoyingly endearing) tone had her almost taking back her offer.

"I could tell your mom my instructions are to feed you kale and blueberry shakes for the next two days."

"I happen to enjoy both." His baby blues didn't lie—he did like both. That she read him so easily had her scratching her head. "Want to try something else?" he asked.

"Spinach and pineapple?"

"Love 'em."

Grr. She stepped off the porch. She had a feeling he'd win this battle no matter what she said. But that was okay, because she planned to win the competition that mattered.

A couple of minutes later, she opened the back door to the kitchen. Mary Rose stood at the counter, stirring something inside a large bowl.

"Good morning," Callie said.

"Hi, sweetie! Come on in."

As always, the room smelled delicious, like butter and sweetness and something spicy. It was also wonderfully warm, so she slipped off Hunter's jacket and hung it on the back of a chair. She peeked into the bowl next.

"Almond crunch cookies," Mary Rose said. "They're Hunter's favorite. Thank you again for staying with him. How's he doing this morning?"

"He's okay. Hungry, though. His fridge is bare so I'm here for eggs and bacon. Do you mind?" She'd run to the market later to stock them with food.

"You know I don't. I saved him some bacon from earlier, just in case, and I'll whip him up some eggs right now."

"I can do it."

Mary Rose opened a drawer and pulled out an ice cream scoop. She handed it to Callie. "How about you drop this dough onto the cookie sheets for me instead?"

"Happy to."

"It's so good to have you home." Mary Rose wrapped her in a hug. "And not because you're helpful in the kitchen or keeping an eye on Hunter."

"I missed you, too." Just as much as her own mom. Mary Rose had always been like a second mother to her, available whenever she needed her.

"So, Africa was everything you hoped it would be?" Mary Rose cracked eggs right onto a frying pan, then put two pieces of bread in the toaster.

"It was. I loved every minute. I feel like I accomplished something that will have lasting effects."

"If the pictures you sent are any indication, then I've no doubt that's true." Mary Rose paused to look at her. *Really* look at her. "You have a new glow about you. Is it because of a certain someone?"

"No," she quickly answered. At Mary Rose's frown, she added, "Trevor wasn't who I thought he was, so we ended things." She and the agricultural scientist had spent the last three months together—until Callie discovered he had a wife in New

Zealand. "I think what you're seeing this morning is jet lag and lack of sleep."

"Rough night with our patient?"

Hunter's bare backside flashed through her mind before she blinked it away. Not exactly *rough*. "A little. He cried out in his sleep and tossed and turned a lot."

"You're an angel for being here."

"I did need a place to stay, too, so my motives aren't entirely selfless. You know Hunter and I…"

Mary Rose plated three sunny-side-up eggs, waiting silently for Callie to finish her thought.

"We don't really like each other."

The toaster dinged at the same time Mary Rose sighed in clear disagreement. "I hate to break it to you, but Hunter does like you. I think what you're trying to say is you don't know each other well."

"That, too."

"Trust me when I say he loves having you stay with him." Mary Rose lightly buttered the toast and added it to the plate.

"That's exactly what Nova said." One cookie sheet full, she reached for another. "As usual, you're both just being nice, given my situation."

"If you give that wonderful son of mine a chance, I think he might surprise you."

"He's already—" Oops, she almost forgot who she was talking to and spilled she'd already gotten a naked surprise. "Sweeter than I expected."

"I'm not going to take that personally," Mary Rose teased. She added bacon to Hunter's meal and covered the plate with tinfoil. Handing it to Callie, she added, "I'm glad you always share your true feelings with me."

"I'm lucky you always listen." She set down the ice cream scoop so Mary Rose could pick up where she left off.

"I'll stop by later with some cookies, but you know I'm here if you need anything. We've got a ton of prep work for the wedding this weekend, otherwise I'd be more available."

Callie slipped Hunter's denim jacket back on. "Good luck with everything and don't worry about Hunter. I've got him."

A sentence she never in a million years thought she'd say.

CHAPTER SEVEN

On the walk back to the bunkhouse, Callie marveled at the flowers on the property. Her best friend had the greenest thumb on the planet and a special talent for floral arranging—both in the wild and for events at the inn.

She crossed over the small white bridge, a route she rarely took, preferring instead to keep as much distance as possible between her and the horses. She couldn't be near a horse without her heart pounding out of her chest and the terrible memory of her fall making her uncomfortable.

Staying focused on the bunkhouse, she found Hunter sitting on the porch exactly where she'd left him. She watched the rise and fall of his chest, grateful he seemed to be breathing easy with his full lips slightly parted.

"Hunter," she whispered. He didn't budge, so she went inside to put down the plate of food. Returning, she put a hand on his shoulder and with a louder voice said, "Hunter, I'm back with your breakfast."

He opened his eyes. "Hey."

"Hi. You ready to eat?"

"Not really. My stomach is a little queasy. Sorry."

"Don't be. How about we get you back in bed?"

"Yes, please."

She helped him to his feet, although really, he did it on his own, she just kept an arm under his, and they walked clumsily to the bed.

Hunter collapsed onto the mattress, not bothering with the covers, so she helped with that. About to step away, he gripped her wrist with a firm yet gentle hold. "Lay with me for a minute?"

The sweet, powerless look in his eyes and the soft tone of his voice were a killer combination she found impossible to refuse. "Okay."

He scooted over to make room for her. She took off his jacket and then crawled under the covers, glad she wore pajamas that covered her from the neck down.

They lay facing each other, their noses inches apart. He smelled faintly of soap and cinnamon and stared right at her when he whispered, "I was really scared."

Then he shut his eyes and fell back asleep.

His confession slid into her heart with uninvited ease. She knew exactly how he felt.

And she knew better than to let it connect them. *Never again.* She'd never again make herself vulnerable.

Slipping out of bed, she reminded herself she mattered just by being here. No one, least of all a man, would make her feel small ever again. She *was* loved. By friends. Her family (mostly). From now on, her heart would remain safe in her own hands. A string of unfaithful, thoughtless romances convinced a girl of that. Her parents' unusual, often careless union had, too. Watching them so casual with each other's hearts had left an indelible mark.

She sat on the couch with her sketchpad. She'd been toying with the idea of expanding her designs in hopes of creating a wider range of A-line dresses to fit a variety of body types and style preferences.

More than that, she hoped all her bridesmaid offerings felt as though they were infused with a bit of magic, not just her MOH dresses.

Thirty minutes later, she had three new sketches, the overall style effortless with a modern flair and a touch of whimsy. Romantic eveningwear with feminine flourishes. Satisfaction filled her. She hugged the pad to her chest.

Next, she worked on a marketing plan. Call it magic. Call it luck. Call it…matchmaking. *Forget Grandma's meddling and dating apps, a Callie Designs MOH dress brings your perfect match to you!* She smiled.

To the best of her knowledge, no other designer had the kind of built-in success she did with six maids of honor engaged to be married after wearing her designs. And continuing to build on that reputation—continuing the streak—was her best shot at taking her business to the next level.

• • •

Hunter heard her before he saw her. He slowly opened his eyes and there she was, staring down at him like she'd been watching for signs of life.

The second their eyes met, she grinned, put her warm, slightly sticky palms on his cheeks, and smooshed his face. "Uncle Hunter, thank goodness you're awake. We were starting to worry."

"Hey, Pipsqueak."

She dropped her hands and then gave him a stern look. "You are in big trouble with me."

"I am?"

"You slept through our riding lesson."

Ouch. That hurt almost as much as the spider bite. He hated letting her down. "What time is it?"

Jenna turned her cute little face toward the corner of the room.

"Almost four," Maverick said from the armchair. That chair had seen more action in the past twenty-four hours than it had since he bought it.

Jesus, he'd been asleep *all* day. He pushed himself up, feeling better than he had this morning. "Hey, Mav. How long have you guys been here?"

"About ten minutes. Mom stopped in, too, and left you cookies."

"I ate two," Jenna admitted. "Uncle Mav said it was okay."

"I'm sorry about our lesson," he told her. "We'll do an extra-long one when I'm feeling better."

She put out her hand. "Pinkie swears?"

"Pinkie swears." He hooked his finger with hers.

"Can I see your spider bite? At first I didn't tell anyone what happened—" She looked down. "But when Daddy said you should have known it was a black widow and not bothered it, I told everyone it was my fault."

Hunter put his knuckle under her chin and lifted her head. "It was not your fault, sweetheart."

"But I—"

"You did what you're supposed to do. Be curious."

"That's right," Maverick said. "And Uncle Hunter did what he's supposed to do because he loves you."

"I love you, too." Jenna wrapped him in a hug,

pressing her cheek against his chest. Over the top of her head, he and Maverick exchanged a look. This little girl had both their hearts and always would.

Jenna raised her eyebrows at him as she let go. He presented his hand, still red and swollen and a little scary looking.

"Does it hurt?" She kept her arms at her sides, rather than try and touch him, which was unusual for her. It must be *a lot* scary looking.

"Yes."

"I'm not gonna touch spiders anymore. I learned my lesson."

Hunter held back a laugh. She'd come by the "I learned my lesson" words from her dad. Speaking of... "How's Gia and Bethany?"

"They're doing great," Maverick said.

"And Cole? Has he chilled out?"

"Daddy doesn't have a chill bone in his body," Jenna said with authority.

This time Hunter did laugh. Someone had been listening to everything said around her.

"Guess what else?" Jenna asked.

"What?"

"There are two hundred and six bones in your body."

Pride swelled inside him. He had the smartest niece on the planet.

"And you know what else? Your hand has a lot of them." She wiggled her fingers. "If you need a hand while you're getting better, Uncle Hunt, I'll give you mine."

He hadn't thought he could love this little girl more than he already did, but damn. "Thank you. I'll keep that in mind."

Maverick stood. "We've been instructed to make sure you take your meds and eat something healthy before you dig into the cookies."

Jenna skipped out of the room and returned a few seconds later to present him with a plate of food that included a sandwich and apple slices. "Did you know an apple a day keeps the doctor away?" she asked.

"I did know that." He put the plate on his lap. "Where did this—"

"Callie stocked your fridge and made you the sandwich," Maverick said. He doled out some meds and handed them to Hunter with a glass of water.

When he'd woken to find Jenna and Maverick instead of Callie, he thought maybe this morning had been enough for her. Maybe she'd left with no plans to return. "Where, uh, is she?"

He hoped he sounded low key. Maverick knew all about his longtime crush, and Hunter wasn't in the mood for teasing or advice.

"There was a fashion emergency," Jenna said. "I have to go see about it, too, but first we needed to come here."

Hunter had no idea what they were talking about.

"The bridesmaid dresses Kennedy picked out are no longer available." Maverick came around the bed and stood behind Jenna. "So, Kennedy asked Callie if she'd design and make them."

"And my flower girl dress, too," Jenna piped in.

"She's over at the main house with Kennedy and Nova doing some brainstorming."

"That's cool." Hunter took a bite of his sandwich.

It was way more than cool. It meant Callie would be around even after her babysitting duties ended.

Maverick studied him. His older brother had this annoying way of reading Hunter's mind. "Jenna, why don't you run back to the house? I'll be there in a minute."

"Okay. Later, gators." She skipped away in her yellow rainboots, happily singing her favorite song, "Good Feeling" by Flo Rida.

"Don't say it," Hunter said as soon as he heard the front door shut.

"The woman you've secretly loved for over a decade is staying with you and you think I'm not going to say anything? What kind of brother would that make me?"

"The good kind." Hunter took a bite of his sandwich. It tasted better than any he made himself.

"I don't want your heart to get broken."

"Why would it?" he asked, his mouth full.

Maverick crossed his arms and gave him the *Really?* look.

"Fine. You're right. Or you *were* right. But when I heard she was dating some guy in Africa, I decided to move on for real this time. So, while I appreciate your concern, I'll be okay. And to prove it to you, Kennedy can set me up with her new MA, Bella, like she's been wanting to."

"Wow, you are serious. But you know, you could come crash at my place if it helps."

"We both know if I did that, you might lose Kennedy to me." He took another bite of his food.

Maverick laughed. "Good to see your sense of humor is intact."

Hunter finished chewing. "I am the funnier brother."

"Funnier looking."

"Keep telling yourself that." In truth, people often thought they were twins, something Hunter had been proud of as a kid. Any comparison to either of his older brothers had made him happy. Still did on occasion, but now nearing thirty, he craved recognition on his own rather than being called Cole and Maverick's "little brother." The ambassador position would go a long way toward earning him a new kind of respect.

"Seriously." Maverick snagged an apple slice off the plate. "I'm here if you need me."

"I think I said something similar to you when Kennedy crashed back into your life." The absolute happiness that spread across his brother's face had Hunter smiling back. He wanted to feel that same sheer joy so badly, he renewed his vow to move on from Callie. "And you were a big pain in the ass."

"Very different situation, but point taken." Maverick backed away. "You good if I leave?"

"How about I come with?" He shifted to drag himself out of bed. Getting out of the bunkhouse sounded good. He hated being cooped up.

Maverick shook his head. "No. You're to stay put for another day at least. Doctor's orders."

"Fine." The slight movement reminded him his muscles still ached and he also wasn't sure he'd make the walk to the inn without needing a rest. No way in hell did he want anyone seeing that. "But bring me those cookies before you go."

CHAPTER EIGHT

"What do you think of this?" Callie asked, sliding one of the new sketches she'd drawn earlier across the table to Kennedy.

Nova and Mary Rose leaned over for a look as well. The four of them were gathered in the kitchen to talk about styles and fabrics for Kennedy's bridesmaids' dresses, and Callie felt confident this was a design Kennedy would love.

The bride-to-be ran her finger over the drawing. "I love it. What do you think, Nova?"

"I love it, too," Callie's best friend said, bouncing in her chair. "It's beautiful and will definitely compliment the maid of honor's dress." The magical MOH dress they'd chosen had a Queen Anne neckline with a form-fitting bodice and long skirt.

Kennedy already had that engaged-to-be-married glow about her, but it shined even brighter. "I'm getting married," she cooed.

"I'm getting another sister-in-law," Nova said, love and affection clear in her tone. "So, what color are you leaning toward?"

They'd been debating between silver and emerald for the Christmas Eve wedding.

"Silver."

"Woot!" Nova apparently agreed.

"Andrew will be thrilled to wear a silver shirt underneath his black suit rather than green." Andrew was Kennedy's best friend and serving as man of honor beside Ava, Kennedy's younger sister, and the maid of honor.

The back door flew open and cool air, along with an adorable Jenna, swept into the room. She headed straight for her grandmother's lap. "Hi. What'd I miss?"

"Where's your uncle?" Kennedy asked.

"He'll be here in a minute." She cupped her hand over her mouth and leaned toward Kennedy. "He wanted to converse with Uncle Hunt alone." Her whisper was cute and not at all quiet.

Mary Rose put up her hand for a high five. "Good job using one of this week's spelling words."

Jenna slapped her grandma's palm. "Thanks, Nana." Jenna's eyes widened as she noticed the sketch. "Did you draw that, Callie? You're really good."

"She is," Kennedy agreed. "I can't thank you enough for coming to my rescue on such short notice."

The rescue went both ways. She couldn't think of a better way to jump back into her design business after being away for six months. "Thank *you* for this opportunity. I'm honored and excited to be part of your wedding."

"I'll have Ava send her measurements," Kennedy said, "and as soon as Bethany feels ready, we'll get hers, if that's okay."

Callie tucked her hands under her thighs and nodded, mentally calculating how long it would take to make the dresses. Two-and-a-half months left more than enough time. What she didn't have, though, was enough space. Space for more bolts of fabric, all her sewing supplies, room to spread out. Hunter had generously told her to make herself at home, but she couldn't take over the bunkhouse even if she wanted to. The square footage didn't lend itself to all her needs. She moved *find a storefront* to the top of her mental to-do list.

"You can start on my dress first," Nova said with a big smile. "And I hope Ava is ready to meet the man of her dreams after this."

"That's right!" Kennedy brought her hand to her mouth for a moment. "Maybe you could leave the butterfly applique off? I don't know if I'm ready for that."

"It's more than the applique," Nova stated. "It's the dress, made by my BFF's magic fingers."

Nova shared Callie's belief in the mysterious and supernatural power of charms, whether they be trinkets, a person, or a special piece of fabric. Callie had chosen two butterflies rather than one for the applique because when two of the tiny, winged creatures were seen together, it symbolized long-lasting commitment and eternal love. It had to be the main reason half a dozen women had found love after wearing the dress. That, combined with her newly inherited matchmaking abilities, and she believed wholeheartedly in her dresses' mystical significance.

"Ahem."

Everyone looked at Jenna, sitting with a straight back in Mary Rose's lap, as if she wanted to appear more grown up. "Did you forget about me?"

"Never," they all said together. "But a very special flower girl's dress takes a bit more time to design," Kennedy said. "Right, Callie?"

"Right. But I do have an idea…" She glanced at Kennedy for approval. At Kennedy's nod, Callie did a quick sketch of a simple gown with a full tulle skirt and lace bodice. What made it special was the back—a heart cutout and bow. When finished, she lifted the piece of paper to show everyone.

Jenna's eyes lit up with excitement. "I'll be a princess."

"Another perfect design," Kennedy said.

"I think this calls for celebratory drinks." Mary Rose gently set Jenna in the chair as she stood. She returned with stemmed glasses and a bottle of sparkling apple cider.

Mary Rose led them in a toast. "Cheers!"

"Looks like the dress crisis has been averted," Maverick said, entering the kitchen and heading straight for his fiancée. He put his hands on her shoulders and kissed her cheek.

"Look, Uncle Mav. I'm going to be a real princess." Jenna showed him the sketch.

"That you are."

"How is Hunter?" Callie asked him.

"Good. He finished his sandwich and started on his cookies. He's looking better."

Callie pushed away from the table. "I'll walk back now," she said easily, a strange feeling of wanting to check on him coming over her. She'd promised to keep an eye on him, and that's what she'd do. Standing, she looked at Nova and added, "Measurements tomorrow?"

"Sounds good."

Five minutes later, Callie knocked on Hunter's door before entering the bunkhouse. "Hey, it's me," she called out, not wanting to catch him with his pants down or anything. Plus, it still felt weird to be staying in the bunkhouse with him.

"Hey," he called back. "I'm right where you left me."

She'd left him asleep, his handsome face mere inches from her own. She'd been charmed by his gentleness, something she'd never associated with him before. He oozed ruggedness. Easily grabbed attention with his fun-loving and gregarious personality. Maybe she hadn't given him enough consideration in the past, too wrapped up in her own humiliation from all those years ago.

"Maverick said—" She stopped in her tracks at the sight of him, sitting up in bed and reading a book. "You read?"

He put the book down in his lap, an amused expression reaching the corners of his blue eyes. "I did graduate college with a business degree."

"I know. I didn't…I just meant…" She sat in the armchair and hoped she didn't sound too flustered. "I didn't think you read for pleasure."

"There's a lot I do for pleasure." His voice, sexier than usual, broke their flirting rule.

"Hunter."

"Sorry." With one blink, his expression moved from playful to…something she couldn't read. Wary, maybe? She didn't know if she liked it, even though he was abiding by her wishes.

"Maverick said you're feeling better."

"I am. Thanks for the sandwich." He didn't take his eyes off her. "How did the dress thing go?"

"Great. We decided on a design, and I can't wait

to get started." She glanced around the bunkhouse. "Would you mind if I set up a workspace in the other room?"

"Not at all."

"Thanks." She tucked her hands under her thighs, the nervous habit nothing new. "Can I ask you a question?"

"You can ask me anything."

"Do you believe in magic?" She didn't normally talk about it with anyone outside of Nova and Birdy, but after the gathering with Kennedy, she wanted another opinion. She wanted *Hunter's* opinion.

He took his time thinking about it. "If you're talking fate or destiny, then yeah, I do."

"Hmm…"

"Hmm?" he mimicked, but with a clear question mark perched at the end.

"Word on the wedding circuit is my maid of honor dresses are lucky charms."

"I heard Nova mention that. You don't believe it?"

"I do, actually. Your sister thinks it's *me*, though, and not just the dresses."

"You are the designer. There wouldn't be a dress without you."

"True." She'd always been her own worst enemy, never giving herself enough credit. Time to put uncertainty to rest and use this incredible marketing angle to her advantage.

Hunter studied her. He rubbed underneath his chin. "I have an idea."

"Okay."

"How about you make my best man suit for the wedding?"

"What?" Was he implying he wanted to get lucky in love?

"I'll check with Kennedy and see if she's good with you making my suit. If I meet the love of my life after the wedding and am the next one down the aisle, we'll know it's just as much you as your special talent for dressing wedding parties."

"I didn't know you wanted to get married."

Hope, clear as day, washed over his features. "I do. Watching so many weddings on the ranch the past few years has me wanting one of my own. And seeing how happy Cole and Bethany are, and now Mav and Kennedy, it's made me realize how much I want a partner to do life with. I've been ready to settle down for a little while now."

"You just need that someone special."

Something shone in his eyes she couldn't decipher. "Exactly."

Callie's pulse thudded in her ears. "I've never made a suit before." She wasn't sure if the statement was to get him to change his mind or if *she* was trying to wiggle out of it.

"There's a first time for everything." The tone of his voice, a mix of challenge and trust, lit a fire inside her she hadn't felt before. Goodbye, indecision.

"Okay. I'll do it if it's okay with Kennedy and Maverick." Thoughts raced through her mind. The style of suits she liked, but more importantly the style that would look good on Hunter's well-made body. The kind of material. Where to hide the butterfly applique inside the jacket.

Hunter chuckled. "All Mav cares about is Kennedy being happy, so no worries there."

She studied her best friend's brother, both surprised and intrigued by his desire to meet "the love of his life." She hadn't thought he wanted to settle down any time soon.

"Not sure what to make of me, are you?"

"You are a little confusing," she admitted. Silently she added, *Unsettling. Unexpected. Inconvenient. Sexy.*

That last one worried her the most.

CHAPTER NINE

Saturday mornings on the ranch were reserved for private Boot Camp groups. Hunter breathed in the crisp early morning air, grateful to be out of the bunkhouse and among this particular crowd of Boot Camp first-timers. Given his body still ached and his hand still hurt, if anyone else had been scheduled this morning, he may have had trouble co-leading them with Brett.

Not to say this over-seventy group of ladies weren't tough chicks ready to kick some boot camp butt.

"Mrs. Knupp just winked at me," Brett said from beside him.

"Did you wink back?"

"Of course I did."

The twelve grandmothers assembling before them outside the barn on this cloudy morning were affectionately known around town as the Baker's Dozen. If someone was sick, or had a birthday, or needed cheering up, they delivered baked goods. Cole and Bethany had received a basket full of muffins, scones, and cookies to celebrate Gia's arrival—who, by the way, Hunter had finally had the pleasure of holding yesterday.

"Did you get your first ambassador assignment?" Brett asked.

Hunter turned to him. "I still can't believe you applied when you knew I was."

"When your girlfriend tells you to do something, you do it."

"Yeah, yeah. And yes, I did. You?"

"Going wine tasting."

"Courtyards and secret passageways for me." He wondered what Callie had gotten. He'd tiptoed by her this morning, leaving her sound asleep on the couch with a blanket tucked under her chin. Not wanting her to worry, he'd left a note to tell her where he'd gone.

Since he'd issued his best man challenge (approved by Kennedy), he'd done his best to keep things low-key. He wanted what his brothers had—confirmed when he'd held Gia in his arms and stared at her tiny, beautiful face—and what better way than having Callie give him her special brand of good luck? He'd been unsuccessful on his own, and this plan felt right. Helping Callie at the same time felt even better.

"You boys going to stand there lollygagging all morning or get to it?" Birdy asked. To the best of his knowledge, Birdy was the oldest of the group, but you wouldn't know it by looking at her.

"Let's get started." Hunter clapped his hands together.

"And shake our booties!" Mrs. Knupp shouted.

"We're not that kind of boot camp, Mrs. Knupp," Brett said.

"You are now!" Right on cue, the whole lot of them started shaking their butts. Hunter swore he heard Maverick chuckle from inside the barn.

This was just one of the many reasons Hunter loved his hometown so much. These grandmothers were part of the heart and soul of Windsong and lived each day by their own rules.

He and Brett allowed the ladies their fun and then got to work. Still on the mend, Hunter watched the group lift bales of hay, chop wood, pass feed bags, and fast-walk through the trees while Brett did the exercises with them.

When the hour ended, everyone, including Hunter, was exhausted. Instructing and keeping an eye out for proper form to avoid injury had wiped him out.

"I never need to do this again," Birdy said, bent over with her hands on her knees.

Hunter pushed a hale bale over so she could sit down. "You did great."

Birdy sat and patted the spot next to her. Happy to oblige and take a load off, too, Hunter took a seat. Birdy had been a part of his life since he was four years old and she'd caught him peeing on her rose bushes. It hadn't been his fault; his mom was taking too long saying goodbye to a neighbor on the street.

They watched Brett help the rest of the group to their cars before he waved goodbye in their direction. Hunter lifted his chin, too tired to raise his arm.

"You did all right this morning, too, kid."

He gave her a small, closed-mouth smile. He hated that he was too weak to do the exercises.

"Morning!" At the sound of Callie's sweet voice, Hunter sat taller, shoulders back, not that he was trying to impress her or anything. "How'd it go?" she continued, coming to stand in front of Birdy.

"Boot camp isn't for the faint of heart," Birdy answered.

"Good thing you're strong, then." Callie's gaze slid to his. "How'd you do?"

"He was a pain in the ass telling us how to chop wood," Birdy offered, "and hand off hay bales, but his muscles are nice to look at."

"You were supposed to be focused on the wood and hay," he said good-naturedly. He didn't like to think about the senior citizens of his town checking him out.

"I can multitask."

Callie chuckled. "You're feeling all right?" she asked him.

"I'm fine." Mostly. Nothing a nap and some pain relievers couldn't fix.

"If you're okay with it, I'm off to Birdy's for a little while."

"Hunter's coming with," Birdy announced as she got to her feet.

"I am?" He didn't mind the idea of hanging out with them. He was simply curious about why they wanted him to tag along.

"Arm candy gets more likes on Insta," she said to Callie.

"I'm sure Hunter has better things to do today." Callie stepped away, the move a sign she wanted to get going. Without him.

He couldn't have that. *Not* because he wanted to be around her. But because Birdy had inadvertently asked for his help and he never let down a cocktail-making, tracksuit-wearing octogenarian. Even if it meant she'd be checking out his muscles some more. "Actually, our seasonal help started early, and I'm under doctor's orders to take the rest of the weekend off."

Callie looked over her shoulder at him. "I didn't see those orders."

With a shrug, he fell in step beside the two women. "Kennedy texted me." Her exact text said: *After bootcamp you must rest. Tomorrow, too.* Flexing his arm muscles didn't take any effort, so he was good to go with that.

"It's settled, then," Birdy said. "Now let's see how you handle a bottle of gin."

Hunter drove them to Birdy's house, and an hour later, his side hurt from laughing so much. Birdy had him holding a pink bottle of gin in every way possible for her and Callie's Instagram account. What made it funny was their pictures didn't include his face because "they wanted the focus to stay on the bottle and his hands and arms." So he made funny faces to get them to laugh, which led to Callie dishing it right back. In between, Birdy told jokes.

"Last one," she said. "Why do ducks have feathers?"

He and Callie exchanged a quick glance. "I don't know. Why?" they asked together.

"To cover their butt quacks!" And once again, the three of them cracked up. Callie's laugh might just be the best one he'd ever heard. Exuberant and bursting with vitality. He'd never seen her more carefree.

He'd watched her from afar for a long time, but over the past few days, she'd seemed different. Being in Africa for six months had changed her, dulled her modesty and restraint.

Hunter put the bottle down. "I think that's a wrap?"

"Yes. Thank you for being a good sport." Birdy smiled at him.

"Yes, thanks," Callie added before sneezing for the umpteenth time due to her cat allergy.

"Thanks for letting me in on your secret account." They had an impressive following and a new fan. @BirdCall (genius name!) rated as his new favorite.

"You need some fresh air," Birdy said to Callie, leading the way to the front door. "And you, young man, need to take our girl out to lunch."

"No, he doesn't." Callie's protest meant he absolutely would be taking her to lunch. Her objections were damn cute and made him want to do the opposite. Plus, this would give him the opportunity to work on their friendship now that Maverick's wedding and his best man attire were sure to be the turning point in his love life.

"Will do," he said, ignoring Callie's objection. She gave a little huff but otherwise remained quiet as they walked to his car.

He opened the passenger-side door of his truck for her, then strode around the hood to his side. He felt her eyes follow him, and when he hopped up into his seat, her green gaze welcomed him with a mix of irritation and gratitude.

"I'm really not hungry, so…" The lie didn't stand a chance when her stomach growled loud enough for them both to hear.

Hunter leaned back in his seat, looked out the windshield. He'd never make her do something she didn't want to, but… "How about we combine lunch with our ambassador assignments? Mine is courtyards and secret walkways. What's yours?"

"Downtown highlights."

"Sounds like an easy pairing to me." He started the truck; hopeful they could work together even though they were in competition.

"Okay. But you don't need to buy me lunch."

"Worried it would feel like a date?" He couldn't help himself. If he could just sneak under her skin a little bit, he'd be a happy man.

"Not at all."

"Ouch." He put a hand on his chest. "You sure know how to ruin a guy," he teased.

Only she didn't take it as teasing. "That's not true," she asserted. "Pretty much the opposite, actually."

"What do you mean?"

"Nothing." She directed her attention out the passenger-side window. "Forget I said anything."

Too late for that. Jealousy had reared its ugly head numerous times over the years when she'd dated other people. As far as he knew, all her breakups were amicable. Well, as much as they could be.

"Did something happen with the guy in Africa?"

She jerked her head to look at him. "You know about Trevor?"

"I heard mention of him when Mom and Nova were talking, but it sounded good. If you want, I'll fly to Africa and kick his ass for whatever he did wrong."

Her eyes softened, making his wavering heart turn upside down. Several silent beats passed between them. "Thanks, but that's not necessary. I took care of it myself."

"Meaning things ended between you two?" What a dumbass. A smart man would do whatever it took to maintain even a long-distance relationship with Callie.

"When his wife called and I answered his phone, yes."

He almost swerved into a tree, her revelation pissing him off. "What an asshole."

"Unfortunately, I'm a magnet for them." She tugged at the ends of her long hair. She smelled like apples and something floral, and he took a discreet inhale while keeping his eyes on the road. "Which is why I've decided I'm over it."

"It?"

"Men. Monogamy. Trusting my heart to someone only to have him stomp on it like I'm easily forgotten. I watched it happen between my parents, too, so you'd think I would have figured it out before now. I'm never committing to anyone again. Never getting married." Sadness crept into her tone, along with something else he couldn't name, and the punch to his gut hurt something awful.

He also had no idea what to say. If he hadn't already strong-willed himself to stop longing for her and hope she realized the man of her dreams was right under her nose, this certainly cured him of that foolish notion.

"Sorry. I didn't mean to unload all that on you." She blushed, like she wished she could swallow the words she'd unleashed.

"It's okay. I'm happy to lend an ear whenever you need one."

He turned onto Main Street and pulled into a

parking spot in front of Baked on Main. Callie might be stubborn enough to refuse lunch, but no one said no to a glazed croissant or other baked good from the best bakery within a fifty-mile radius. Plus, with a line often out the door, it had to be a downtown highlight—a win-win.

"First stop?" He raised his eyebrows in question after they exited the car.

"Sounds good."

The chill outside vanished the second they walked into the warm, cozy bakery. Hunter held the glass door for Callie, and he couldn't help it; he put his hand on the small of her back. Just for a moment. A moment that sent a rush of pleasure through him. She, of course, appeared completely unaffected. *Quit being a glutton for punishment, man.*

They'd timed their arrival right, and only two people stood in line in front of them. When they reached the counter, the bakery's owner, Claudia, greeted them with her customary wide smile. "Hi, you two!" She sounded like seeing him and Callie together was a normal occurrence. "Hunter, it's good to see you up and around. I'm glad you're feeling better."

"Thanks," he said.

"And Callie, welcome home. I heard you had a great time in Africa."

"Thank you, I did."

"What can I get you?"

"We'll have two pumpkin scones, please," Callie said.

"How do you know I like those?" he asked.

"I remember Nova bringing you one last year."

So, she wasn't always oblivious to him. Good to know, even if it didn't matter anymore.

When they tried to pay for their food, Claudia dismissed it. "It's on the house. Good luck in the ambassador competition."

"You, too," he and Callie said at the same time. Out of the other finalists, Hunter worried about Claudia the most. She'd worked for the local paper before opening the bakery and no doubt knew how to write a strong, persuasive article.

Hunter glanced at Callie out of the corner of his eye as they walked down Main Street eating their scones out of white paper bags. Bundled in a coat and scarf, and even with her declaration of anti-marriage at the forefront of his thoughts, she still made him think impure thoughts.

Pumpkins and fall foliage decorated many of the shop windows and doorways. The gold, yellow, red, and green leaves on the trees informed locals and tourists alike that Windsong did change seasons.

"Turn here." He nudged Callie to the right, down the small, bamboo-lined passageway that connected Main Street to Sea Breeze Avenue.

Callie sighed. "I haven't walked this way in forever. Where are we going?"

"It's a secret," he half whispered. Not many people knew about the garden Nova had started a few months ago. She may have mentioned it to Callie, but given Callie had only been back for a few days—and practically glued to his side during those days—he knew she hadn't seen it.

The peaceful sound of a wall-mounted fountain filled the space. Copper and bronze figurines peeked out from dark green ivy at the base of the buildings. Halfway down, Hunter opened the small iron gate that most people walked past without a second glance. With a curious smile that nearly knocked him off his feet, Callie quietly stepped through. He loved that she didn't question him further.

They followed the aged redbrick path through low-hung greenery, the vines twisted and gnarled. Spots of sunlight dotted the way until they came to a fork in the path and a courtyard where a watercolor blue sky opened above them, immediately bathing them in warmth.

To the left beckoned Marvin's glass-blowing shop, to the right, The Last Word Bookstore. But in front of them, Nova had created a garden befitting a storybook cottage. Hunter couldn't name all the flowers, but it didn't matter. The reds, yellows, pinks, and oranges were spectacular.

Like heaven's very own garden, a clear spot for the sun to shine without interference.

Callie stepped closer to the blooms, her red hair catching the light and glistening as she took in the beauty before her. "How did I not know this was here?"

"It's new."

She turned her head to meet his eyes. "Nova." A statement, not a question, because of course she'd recognize her best friend's talent.

It took him a minute to nod, her beauty short-circuiting his brain. He took in the soft sweep of her eyelashes when she blinked, the tiny parting of her full lips. The natural sparkle in the green depths of her gaze.

He hooked a finger inside the collar of his shirt

and gently tugged the cotton away from his neck.

"Is something wrong?" she asked. "Is your fever back?" She pressed the back of her hand to his forehead.

Do not say, "I'm burning for you."

"You feel a little warm."

Do not say it. Say anything else.

"Fivvergloven." What the hell? He had no idea what he'd just said, other than it sounded German. Maybe he *was* feverish. Maybe his brain had swelled from the antivenin. Maybe his great-great-grandmother hailed from Germany and her ghost had decided at this moment to pass through him.

"What?"

"Nothing. I'm okay." He stepped back and turned his attention to the garden. "This won't be a secret anymore after I mention it in my winning article."

She looked like she was about to argue—whether about his being okay or his confidence he didn't know—before bending to smell a rose and saying, "Our girl is insanely talented."

"So is her best friend."

Callie slowly straightened. "That's nice of you to say, thanks."

"Come on." He canted his head to the side. "We've got more courtyards and secret passageways to check out."

"But first, glass blowing," she said, taking the pathway toward Marvin's shop. Her article on downtown highlights wouldn't be complete without his store and workshop.

Hunter followed her lead.

He'd follow her anywhere.

CHAPTER TEN

Callie had missed her picturesque hometown with its local restaurants, fanciful shops, and enchanted feel. So much so, she hadn't given a second thought to dragging Hunter around with her, even though he was the enemy.

Okay, not enemy. Competition.

Handsome, friendly, and funny competition who said nice things and *oh my God…*

"Hey, Doc Howser, let me help you with that," Hunter said, jumping in to help the older man with an oversize shopping bag.

…he helps townspeople with packages, too.

"Thank you," the town's retired doctor said, opening the back of his car with ease now that his hands were free. "I'm glad to see you're feeling better."

No joke, Doc Howser had to be the fifth person to tell Hunter that. In their small town, not much went unnoticed, and especially not anything out of the ordinary or having to do with the beloved Owens family. Callie was convinced the saying *a little bird told me* started with Birdy some sixty years ago.

"I am." He *had* recovered quickly from the heat flash he'd suffered while looking at Nova's courtyard garden, and over the past few days he'd gotten stronger and stronger. It was probably time she started looking for an apartment.

"Good to see you, too, Callie," Doc said. She responded in kind before he drove away.

"I think I've seen enough of the town for one day." Hunter's hand brushed hers as they walked down the sidewalk. The contact teased her insides with a fleeting moment of butterflies. *It's nothing! He's just charmed more than one person today*.

From the looks on the faces of the two women walking toward them, he didn't even have to say or do anything to be charming.

"Hi, Hunter," Krysten said, a coy smile following.

"Hey, Hunter," Tracey drawled, her smile brazen. She and Krysten were partners in a successful interior decorating business. "It's really great to see you." Tracey put her hand on his arm. "We heard about what happened."

"Hello, ladies. You know Callie, right?" He itched the back of his neck.

"Of course. Hey, Callie!"

Callie said a friendly hello in return. She knew them through Brooke, and they'd always shared a kind word with one another.

"And of course, we heard that you're making Hunter's best man suit." Tracey's attention flew back to Hunter. "That's exciting news."

"It is," Hunter agreed, and an unwelcome knot lodged itself in the pit of Callie's stomach. Clearly Tracey would like to be on the short list of potential soul mates should Callie's magic touch work on Hunter's suit.

"So, it's true? You're hoping for the wedding magic to work on you?" Krysten bit her lower lip. Callie didn't know if she did that regularly, but either way, it took flirting to a level Callie had never achieved.

Hunter glanced at Callie out of the corner of his eye. For a second, she thought he might change his mind about their agreement. She looked away, not wanting him to see her own indecision and how much it bothered her all of a sudden.

She hoped he fell in love, right? Just like she hoped Kennedy's sister would after wearing her maid of honor dress.

Her thoughts strayed to her earlier conversation with Hunter and her own unsuccessful love life. Every time she fell hard, she had her heart broken. Before Trevor, it was never anything awful, like a big fight or cruelty, but more a gradual decline in attention. Forgetting about plans. Not offering her his jacket if she forgot hers. Forgetting about *her. It's not you, it's me* followed. Then a breakup.

Trevor's deception had pulled the ground out from beneath her feet. He'd fooled her, lied to her face. Humiliated and hurt, she'd never allow it to happen again. That she confessed it all to Hunter had surprised her as much as it comforted her. He was easy to talk to. And he didn't judge, which was such a relief.

Her only wish now focused on making Callie Designs the most sought-after bridesmaid dress design business on the West Coast.

"He is," Callie asserted when Hunter remained quiet. She wrapped her arm around his and bumped his side like they were best buds while working together to find him the love of his life. "Who knew Windsong's most eligible bachelor was ready to settle down? I, for one, am here for it and excited to help make it happen. The entire wedding party is going to look amazing."

"Your unique reputation is definitely growing," Tracey said.

"We're having a cocktail party at the store tomorrow night. You should come," Krysten said directly to Hunter before kindly adding, "You, too, Callie."

"Thanks, but we have plans already." Hunter rubbed his chest, then keeping her close, maneuvered them around the women. "Catch you two another time."

"Bye!" Callie called over her shoulder, not particularly liking her curiosity about *their* plans, but not hating it, either.

Hunter hurried them down a narrow side street. Strings of tiny lights hung between the buildings. A mural of the forest meeting the sea decorated one wall.

"What's your hurry? I thought you'd like to—"

"Something's wrong." He steered them onto Pine Grove Avenue, a direction opposite from where they'd parked.

With him, she quickly realized, noticing he held onto her for support, not because of their new buddy status. He scratched at his stomach, took a deep breath.

"Hunter, what is it?"

"I don't know, but Kennedy will."

Her heart pounded. "She's in her office today?" Fingers crossed she kept Saturday hours.

He nodded. Callie told herself everything would be okay as she kept pace with his long strides. At least he walked like he felt well. There were two people in the waiting room when they entered. She took a seat by the window while Hunter checked in at the front desk.

The pretty front office person—"Becca" was stitched in the top left corner of her scrubs—gave her full attention to Hunter. Rather than watch yet another female adore him, Callie turned her attention out the glass and to the tree-lined street.

And there it was.

An absolutely adorable cottage with a…could it be? A *For Sale* sign on the small patch of overgrown grass.

She jumped to her feet, eager to check it out, and bumped right into Hunter as she turned away from the window. "Sorry!"

"S'okay. Kennedy is going to squeeze me in right now. Will you come with me?"

"Oh, uh, sure." His weak smile made her forget all about her dream cottage. She didn't like that this morning he'd been laughing and flexing his muscles, and now he looked sick again.

Inside the exam room, he sat on the table and she took the chair. He scratched his neck, then his arm. Red blotches marred his skin.

Kennedy came in wearing scrubs with medical cartoon dogs all over them. Hunter greeted her with a sheepish, "Hi, Dr. Conway."

"Don't Dr. Conway me, Mr. Owens. You're not feeling well?" She scanned his body, then added, "Let's have you take off your shirt, please."

He grinned as he reached one hand over his shoulder. "I knew you'd tell me that one day."

Kennedy rolled her eyes. "You must not be feeling *that* bad."

"I won't tell Mav if you don't tell Mav," he continued to tease. With a slightly jerky motion, he pulled the shirt over his head and placed it beside him.

And oh my. His bare chest looked a lot different than it had the other day. Hunter's eyes moved to hers, so she did her best not to appear alarmed.

Kennedy didn't say a word about the rash all over his body. She put her stethoscope to his chest and listened to him breathe. She looked in his mouth and ears. Took his temperature. All the while, his baby blues stayed on Callie.

"Are you having any muscle or joint pain?" Kennedy asked.

"Yes." He broke eye contact, noticing for the first time that redness and spots covered his torso and arms. "Jesus, what is happening to me? Besides the obvious."

"You've got serum sickness."

"Is that bad?" Callie asked, hoping she didn't sound too alarmed.

"It's a delayed reaction to receiving the antivenin. The good news is your lungs are clear."

"And the bad news?" Hunter asked.

Kennedy put her hands on the sides of his neck and gently felt around. "Your lymph nodes are a little swollen and you have a fever. Both are normal," Kennedy assured, "and should go away within a few weeks."

Hunter itched his arm. "*Weeks?* And the itching?"

"Same. Continue with the medications and cream you're already using. In addition, I'm going to prescribe a corticosteroid to help with the inflammation. You're not contagious, but I would like you back in bed resting until your fever is gone. Callie, you'll make sure he's a good patient?"

"Yes."

"Any questions?" Kennedy handed him his T-shirt.

"I'm still not dying, right?" Hunter asked, pulling his shirt on. He sounded so sincere and sweet that Callie wanted to give him a hug.

"No, you're not dying." Kennedy gave him a sisterly look of love. "But you know where I am if you need me."

"Thanks, Ned." His using Kennedy's nickname turned Callie's insides to mush.

"You're welcome. How about I take Rebel for a ride for you tomorrow?"

"That'd be great." Hunter slid off the exam table to stand, disappointment weighing down his posture. He clearly missed riding his horse. He'd been out to the barn the past two days to talk to her while Callie did some sewing. When he got back to the bunkhouse, he'd tell her about their discussions, making her smile despite her uncomfortable feelings toward the animal.

Making her feel things for Hunter she didn't want to feel. Like affection. Admiration.

Tender emotions she couldn't afford to have if she had any hope of walking away unscathed.

CHAPTER ELEVEN

On the sidewalk outside the office, Callie paused to write down the phone number for the sale property. Hunter looked from her to the cottage and back to her. "You interested in that place?"

"I'm not sure I can afford it, but I'm curious, yes. I want to open a store, and it looks like it might be the perfect place." Her grandmother had left her a nice inheritance with a note to use it for a life-changing purchase only. This seemed like it could be that.

"Come on." Hunter started to cross the street.

"Wait. We need to get you home. I can come back for a closer look later." She followed a step behind him.

"Closer look? I'm taking you inside."

"We're not breaking in."

"That you would think that wounds me." He brought his palm to his chest for the second time today.

She jogged around him, ashamed of herself for implying anything unkind. She stopped him with a hand up in front of his chest. "I didn't mean it like that. Do you have a key?"

"No."

"Then how—"

"It looks like there's someone inside." He raised his eyebrows. *Now what do you say?*

"Oh. Well, what are we waiting for, then?" She

spun around and marched to the front door. She felt his eyes on her backside and for some inexplicable reason added a little sway to her hips.

Before she could knock, someone opened the door. "Hello," a well-dressed forty-something woman said. "Can I help you?" The woman's eyes slid to Hunter as he arrived at the doorstep beside Callie. "Hunter Owens, is that you?"

"It is. Hi, Mrs. Chapman."

"How are you…" Mrs. Chapman didn't stop talking for a solid thirty seconds, mostly because she talked about her daughter, Addison, and how she and Hunter should get together when Addison visited next. When Hunter was finally able to get a word in, he introduced Callie.

"You're the good-luck-charm dressmaker! It's a pleasure to meet you." She gave a firm handshake.

"You, too," Callie said around a smile. "We—I was wondering if this cottage is still available?"

"It is. But most likely not for long. I've had several interested inquiries. Come in, come in." Mrs. Chapman waved them over the threshold. "The owner lives in Hawaii, and I manage the property for him. Please look around and let me know if I can answer any questions."

"Thank you." Hunter hung back while Callie walked through the cottage. The space was large enough for her to set up a work area, have a dressing room, and display some of her designs. The hardwood floor had seen better days, but a few rugs could help with that. The walls were white and looked recently painted. Crown molding added warmth and sophistication.

At the back, French doors opened to living quarters with a modest kitchen and bathroom. She loved it. All of it.

"I'm very interested," she told Mrs. Chapman as she rejoined the realtor and Hunter.

"Wonderful. Here's my card. You can go to my website for all the information on the cottage and click the link to get started on the application process if you want to proceed. I should warn you, though: one other party in particular is very interested as well."

Callie put the card in her pocket, worried about the other interested person but telling herself if it was meant to be, it would be. Fate, and all that.

The three of them left together, parting ways on the sidewalk. "Scale of one to ten, how badly do you want that place?" Hunter asked.

"Nine. But it's the first place I've looked at, so maybe I shouldn't rush into it."

"What's your gut say?"

She thought about it for a minute. "To at least try. I had a good feeling being there."

"I have a feeling your gut is rarely wrong."

"What makes you say that?" Her gut had definitely screwed her over where men were concerned. Good thing she'd written them off.

"My instincts." He pulled her to his side so she'd avoid stepping on a piece of pink bubblegum stuck on the sidewalk.

She laughed. "Thanks for the save and one-upping me with your talent for hunches. Should we go buy a lottery ticket? It might be the only way I'm able to afford the purchase."

"Not one-upping. I have confidence in you."

His sweet words were going to be the death of her.

"Besides, Mrs. Chapman will go to bat for you."

They turned the corner, walking in the direction of the car. "She will?"

"Here's my theory. If you get the cottage, then she can lay claim to helping find the perfect spot for Callie's Designs. And if I have dinner with Addison when she comes to town, then wear the best man suit you design, it's a six-degrees-of-separation type thing where Mrs. Chapman will get some bragging rights about the situation, whether it's Addy I end up with or someone else."

"That's some interesting and confusing logic." It made her belief in kismet sound much more reasonable.

He shrugged.

"Addy, huh?" It pained her to think about him being with someone, yet that's exactly what she was counting on to increase her business.

He tossed her one of his mischievous smiles. "We're friends and nothing more. She's got a girlfriend."

Callie's mouth eased into an *O* shape.

"I'm pretty sure Mrs. Chapman knows, but that hasn't stopped her. So bottom line, lottery ticket or not, you should at least try. What have you got to lose?"

"You're right."

"Usually am," he teased.

She gave him her best eye roll. "The cottage really was a nice surprise."

Hunter's hand brushed hers, his skin hot to the touch. He said something under his breath that sounded like, "You're a nice surprise."

It had to be the fever talking—which she felt terrible about. She needed to get him home and tuck them into bed immediately.

Him.

Tuck *him.* There was no them. Not like that.

CHAPTER TWELVE

"You still awake?" Hunter asked from the comfort of his bed. He and Callie had said good night a while ago, but a tiny glow of light from her area of the bunkhouse clued him in to her wakefulness.

"Just one more chapter," she said softly.

So, she was reading. He'd noticed a romance novel on the couch when she grabbed a shower earlier and he'd read the back cover copy. "Has Archer won back Bridget yet?"

In the silence, Hunter pictured her brows creasing as she wondered how much of the book he'd peeked at. "Not yet. Would you like to read it when I'm done?"

Good comeback. "That's okay, but if you want to tell me about the sexy parts, go right ahead." He put his hands behind his head, hoping she'd take the bait even though he knew she probably wouldn't.

Dirty talk from Callie would cure all his ailments and kill him at the same time.

"You'd like that, wouldn't you?" Her frisky tone of voice also had the potential to kill him. *Huh.* They should talk in the dark more often.

"I'd love it," he fired back. When she didn't respond right away, he added, "But maybe we should get to know each other better first."

He couldn't explain how he knew, but he sensed her smiling. When she didn't say anything, he took the initiative. "I'll go first. My middle name is

Calrissian. My dad won a bet with my mom so he got to name me after one of his favorite Star Wars characters."

"I didn't know that. Mine is Chanelle, named after my grandmother on my dad's side."

"It's a beautiful name."

"Thanks. She passed away when I was seventeen."

"Do you ever feel like she's with you?" He believed in ghosts and spirits, having seen his fair share of unusual shadows out of the corner of his eye or discovering things moved around in the barn that nobody owned up to. He liked to think it was his great-great-grandmother keeping an eye on all of them. The one who may be German.

"So weird you should ask that, because yes, I do. Every once in a while, I feel like someone is with me and pushing me in a certain direction, and I think it's her. She was a seamstress, too, and did alterations on wedding gowns. She also believed in magic."

"It's definitely her, then. And she'd be really proud of you."

In the quiet of the bunkhouse, he heard her sigh. He didn't give false compliments and always meant everything he said. God, he wished she were close enough to touch. To run his fingers through her hair. To press his lips to hers and learn how she liked to be kissed. *Stop going there, Hunter.*

"What's your least favorite food?" she asked, roping them back into superficial territory.

"Don't have one. I pretty much like everything. If it's put in front of me, I'll eat it. Yours?"

"Peppers. I don't even like them on my plate."

"Peppers everywhere are mourning the pleasure of your mouth." Jesus, did he just say that? Apparently, he still bumbled his words around her. "Do you want to go back to Africa some day?" he rushed to ask, the question the first thing to pop into his head. "Or someplace else?"

"If given the opportunity, I'd love to. I know Maverick loves to travel; do you?" she asked.

"It's not in my blood like it is in his, but seeing other parts of the world would be great. Especially with the right person."

"Well, she could be just around the wedding corner."

"I've no doubt." With Callie's magic touch and Bella's phone number in his phone, he was out of the gate. Kennedy's medical assistant had been sweet to text him to see how he was feeling, and they'd struck up a conversation that ended with some flirting. Plus... "I refuse to be the first person to break your streak."

"So, you're a 'take one for the team' kind of guy."

"Yeah." For her, he'd do anything. "Growing up, I took one numerous times for my brothers to get them out of trouble. Being the baby boy, my parents allowed me to get away with more than they'd ever allowed Cole or Maverick. And being that I always wanted my brothers to think I was cool, I didn't mind."

"Not to mention the times you bailed Nova out of trouble."

"That was different. I'll protect her until my last breath."

"She's lucky to have you."

You could have me, too.

"All three of you," Callie continued. "My sister looked out for me in her own way, but she never took any blame for me, that's for sure. Okay, important question, would you wait for me to watch the next episode of a TV show we started together?"

He loved that she said, "me" and "we." "How long do I have to wait?"

"That's irrelevant. It's a show we both love."

"Then it's a no-brainer. Of course I would wait. It sounds like you're asking from experience. Who is he and what streaming service do I need to hack into and cancel?"

She laughed. He rolled to his side so he faced her direction and wished he could see through the barn door. Her reading light, still on, gave a tiny bit of illumination.

"Sadly, it's happened more than once."

"Those guys were boneheads."

"Selfish boneheads," she amended.

"Dumbass selfish boneheads," he continued on her behalf. He hated that those guys had helped build the wall around her heart.

She turned off the light, and the sound of rustling met his ears. "Who was your first kiss?" she asked curiously.

Now they were talking. For the first time ever, she was asking an intimate question. "Natalie Shoemaker. We were thirteen, and as far as first kisses go, it was good."

Callie let out a breath like she'd been holding it. "She was best friends with Brooke."

"You sound relieved. Did you think because we

were in the same grade it was your sister?" He rolled over onto his back as he tried not to laugh. He and Brooke never clicked, even as friends.

"Maybe."

"The first time I met your sister was when the two of you came to the ranch for a riding lesson. By then, I'd kissed a few girls." None he'd wanted to kiss more than Callie at first sight. "Who was yours?"

"Ashton Weeks. I was older than you were."

"How old?"

"Seventeen, almost eighteen."

"You dated him for a while, right?" he asked nonchalantly. In reality, he'd called the guy Asston Reeks (not to his face, of course) because he hated the guy on the spot. He'd really hated the guy when he'd failed to attend Nova and Callie's graduation party and he'd seen how upset it made Callie. Come to think of it, her parents had failed to attend that night, too, so that probably played into her sadness as well.

"Right." She yawned, the sound easy to decipher in the warm, quiet confines of his home.

"Last question," he said. "If you knew the world was going to end in a week, what would you do?"

"I don't know."

"Come on. You have to pick something."

"Be with my family and friends. Sail to Catalina. And sew something outrageous to wear to Disneyland."

"For someone who didn't know a second ago, those are pretty specific. I like it."

"Now it's your turn."

He'd confess to her about his long-time crush.

"I'd be with my family for sure. Ride Rebel repeatedly. And eat burgers and fries for breakfast, lunch, and dinner."

"*Mmm*. I could do that, too."

"Let's do it tomorrow," he suggested.

"I think that could be arranged. As long as you feel up to it."

She had a point, given he'd not been hungry at all this evening. He'd only downed a small cup of chicken noodle soup to follow the "take with food" instructions on his medication. Given the chance to spend more time with her, though? He'd be up for it, no matter how he felt.

CHAPTER THIRTEEN

The next night, Callie snuggled into the couch under a blanket, her book and reading light put away, but her body—and mind—not ready for sleep. "You still awake?" she said into the quiet. Once asleep, Hunter slept like the dead, so she wasn't worried about her question waking him up.

Disappointment flooded her when he didn't answer. Last night had been…

"I am," he finally said. "Sorry, I was doing a calculation in my head. I need to order feed tomorrow and we're helping another ranch, so it's not the usual order. You having trouble falling asleep?"

Hearing about him help others and then insinuating he'd like to help her fall asleep were a killer combination. If she were anyone else, she'd be crushing on him by now.

"I'm anxious to hear back from Mrs. Chapman about the cottage." Callie crossed her fingers under her pillow. She couldn't afford to buy the building so asked if she could rent it with an option to buy after six months. She'd come up with a generous rental fee and hoped the owner agreed. Was she worried six months gave her enough time? Yes. But nothing motivated her more than a deadline.

With some more luck, her dressmaking business would soon take off. She had a feeling Hunter's future engagement was the key.

"When will you know?"

"This week, I hope."

"I have a good feeling about it," he assured her. "How are things going with Archer and Bridget?"

Her pulse skittered. Did he want her to tell him about the dirty parts? She'd thought about their conversation from last night all day and earlier swore Hunter had undressed her with his eyes. His deep, sexy voice seemed to do the same right now. Was he picturing them exploring each other's naked bodies?

The man could no better stop flirting than he could stop breathing.

She wanted to be furious with him for breaking their rule, but that would make her a hypocrite because he had her most intimate parts tingling, her mind thinking about the sinful positions they could get into together. In the darkness, inside this small, warm space he'd turned into a home, her body reacted to him whether she liked it or not.

"She's mad at him." And lusted after him. Pretty much exactly how Callie felt at the moment. Somewhere between a BW bite, the ambassador competition, and designing his best man suit, Hunter had piqued her interest without her approval.

"And what did Archer do?"

"He made a bet with her and won."

"I think I'm going to leave that alone and ask if you're available for dinner tomorrow night. My dad will be back from his trip, everyone from the wedding this weekend will be checked out, and my mom is planning to have the whole family over."

"Actually, Nova already invited me."

"Oh, cool. You'll be there, then."

There it was. The boyish, slightly awkward manner that had dictated the majority of their interactions over the years. *That* behavior she knew how to handle. The trouble was, she no longer wanted to respond with quiet disregard. She'd rather flirt, laugh, get to know him better. She'd rather replay the inappropriate thoughts in her head than neglect them.

She blamed his very nice butt. She couldn't unsee it!

She'd miss this when she left the bunkhouse. Miss feeling this unanticipated camaraderie with her best friend's brother. Hunter Owens's companionship had turned out to be a nice two-way exchange of support.

His bed creaked as she heard him shift, then groan.

"You okay?"

"Yeah, it's just a cramp in my calf. It'll pass." He'd suffered joint pain earlier, reminding her he had more healing to do.

Several quiet seconds passed where she debated getting up to massage his leg for him. Instead, to get his mind off the muscle spasm, she said, "If you could no longer see, what's the one thing you'd picture all the time so you never forgot it?"

"Did you ask yourself that after your accident?" Care and sincerity made the question easier to answer.

She nodded even though he couldn't see her. She'd asked herself the question dozens of times. "I still do. Those few weeks were the worst of my life, and to this day I ask myself that question to make sure I commit important things to memory. Not just how they look, but how they smell and make me feel."

"It's impossible to pick just one thing, then."

"I guess it is."

"Have you ever thought about riding a horse again?"

"No." She knew it had been a fluke accident, but she couldn't even look at a horse without fear.

"Because you're afraid of it happening again?"

When she didn't answer right away, he continued. "If you ever want to start slow, let me know. I could take you to Rebel's stall and you could feed her a carrot. Pet her. There's also George, who is friendlier than you can imagine, closer to the ground, and very gentle with new riders."

Tears pricked her eyes. She hated that fear still gripped her, and for the first time since that awful day, a tiny part of her wondered if she could do it. Hunter's kind voice and knowledge of horses were hard to ignore… But he'd been there that day. He'd seen her damaged body and terror.

She wiped the corner of her eye; humiliation once again overpowered every other emotion. She hated that he'd witnessed her embarrassment. Her weakest moment.

"I fell off a horse once," he said into the stillness. "I was Jenna's age and too cocky for my own good."

The invisible weight pressing Callie into the couch lessened just a little.

"I landed hard enough to break a finger and give myself a black eye. To this day, I can't properly flip anyone off with my left hand."

She laughed.

"It's not the same thing, I know, but you're not alone, Triple C."

"Triple C?"

"Callie Chanelle Carmichael. I can't have you contemplating riding without a nickname. It's sacrilegious. Now quit talking, would you? I need to get some sleep."

No one had ever called her anything but Callie or Cal, which apparently didn't count as an appropriate nickname. Once again, Mr. Fab Ass—his nickname in her head—caught her off guard in a really nice way.

She smothered a smile into her pillow before whispering, "Good night, Hunter Calrissian Owens."

CHAPTER FOURTEEN

Dinner with the Owens family equaled a loud, boisterous, and joyful time. Fall flowers, white and
orange baby pumpkins, and dark, jewel-toned throw
blankets decorated the inn's dining and living rooms
where they'd gathered to eat. Mary Rose had added
a leaf to the table so they could all squeeze around
it. Callie sat between Nova and Kennedy. The sun
had long ago set, and Jenna, seated next to her uncle
Hunter, currently captivated the room.

"We're going to be bank robbers," Jenna said.
"Me, Mommy, and Daddy are going to wear black
pants, a black-and-white-striped shirt, a black bean-
ie, black gloves, and a black eye mask. My
trick-or-treat bag is going to be the *giant* bag of
money only it will have candy inside it. Rumi is going to dress up, too, as a police dog."

Upon hearing her name, Rumi barked from underneath the table where she'd been quietly sitting.

"What about Gia?" Maverick asked.

Jenna shrugged and made an I-don't-know-and-I-
don't-care face.

"How about I babysit her while you three trick-
or-treat?" Hunter suggested. "Are you guys still
going to be here?" he asked Bethany's mom and
sister.

"I think so," Bethany's mom said.

"You can trick-or-treat, too, then."

Jenna whispered something in his ear. He

whispered something back. Jenna whispered again. Cole cleared his throat. "Jenna, it's not polite to tell secrets at the table," he said.

"Sorry, Daddy. Me and Uncle Hunt are plotting."

"What are you plotting?" Mary Rose asked with grandmotherly curiosity.

"I guess the cat's out of the bag, Uncle Hunt."

Hunter—and everyone else around the table by Callie's calculations—tried not to smile too hard at Jenna's matter-of-fact tone and almost on-target colloquialism.

"Technically it's not yet," Hunter said. "But it will be once you share with everyone." His eyes landed on Callie's from across the table. She couldn't look away, a sparkle in those blue depths of his full of appreciation and joy.

"Me and Uncle Hunt are going to dress up Rebel for Halloween! It was my idea, and he said it was great." She glanced around the table with a huge grin on her face. "Callie is going to help us!"

From afar. She planned to help them from afar. She didn't have to get close to the animal to sew what Jenna had in mind.

"What's she going to be?" Nova asked.

"A superhero. She's going to have a purple cape and a sparkly purple eye mask that won't hurt her eyes. And guess what her superpower is?" Jenna bounced in her chair. "She can run faster than any other land animal and find buried treasure by sniffing it out with her nose."

"That sounds terrific," Bethany said. "Thanks for sharing with us, sweetie."

"You're welcome." She forked a piece of potato

on her plate and ran it through the gravy from the pot roast before popping it in her mouth.

"You know," John said, addressing his granddaughter, "there's buried treasure here somewhere on the ranch."

Jenna's eyes and mouth widened like saucers.

"*Supposedly*," Mary Rose amended.

"You never told us that," Maverick said.

John and Mary Rose exchanged a look. "If we'd told you as kids, you would have searched and searched and driven us crazy," John said lightheartedly.

"If there's one thing you all have in common, it's determination." Mary Rose squeezed Cole's hand, the closest seated child.

"What's the story?" Cole asked.

"The story goes that back in the late 1800s, just before my grandfather bought the land, a Mexican ranchero sold off his cattle and received payment in silver," John said, "The ranchero didn't trust banks or anyone else, so he buried the six chests of silver he received. He drew a chart with the spot where the treasure was so he could return for it one day. Then wanting a better life he believed he could have in a new settlement, he gathered his dependents and vaqueros—"

"What's a vaquero?" Jenna asked.

"A cowboy," John said with a wink.

Everyone remained riveted on John, the room so quiet you could hear the antique wall clock in the next room ticking. Even Gia, who had been a bit fussy, had quieted. John's rich and compassionate voice soothed as much as it informed.

"He gathered his dependents and vaqueros and headed north, but before they'd gone very far, they were attacked by bandits. The ranchero fell from his horse and was badly wounded and left for dead while the others in his party were rerouted."

Callie lifted her gaze from a small stain on the tablecloth and found Hunter's attention on her. She slowly blinked at him—a *yes, I heard the part about falling off a horse, but I'm okay* blink.

"He laid by the side of the road helpless for two days before a priest found him. The ranchero was delirious and dehydrated and told the priest about the buried treasure, but he didn't have the chart on him and he couldn't describe the location with any accuracy. Just before he died, though, he woke with a small degree of intelligence and tried to tell the priest where the chests were buried. The priest, believing the ranchero to be feverish and incoherent, didn't think much of it. Still, he made a casual search of the land but didn't find any trace of the silver."

"Where do you think the treasure map is, Papa?" Jenna asked.

"No one knows. Most people today believe the story is nothing more than a rumor."

"What do you believe?" Hunter asked.

"It's fun to think there might be buried treasure on the property, but if it were true, I think my grandfather would have found it."

"Maybe Rebel will find it!" Jenna said.

"Maybe," John agreed.

Multiple conversations took place after that. Every few minutes Callie caught Hunter looking at her again, giving her a different face each time—silly, happy, contemplative. And each time she softened toward him more.

He wasn't at all what she expected, each layer he shared another reason to fall under his charms.

After everyone had finished eating, the guys cleared the table and brought dessert out. Fresh baked pumpkin and apple pies that smelled divine, along with vanilla ice cream and Mary Rose's famous hot chocolate.

"What's going on with you and my brother?" Nova asked under her breath, a hint of delight dusting her words.

"We've become friends. Good friends, I guess."

"You know, he's had a crush on you forever."

"*What?* No, he hasn't. He's always acted weird around me."

"Because he was tongue-tied."

"You're being ridiculous. How many glasses of wine did you have?" She took a sip of her hot chocolate to ease the growing lump in the back of her throat.

"One. And why is it ridiculous? You're a catch."

"Your brother is just a friend. We wouldn't even be in each other's orbit if not for my helping to keep an eye on him."

"You're in my orbit and my family's, Cal, which means you've always been in his." Nova eyed her more closely. "He's turned on the charm, hasn't he?"

Nova was more than a best friend, she was a sister, and Callie had never lied to her. "He has, yes, but nothing is coming of it."

"Why not?"

"You really think that's a good idea?"

"I think Trevor hurt you. And guys before him, too, and you deserve to be with someone you can trust."

Callie threw her head back and laughed. "No offense, but I can trust him to leave, just like everyone else, and that's about it. Besides, after Kennedy and Maverick's wedding, I need him to find the woman he's going to marry, and you know I have no plans to do that."

"I respect your choice, I do, but I also think you're too young to decide you never want to get married. Not that I'm implying you and my brother—"

"Why are we talking about this now?"

"Because it's clear there's *something* going on between you two." She bumped Callie's shoulder with hers. "I'll drop it if that's what you want."

"Please." Had anyone else noticed this new awareness between her and Hunter? She hoped not.

Though if they had, so what? Everyone knew he was a flirt. Add in his feverish state for most of the time they'd spent together and the *something* could be easily dismissed.

To be sure, though, maybe she needed to try matching him with someone before the wedding. Help fate along, as it were...

"Hey," the man himself said, sliding into the chair vacated by Kennedy. Eyes tired. Forehead creased. Shoulders slumped. "Sorry to interrupt, but I'm going to head home now."

Without a second thought, she put a hand on his arm. "I'll go with you." Seemed like he needed some TLC right now.

"No, you should stay."

Nova slung an arm around Callie's shoulders. "Yes, stay. We can talk more and spike our next hot chocolate."

"Raincheck?" Callie said to Nova, needing zero time to think about the right thing to do. What she *wanted* to do. It didn't make sense. She loved spending time with Nova over anyone else, and yet she couldn't fight the pull to go with Hunter. "I think I should go with Hunt."

"Of course." Nova pressed her lips together, obviously trying not to smile. "*Hunt* still needs looking after."

Oops. The simple act of shortening his name — which many people did — was new for her and her best friend obviously thought it noteworthy.

Callie rolled her eyes, then turned to face Hunter. "Let's go."

"Only if you're sure."

She pushed her chair back to stand. "I am."

They thanked Mary Rose for dinner and said their goodbyes. Callie bundled inside her winter coat for the short walk back to the bunkhouse. Stars sparkled in the pitch-black sky. The cold, crisp air felt nice on her cheeks.

Hunter picked up her hand. "Thanks, Callie."

Shocked with the handholding, she stiffened and almost came to an abrupt stop. Was he going to let go? Keep hold for the entire walk? Her hand fit nicely against his, and she thought to run her thumb over his knuckles, explore further. His slightly callused and warm skin sent a tingle up her arm.

Okay, many tingles. It was disturbing.

And interesting.

He squeezed her hand. "I don't think I've said that enough." His grip lightened. She readied herself for him to let go. In three, two...

"Uncle Hunt! Callie!" Jenna shouted from behind.

Callie pulled free of his hand so fast she almost dislocated her shoulder. The two of them spun around.

"Hey, pipsqueak. What's up?" Hunter asked.

"Can I have a sleepover with you?" She steepled her palms together and placed them under her uplifted chin.

"Don't you have school tomorrow?"

"Yes, but it's conference week so the schedule is different. I promise I will pop right out of bed and won't be any trouble." She batted her eyelashes. "Pretty please?"

Hunter bent to eye level with his adorable niece. In Callie's head, she'd already said *yes*. Mostly because she needed some space from Hunter. They'd grown too close, too fast, and Jenna provided the perfect distraction.

"What did your mom and dad say?"

Jenna dropped her arms. "That I could if it's okay with you. I really need this, Uncle Hunt. Gia cries *all* the time at night. My brain is suffering from lack of sleep."

"Well, we can't have that. Hop on." He shared a quick, amused look with Callie before he canted his head for Jenna to hop onto his back for a piggyback ride. The young girl's shenanigans were too cute for words.

"Yay!" She jumped onto his back, a brief wince crossing Hunter's face.

Callie never doubted he'd say yes. He'd say yes no matter how much discomfort he was in. Jenna had him wrapped around her finger.

The moment they stepped inside the bunkhouse, Jenna slid to her feet. She immediately walked over to the bolts of fabric leaning against the wall to feel the material.

Hunter continued to his bedroom. "Come on, let's get your pajamas." He opened the bottom drawer of his dresser and pulled out a pair of pale-yellow jammies.

Jenna glanced over at Callie. "I have a drawer at Uncle Maverick's house, too. And at Nana and Papa's. I'm welcome everywhere." She skipped to her uncle, took the clothing, and darted into the bathroom.

"Make sure to brush your teeth," Hunter called out.

She poked her head out. "Duh."

He sat on the edge of his bed, phone in hand, texting. "Just letting Cole and Bethany know we're home and we've got Jenna."

Callie didn't know what to do with herself. She watched Hunter, watched for Jenna to come out, then finally removed her coat. Hunter looked up, his focus landing on her mouth, then dipping lower, taking in the curves underneath her sweater dress with undisguised interest.

She quickly spun around and moved out of eyesight. (Thank you, sliding barn door.) Sitting on the couch, she tossed her coat to the side and took off her boots. "We agreed no flirting," she said.

"When did I flirt?" he asked.

"Just now."

"I didn't say anything."

"You didn't have to. Your eyes did the talking." She leaned back and closed hers.

"Really? What did they say?" His come-hither timbre did not help matters. And the thing was, he didn't even realize how sexy he was no matter what he did.

"What do you think they said?" Rather than shut him up, she wanted to hear him talk more. She didn't know what was happening to her.

"If I told you…"

Her head snapped to the left where he stood leaning against the barn door, one jean-clad leg crossed over the other. His arms were over his chest, casually showing off his muscular biceps beneath his long-sleeve Henley.

"All done!" Jenna called out. She popped up next to Hunter a second later. "Wanna play cards?"

Eight-year-olds had perfect timing.

Three games of Go Fish later, Jenna lay tucked in bed next to her uncle and Callie was conked out under a blanket on the couch, her eyelids heavy with exhaustion. Just before she fell asleep, she heard a soft, "Good night, Triple C."

Needless to say, she dreamed about one very hot, confusing cowboy.

CHAPTER FIFTEEN

"You made me a Damn Aussie pie?" Hunter asked, confused by the name of the delicious-looking baked good Bella handed him on his doorstep. Her unexpected visit was just what the doctor ordered. Literally, so to speak, since Kennedy had no doubt prompted Bella's visit. Hunter had promised himself to have an open mind where the cute medical assistant was concerned.

She laughed. "No, but that's funny. I said Banoffee. Baaan-off-eee. It's a combination of bananas and toffee."

He nodded. "That makes much more sense. Thank you."

"You're welcome. I hope you don't mind me stopping by on my lunch break. Kennedy mentioned you'd be home."

Yep. What the doctor ordered. *Hunter, you smart devil, you.* "Not at all. Want to sit?" He gestured toward the cushioned armchairs.

"I'd love to." She wore a puffy jacket over her scrubs so she should be okay in the cool afternoon air.

"Great. I'll go grab two forks and be right back." He returned half a minute later. "It's a perfect day to have pie for lunch." The smell alone had his tastebuds singing. He didn't bother with plates, figuring they'd share right from the plate. Bella seemed to like the idea, her eyes sparkling when he handed her a fork and nothing else.

"It's not my first time," she said.

"Not mine, either. I've never had baaan-off-eee pie before, though. Did I mention it looks and smells great?" He dug his fork in at the same time she did.

"I'm glad you think so. It's my favorite thing to bake."

He moaned as his first bite tasted better than anything he'd had in a long time. Except for the sandwich Callie had made him. And the Pop-Tart she'd warmed up. "You could weaponize this and end hate in the world." The flirty compliment helped remind him he was moving on from Callie and on a mission to find love *and* help her business thrive at the same time.

"You think?" she said around a smile.

"If anyone who eats this isn't immediately full of happiness, then they're not human. How come I've never heard of this pie before?"

"It's popular in London, not here."

"Is that where you're originally from?" Every now and then, he detected a faint British accent from her. He liked it. Not as much as he liked Callie's voice, but— *Dude, can you stop thinking about Callie for one second?*

Bella leaned back in her chair, content to let him keep eating without her. He appreciated her kindness considering she had made the dish especially for him. "I am. Moved to the States when I was seven, but we often go back to visit family."

"'We' being your parents?"

"My mum and brother. They live in San Francisco."

He set the pie on his lap, thinking he'd save the rest for later to share with Callie. "How did you end up in Windsong?"

"Funny story. I was driving to Santa Barbara to visit my roommate from college when I saw the sign for Windsong. I thought it sounded like a town I'd like to visit, so I took a little detour. I was in the bookstore when I met Kennedy and we struck up a conversation. And longer story short, here I am." She spoke with her hands and dropped them in her lap when finished.

He was interested in the longer story but let it go. "Kennedy sings your praises."

"She does the same for you. How are you feeling, by the way?"

"Better, thanks to your pie." He hadn't meant for that to sound flirty, but the blush filling her cheeks told a different story. "And the company," he added with sincerity. "Callie's been keeping a good eye on me, too."

"I heard that. She's the woman who was with you when you came in the other day?"

"That's her."

"Are you two…?"

"No." He shook his head. That wish would remain just that. Thinking it and feeling it were two different things, though, and no matter how much Bella presented the perfect opportunity to move on, he couldn't make himself go there. *Yet.*

Restless silence passed between them.

"Have you ever done a corn maze?" he asked, determined to end this impromptu visit on a good note.

"I haven't, no."

"A group of us is planning to go. They do one at the Brand ranch every year. Would you like to join us?"

"I'd love to."

"Great. It's a date." He ignored the sour feeling in his stomach from the word "date" and took another bite of pie.

• • •

All Vivian Fisher wanted to know about was the best man suit, and it pissed Hunter off—not because he minded talking about it, but because she'd lured him to this interview under the pretext of discussing the ambassador competition.

"You're saying you believe in Callie Carmichael's luck with wedding party attire?" the reporter from the *Windsong Gazette* asked.

He believed in Callie. "Yes."

"The single women of Windsong are already lining up given your reputation as the town's most eligible bachelor."

"I haven't noticed." He had, but he didn't need to feed into his least-favorite status in town.

Miss Fisher leaned back in her chair with her brown eyes narrowed like she didn't believe him. They were sitting by the window in Baked on Main, the only good thing about this scenario the smell of Claudia's baked goods and the two glazed donuts he'd scarfed down to settle his nerves. The *Gazette* liked to embellish, and he didn't like his love life exaggerated.

"Modesty makes you more appealing, Hunter."

He shrugged.

"I did some digging, and Callie's track record with maid of honor dresses is interesting, to say the least. Does being the first best man to wear her clothes add any pressure?"

"Some I suppose." He wanted the best for her, no matter what.

"I imagine it's going to take a special girl to date you after the wedding, what with all eyes on the relationship."

His stomach roiled. He did want a relationship, but the thought of truly moving on from Callie hurt. "I thought this interview was about me and the ambassador position?" He felt bad about his gruff tone the second after the question left his mouth.

"You're right. I'm sorry. Why is the ambassador position so important to you?"

"Because I love this town." And being ambassador would give him the respect he craved. It would allow him to serve his hometown with distinction and seriousness. "I want to make a difference and be looked at differently."

"All the finalists love the town. What sets you apart?"

He thought about that. "I'm a fourth-generation Windsonger, and I think that qualifies me to speak about the past as well as the future. I want to keep our town's unique and interesting attributes alive and well. And I embody small town pride and values."

She smiled. He'd never met her before today, a recent transplant from Los Angeles, she'd told him.

Around his age, he guessed. A glint in her eye that told him she wasn't all business. He also had to admit her smile was friendlier than he'd given her credit for earlier.

"The ambassador is expected to represent Windsong in an unbiased manner and not use the position to advance their own endeavors. You recently started a boot camp?"

"That's correct." He wasn't about to justify her rude remark with anything but a positive response. She was just doing her job. "We're planning to offer free weeklong camps to underprivileged kids soon. You're welcome to come see what that's about when we do."

He meant it. Kids brought out the best in everyone and bonus points if she decided to write about it.

"Thank you. I just might." She leaned forward, her elbows on the small, round table. "Aside from the boot camp, you help your family run the ranch and inn. It's impressive moving from cattle to one of the most premier guest houses on the West Coast."

"I'll pass along the compliment."

"What do you do just for you?"

He blinked.

She chuckled at his blank expression. "I've met your type a few times. You work hard. Put others first and are loyal to a fault. Am I right?"

"I ride my horse," he countered, not sure he liked that she'd pegged him so well.

"I should have guessed that. What's his or her name?"

"Her name is Rebel. You ever ride?"

"Are you asking me to go riding with you?"

In his periphery, someone bumped into the table next to them before taking a seat. The flash of red hair told him who it was. She also made his pulse speed up. "Hi, Hunt," his sister said, sitting across from Callie at the other table.

"Hey, Nova. Hey, Callie." Callie smiled back in acknowledgment. "This is Vivian Fisher." He gestured toward his tablemate. "She's a reporter with the *Gazette* doing a piece on the ambassadorship."

"Callie Carmichael?" she asked.

Callie turned to look at Vivian. "Yes."

Vivian sat taller. "This is great. Do you mind if I ask you a question or two? I'm so intrigued by your dressmaking business and reputation. You're also in the ambassador running, correct?"

For a split second, Callie's eyes met his. They'd talked this morning about their friendly rivalry and their next assignments. Even gave each other a high five for luck. He flexed his hand underneath the table, remembering the feel of her soft fingers against his rough ones. "That's right," she said.

"It's common knowledge you're making your first best man suit for Hunter. How does it feel?"

"Good. It's easy to dress someone like him."

"How so?"

"He's very agreeable is all." She focused back on her glazed croissant. "Not that bridesmaids aren't, too, but they can be more challenging."

"I'm sure. Will you be putting the same butterfly applique in his suit as you do your maid of honor dresses?"

"I will, yes."

"Do you think it will work?" she asked.

Callie took her time before answering. "I believe in magic myself, but nothing can be counted on to work every single time."

"It will work," Hunter said.

Vivian turned her attention to him. "Sounds to me like that's the magic—the wearer's willingness to find love."

"Definitely," he and Callie said at the same time. He couldn't help it; he grinned at her.

"Did you two know each other before this?" Vivian asked, even though it was obvious, wasn't it? And if she were any kind of reporter, she knew about his spider bite and arrangement with Callie.

"We've known each other since we were teenagers," Hunter said. He'd almost spouted fourteen years, three months, but that would make him a total creeper.

"Callie is my best friend," Nova offered. "And Hunter is my brother, so she's been part of our family for a long time."

Vivian turned in her seat to face Callie and Nova more fully. "Interesting. Callie, you must feel some extra incentive, then, to help Hunter find the woman he's going to marry."

"Yes and no." Callie glanced down at Vivian's cell phone, face up on their table and recording the conversation. "Yes, because Hunter does want to get married and settle down. But no because he has no trouble meeting women."

"I can't help it if they find me irresistible," he teased, owning his reputation for a moment, mostly because he wanted to see Callie's reaction. She rolled her eyes.

"You sure don't seem to be lacking in confidence." Vivian took a sip of her coffee. "One last question, if you don't mind me asking."

"Go ahead," he said.

"What does this soul mate of yours look like? I'm sure our readers would be interested to know who might finally lasso Hunter Owens."

Red hair. Green eyes. Unforgettable laugh.

It took superhuman strength, but he did not glance at Callie. "I'm not sure, but I'll know her when I see her."

Vivian stopped the recording. "Thanks for taking the time to speak with me, Hunter." She slid her business card across the table as she stood. "Call me if you change your mind about that ride. I love horses." She gave him a look that said she'd be up for more than one kind of ride before turning to his sister and Callie. "Nice to meet you both. Callie, I'm super interested in the story developing with Hunter's suit. I also assume you're designing the maid of honor dress?" Callie nodded. "Could we set up another time to talk? I could highlight your business and the touch of magic everyone seems to believe in."

"That would be great. Thank you." She accepted a business card from Vivian.

"Wonderful. I'll reach out soon." She set her eyes back on him and bit her lower lip just a little before turning to go. Her high heels click-clacked and her hips swayed as she walked away.

"Seriously?" Nova said. "Is there not one woman alive who doesn't want to see you naked?"

When Callie didn't say "me," he took it as a win

and puffed out his chest. "I can't help it."

"That's it. We're doing it," Nova said. "And you're helping," she told Callie.

"What are we doing?" Callie asked. She carefully tucked Vivian's card in her purse.

"We need to act fast so we can have it ready for Christmas."

"What are we doing?" Callie repeated. Her eyes met his for help, but he had no idea what his sister was talking about, either. He shook his head and lifted a shoulder.

"A calendar. I've been wanting to help raise funds for the Botanical Society, and this is how we can do it."

"Flowers are pretty, Nov, but kind of boring for a calendar," he said.

"Not if shirtless guys are holding the flowers." She grinned from ear to ear.

Aw, shit. He knew that grin. It was the one she gave right before asking him to do something he didn't want to do. "No."

"Yes."

"I'm not doing it." He had a serious image to cultivate that did not include taking his shirt off for a calendar, even for a good cause.

Nova ignored him and addressed her best friend. "We can totally do this, Cal. We just need twelve guys who will wear jeans and nothing else and hold a flower. In their hand or their teeth. In their pocket." She waggled her eyebrows. *Eww*. This was his cue to leave. "I saw Caleb the other day. He asked me about you."

"He did?" Callie asked.

Hunter watched Callie's cheeks turn a light shade of pink, and he in turn kept his butt in the chair, no longer in any hurry to leave.

"I can't believe I forgot to tell you. That man is *hot*. I bet if you ask him to be in the calendar, he will. Then he could ask a couple of his fireman friends."

"Fine. I'll do it," Hunter said.

Nova caught his eye, and something told him he'd just walked right into her evil plan. "Great! I'll get Maverick in, too, even though he'll hate it. Cole maybe." She kept talking, and Callie took out a small notebook and pen to take notes.

A knock on the window drew his attention. Maverick waved to him to *come on*. His brother had delivered glazed donuts to Kennedy, and now they had work to do.

"See you later," he said, not accidentally brushing Callie's arm as he left. The urge to touch her refused to diminish, especially when they were in the same space, and he wondered if the innocent touch would leave her thinking about him like he'd be thinking about her.

CHAPTER SIXTEEN

"Good morning, Tom," Callie said to the bolt of dark fabric leaning against the wall. She ran her hand across it in a caress, and Hunter had never wished to be a bolt of fabric before, but he did now.

"Good morning, Vera," she said to the next bolt. "Happy Friday, Giorgio. It's going to be a busy day for you," she said to the third fabric ream, silver in color. "And hello, Oscar." She completed her daily ritual with a stroke over Oscar.

Hunter wondered if she'd consider adding him to her routine. The fact that watching Callie touch fabric she named after famous designers turned him on proved how much he wasn't over her. Damn it. He adjusted himself.

Get over it. Everyone expects you to meet the love of your life after the wedding. No way in hell would he be the one to break Callie's good-luck streak. Especially now that Vivian planned to continue to report on it. The positive exposure for Callie's work might be the boost she needed to secure the cottage as her permanent place of business in six months. That's right. Her offer had been accepted, just as he'd predicted.

He cleared his throat before he took creeper status to an uncomfortable level. Was he creepy, though, if he did it in his own house? Anyway…

"Morning." He stepped into the living room, careful not to disrupt the sewing stuff on every available surface. He loved that she'd made herself comfortable.

"Good morning, how are you?"

"Better, thanks." He'd worked a little too hard yesterday, and last night he'd spiked another fever, a side effect Kennedy said could continue for a couple more weeks. At least his rash had dissipated. Because nothing said *sexy* like a rash.

"You ready for your fitting, then?"

"I am." He inwardly high fived himself. Her hands *would* be all over him this morning. Not a caress, but he'd take it.

"There's coffee if you want a cup first." She picked up a cloth measuring tape.

"You beat me to it this morning." He poured himself a mug, adding milk and a little sugar. He let out a sigh after his first sip. It tasted much better when she made it.

They'd fallen into an easy rhythm this week with zero flirting. It took herculean effort on his part, but he'd agreed to keep things platonic and continuing to break that rule made him a jerk. They still talked every night before falling asleep, sans anything provocative, and those ten or so minutes were the best of his day.

He leaned against the small counter to sip his coffee. Trees swayed outside the small window above the sink. Inside, the prettiest girl he'd ever laid eyes on gathered her long, curly hair and piled it on top of her head in a knot. He admired the long slope of her neck and her hourglass figure before looking away, lest he get caught. Feet bare, toenails painted white, soft beige joggers and a matching pullover.

He could stare at her all day.

"Ready?" she asked, drawing his attention back to her face.

"Yep." He put his coffee down and stepped in front of her.

She measured around his chest first, reaching behind him and then coming around under his armpits. "Relax your arms," she instructed. She had such a pleasing voice she could have said *drop and give me fifty* and he would have without question.

Next, she measured his neck, bringing the tape together at his Adam's apple. He breathed in her sweet scent before she backed away to note the measurement.

"Turn around, please." She put a hand on the top edge of his left shoulder. His body heated at the innocent touch. Almost as much as it had the other night when he'd taken her hand. He would have held on all the way home if Jenna hadn't interrupted them.

He glanced down to his right shoulder when she placed the measuring tape there. His eyes connected with hers, held, until she looked away to measure down his arm, shoulder to elbow and elbow to wrist. When she wrapped the measuring tape around his biceps, he flexed his muscle there.

"Relax, Show Off."

"I have no idea what you're talking about," he teased, doing as she asked.

"And I'm Margot Robbie."

"You're way prettier than she is." He meant it inside and out.

Wordlessly, she shook her head and continued.

When she knelt to measure around his hips, his mind went straight to the gutter. Her mouth lined up perfectly with the part of his anatomy he concentrated very hard to keep under control.

"Place this right under your crotch, please." She handed him the end of the measuring tape. "And do not say a word," she added. She knew him so well.

She brought the tape down the inside of his leg to the floor. His dick stirred mercilessly. Jesus, at this point if she talked to it, he'd probably go off like it was his first time.

"When do you move in to the cottage?" he asked, needing to divert his thoughts.

"As long as everything is cleaned up and refurbished, on the first."

"At least the pipe burst before you moved in." While they'd celebrated her renting the property with a special cocktail at Birdy's, a water pipe had broken and flooded the place.

"That's true. Spread your legs a little." She measured around his thigh while he pictured spreading her thighs. Licking his way from the back of her knees up to—

"There's no rush, you know," he managed to say, ridding his mind of inappropriate thoughts. *She does not want the same thing you do. Stop torturing yourself.*

"No rush?" She rose to her feet, thank the Lord.

"For you to leave. You can stay here as long as you need, even after I'm back to my normal self."

She sat on the couch with her computer in her lap and typed. "Thanks, but I'm sure you want me gone as soon as possible."

Where was that coming from? He'd given no indication of any such thing. He rubbed the back of his neck, took a deep breath.

"You know, in case there's any more pie deliveries," she added. She gave him the same encouraging look his buddies did when they thought he wanted to get lucky.

"I'll just hang a horseshoe on the front door if I need privacy," he said cheerfully, playing along.

"That could work or…"

"Or?"

"I move into the cottage as soon as possible. I really do need more space than I have here. And it's not like I'll be that far away." She put her computer aside, tucked her hands under her legs, and looked up at him with warmth in her eyes. "I mean it when I say if *you* need anything after I'm gone, I can be here in five minutes."

"I appreciate that."

"And so can your family. We've all got your back."

He knew he'd lucked out in the family and friend department. "I've got yours, too, you know."

"I do. Which is why I know you're going to wear your best man suit like a boss and meet your match."

"We'll both be the talk of the town."

"I like the sound of that."

Saying, "Me, too" sat on the tip of his tongue — where it stayed.

CHAPTER SEVENTEEN

Callie wandered around Windsong's Art Walk the next morning for her second ambassador assignment. She couldn't remember the last time she had visited the weekly event in Pine Park where local artists sold their wares, and she couldn't have asked for a more perfect day outside. Blue sky, warm sun, birds chirping in the countless trees along the bluff, the scent of the sea mingling with pine and earth.

She took photos with her phone, talked to artists, admired the many different forms of art. "Good morning," she said to Marvin, admiring his glass vases, sun catchers, windchimes, small figurines, and wall art.

"Hi, Callie. Thanks for stopping by. Let me know if I can answer any questions."

With a nod, she ventured toward some tiny glass animals and discovered a glass-blown spider, black with a red heart on its underbelly. She carefully picked up the delicate art piece with a certain cowboy in mind. As of late, he filled her head way too often.

She put the glass spider down. Picked it back up. Put it down. Picked it up. *Stop overthinking it and buy the figurine to thank him for letting you stay with him.* "I'll take this, please," she told Marvin.

She could already picture Hunter's smile when she gave it to him.

"Callie?"

Turning her head, she found Mrs. Chapman and another woman who, from the resemblance, must be a family member.

"I thought that was you," Mrs. Chapman continued. "This is my sister, Luella. Lu, this is the dress designer I was telling you about."

"Nice to meet you," Callie said, accepting a small bag with her purchase inside it from Marvin.

"Before my sister talks shop," Mrs. Chapman guided them away from Marvin's booth, "I've got good news about the cottage. There's no mold, so we're moving ahead with reconditioning the floors and remodeling the bathroom."

"That's great. Thank you." Grateful for the update, her mind raced with ideas for the shop—her very own storefront! Now came the hard part: growing her business to where she could afford to buy the building when the time came in a few short months.

"On to dresses," Luella said, "I'm getting married in April and my daughter is my maid of honor. She recently broke up with her longtime boyfriend—"

"Who no one especially cared for," Mrs. Chapman interjected.

"Right. And she's one of those girls who is in love with love and wants to settle down."

Doc Howser and his wife passed by them with a smile and a hello.

"I'd like to hire you to make her dress. Your reputation as a good-luck charm is one I can't ignore, and I couldn't think of a better wedding gift to myself than to have her wear your design."

"She could be one of your first clients in your new store," Mrs. Chapman said with a clap of her hands.

"I'd love to make her dress." If word could keep spreading and maids of honor continued to find their own HEAs, then that got her closer to her dream of owning the cottage by summer.

"Fabulous. We're in San Francisco but can drive down anytime."

Callie pulled her appointment book out of her bag. They set a day and time for early December.

"Hello, Cicely," Mrs. Chapman said warmly as the mayor of Windsong approached.

Always well dressed with a friendly expression on her face, Mayor Garnett had several bags hanging off her arm. "Hello! You three look like you're conspiring about something."

She was also very intuitive.

"I've just booked Callie for my daughter's maid of honor dress." The delight in Luella's voice filled Callie with joy. She loved being part of weddings and making the bridesmaids feel beautiful in a dress they'd want to wear again. Loved the magic she'd been blessed with when designing the MOH dresses. She crossed her fingers her good-luck streak lasted for many more years so she could keep helping people find their happily ever afters. Not having to stress about a mortgage payment would be pretty nice, too.

"Congratulations on your engagement. And best wishes to your daughter."

Mrs. Chapman looked at her wristwatch. "I'm sorry to rush off, but we have lunch reservations in five minutes."

"Of course," the mayor said.

"I'll see you soon, Callie," Luella called over her

shoulder after they all said goodbye.

"I'm guessing you're here for your ambassador article," Mayor Garnett said now that it was just the two of them.

"I am." Last night she'd dreamt she won. She'd stood at a podium to give a thank-you speech with a crown on her head (in reality there was no crown) and a standing ovation. Her sister was there clapping, but she had on her own crown, and a sash across her chest, and a First-Place ribbon pinned to her dress and a key to the city dangling from a gold necklace because she'd built a home for a family in need.

Callie shook off the dream and resolved to forget it by the time her head hit the pillow tonight. *Comparison is the thief of joy.*

"It looks like this is one of your favorite places." Callie gestured toward the mayor's shopping bags.

"Early Christmas shopping." She quietly studied Callie for a moment. "You're becoming something special and unique to Windsong."

It took Callie a second to realize she meant with her dressmaking business. "Thank you. I can't think of anything better than being part of the fabric of this town. Even if it is a little stressful at times," she admitted. "I don't want to let anyone down."

"That's not possible when you do your best."

"Easier said than done."

"True." The mayor's kind eyes blinked in agreement. "I'm looking forward to seeing what the next year brings for you." She glanced over Callie's head. "There's my husband, waving for me. Good luck with everything."

Callie's imagination ran wild as she watched the mayor walk away. She'd pinned her hopes on the ambassador position freeing her from more than her sister's shadow. It would also give her an escape from the pressure of being a business owner. She could use her magic touch for the benefit of the whole town.

Similar to her time in Africa, she'd be an integral part of the greater good, just like her parents and sister were in their pursuits. This opportunity might finally be the thing to get her over her mistrust of them and create a bond they could build on.

CHAPTER EIGHTEEN

"You look yabba-dabba-dynamite."

"Right back at you," Callie said to Nova as they stood on Main Street ready to partake in the annual Windsong Pumpkin Crawl.

"I think Wilma and Betty should find a couple of cavemen, and if the cavemen play their clubs right, we do some bedrocking."

"Would you stop already?" Callie bumped bare shoulders with her best friend.

"Hey, we look hot, and there is no Fred or Barney in our lives, so let's have some fun."

Every year on the Saturday before Halloween, the streets of their small downtown turned into a costume party and pumpkin crawl where restaurants and bars offered up specialty pumpkin dishes and drinks.

"Let's take a selfie." Phone in hand, Nova extended her arm in front of their faces. "Say cheese!"

"Did they have cheese in the Stone Age?" Callie teased.

"Okay, meat then."

"Meeet," they sang out as Nova snapped the picture. "Where to first? Sutter's?"

Callie vividly remembered how delicious their pumpkin mac and cheese with bacon tasted. "Do you even have to ask?"

The late afternoon sun shined, but their skimpy costumes offered little warmth, so they fast walked to the town's oldest and most beloved tavern. On the way there, they said hello to vampires, witches, superheroes, and fairy-tale characters.

"Lookin' good, Wilma and Betty," a guy in a *Scream* mask said before he crossed the street in front of them.

Nova hip checked her. "Told ya." Callie had quickly made their white and blue cavewoman dresses this morning after Nova had popped into the bunkhouse with the fabric and accessories to make their matching costumes.

The second they stepped inside Sutter's, a heat wave and celebratory racket greeted them. The restaurant hadn't decorated for the holiday but for one lone jack-o'-lantern sitting atop the bar where zombie bartenders made drinks. She and Nova showed the wristbands they'd purchased earlier and then wove through the main room to find a spot at a high-top table. A server came by and dropped off pumpkin mac and cheese inside small paper containers. "Can I get you something to drink?"

Nova slid over two drink vouchers. "Two pumpkin beers, please."

"There is a party in my mouth right now," Callie said around a mouthful of food. As another server walked by, she snagged a second helping. A girl could never have too much mac and cheese.

"It's a crime they don't serve this all the time." Nova enjoyed her own bite. "You know what else we need?" She looked around, and when a server dressed as Thor approached carrying a tray, she smiled and held up her pointer finger.

"Pumpkin mashed potatoes?" Thor asked.

"Please." Nova made room on their round top for the additional dish.

"I love that we speak the same food language." Callie clinked forks with her best friend. "Where should we go next?"

"I was thinking Baked on Main."

"Oh yes, I need a pumpkin whoopie pie." Callie noticed an attractive man dressed in a business suit sitting at the bar. He stuck out given everyone else wore a costume. Unless that was his costume? His eyes were on Nova. Zeroed in on her like there was no one else in the room. Callie turned back to her friend, then glanced back toward the man a minute later. He remained focused on Nova.

"Suit, three o'clock, has not taken his eyes off you."

Nova boldly stared in the man's direction. Callie swore she saw an electrical current flare to life between them when their eyes met, like they'd both been struck by lightning.

"Do you know him?" Callie asked.

Without taking her eyes off Mr. Suit, she said, "No. But I think I want to." She turned her head to look at Callie. "Do you mind if I walk over there?"

"Don't you usually like the man to come to you?"

"Yes, but…" She glanced back over at him. He put down his drink—probably a pumpkin old fashioned from the looks of it—and met her gaze. "Something tells me he won't make the first move."

"Okay. I'll wait here. Give me the signal if you need me." Callie watched Nova stride to the bar with confidence and take the seat next to the mystery man.

"Guess I get the rest of you," she happily said to the mac and cheese and mashed potatoes.

"Hello, Wilma." The soft whisper on the back of her neck sent a shiver down her spine. "Mind if I join you?" The achingly familiar voice, not to mention Hunter's warm breath, touched her skin like a velvet caress, so yes, he could join her, please and thank you.

He popped into view and took the spot vacated by his sister. "Hi," she said like his nearness did not make her weak in the knees. "Where's your costume?"

"This is it." He tipped his cowboy hat and one corner of his mouth lifted.

"You always dress like that." Jeans. Flannel shirt or Henley. Boots. Tonight's shirt brought out the blue of his eyes. Like they needed to be any bluer. She pretended her food was much more interesting than him.

This past week she'd tiptoed around her growing feelings for him. Avoidance, however, only served to make her more aware of him when they were together. It was like the spider bite had not only poisoned him but caused him to release pheromones with her name on them, and unscientifically speaking, they'd had a direct impact on her brain and body.

Not to mention the effect he had on her at night before bedtime. With no lights on in the bunkhouse and feeling safe to let down her guard—their nightly tradition of talking before falling asleep had become her favorite part of the day.

"Which makes it the greatest costume there is."

Both sides of his mouth lifted to show off his straight, white teeth and dimples. "I've never liked dressing up. You, on the other hand, look fantastic." The beers arrived, and he took a drink of Nova's.

She downed a big gulp of hers.

"That was just a compliment, by the way. I'm not flirting."

"You're not?" The question sounded far more disappointed than she'd intended.

He narrowed his eyes in confusion. *Yeah, join the club, cowboy. Confusion is my new middle name.* "I thought I wasn't allowed to flirt with you."

Callie toyed with her chunky "bone" necklace. Hunter wasn't a caveman, but if she were going to let go and have some fun tonight, she wanted it to be with the handsome cowboy standing across from her.

"You're not. But tonight, I'm not me, I'm Wilma."

He ran a hand over his jaw. Indecision furrowed his brows, and she wished she could rewind the last twenty seconds and take those words back.

"Okay," he finally said. "And who would the beautiful Wilma like me to be?"

"Hey, you two," Brett said, arriving at their table with his girlfriend, Janey, and saving Callie from admitting she wanted *him*. "Dude, that is the worst costume ever." He eyed Hunter top to bottom.

"And yours is better?" Hunter made a face at Brett's onesie cow costume.

Brett put his arm around Janey. "It is. Because I have my very own milkmaid." He waggled his eyebrows.

Callie almost spewed her beer, Brett's innuendo

striking her funny bone just right.

Janey swatted Brett in the chest. "Don't be rude."

"Like that's possible," Hunter said kindly. "I think it's his default setting." Hunter's gaze caught on something over Janey's shoulder. "Who's my sister talking to?"

"I don't know," Callie said. "But she's got it handled." Her best friend didn't need rescuing or her big brother interfering, even though Hunter's protectiveness came from a place of love. Plus, the fact that she hadn't given Callie the signal—a tug on her right earlobe—meant she was having a good time.

Hunter narrowed his eyes, deciphering for himself if his sister had it under control. Seeming satisfied, he gave a small nod and returned his attention to their table.

"Oh, hey! We'll take some of those." Brett waved over a server—this one offering a great impression of Britney Spears—carrying a tray of shots, each with a dollop of whipped cream on top.

"Hi, everyone," the waitress said with her eyes directly on Hunter. She put down four shot glasses. "Start you a tab?"

"Sure." Hunter flashed her a smile.

"What are they?" Callie asked.

"Fireball pumpkin pie shots. It's Hunter Owens, right?"

"Right." It was just one little word, but it sounded like, *That's me and how about we get to know each other better later?* to Callie. She didn't especially like it.

"I'll check back in a few and see if you need anything else," she said directly to Hunter before drifting away.

"Bro." Brett put a hand on Hunter's shoulder after the waitress was out of earshot. "I'm pretty sure she's on your menu."

"Every single girl in this bar is on his menu," Janey added.

Callie glanced around. More than one set of female eyes were on him, some obvious, others more subtle. She pushed a shot glass in front of each of them. "Let's do this."

"On three," Hunter said. "One, two, three."

Oh wow, that tasted good. Callie put her empty shot glass down and ran her tongue along her upper lip.

"You missed a spot." Hunter gently wiped the corner of her mouth with the pad of his thumb. His warm touch had her cheeks heating. When he sucked the bit of whipped cream off his finger, heat flooded other parts of her.

"Callie, I hear you're opening your own dress shop." Janey snagged some pumpkin mac and cheese from a passing tray. "Congratulations."

"Thanks. I'm excited *and* nervous. It's a big step for me."

"We also heard you're dressing this guy for his brother's wedding." Brett gave a chin up to Hunter. "That true, too?"

"He's my first best man, yes, but I don't plan to make it a thing. It's more of a favor."

Brett laughed. "Yeah, he needs all the help he can get. Poor guy, no one ever wants to date him."

"The struggle is real," Hunter said. The sincerity in his voice surprised Callie. When had he struggled? For as long as she could remember, girls lined up to be with him. From the glance around the restaurant, they still did.

"The suit isn't about dating," Janey said. "It's about finding his one true love."

"Another round?" Flirty Britney Spears asked, already placing shot glasses on their table.

"Hey, you know my name, but I don't know yours," Hunter said with clear interest.

"Brittany."

"For real?" Hunter asked.

"For real. I spell mine with two *T*s and an *A*, though."

"Shot time!" Callie picked up her glass and downed it before everyone else. The second taste went down even smoother. She scooted closer to Hunter and smiled at Brittany, who took the hint and stepped away to another table. Twenty minutes and another shot later, Brett and Janey moved on to other friends, and was it her imagination or had Hunter moved closer, too? More than a little tipsy, she couldn't be sure. He did smell better than any man had a right to smell.

She looked up into his bright blue eyes. "You smell really good."

"Yeah?"

"Uh-huh." She pictured running her cheek along his clean-shaven jaw and breathing him in. "Your aftershave is making my nose nosey."

He grinned. "I have no idea what that means, but I hate to tell you I'm not wearing aftershave. This is all me, sweetheart."

She braced her arms on the table and leaned back. "No."

"Yes."

A server who was not flirty what's-her-face dropped off two more shots.

"That'll do it for us," Hunter said, handing over his credit card. He lifted his shot glass and held it in front of his face. Callie did the same with hers. They took a moment, and then he said, "Bottoms up."

"Down the hatch," she countered, drinking the flavored whiskey in one gulp before slamming the glass on the table and licking her lips. "Who knew whishkey tasted so good?"

"Whishkey?" Hunter said, amused.

"That's what I said."

"Has anyone ever told you your pronunciation is cute when you're drunk?"

"It's my lips." She pouted.

"Why the face? Your mouth is gorgeous, Cal." Voice husky, he cleared his throat before seeming to backtrack and adding, "I mean some mouths are functional looking and some are thin and forgettable, but yours is...yours is noticeable. Again, I'm just stating a fact."

She swung her head back and forth in an exaggerated "no." *Ouch, no more swinging of heads.* "In elementary school, kids called me Fish Lips."

"Stupid kids."

"I ended up punching one of them in the mouth, I was so mad. I got suspended for the day, but I didn't care."

"Huh."

"Huh, what?" She put a hand on her hip.

His gaze moved there, then took a slow tour over her torso, up to her chest, her neck, her *mouth*, before connecting with her eyes again. "I pictured you as this sweet little thing and here you were fighting and getting in trouble."

"I can be tough if I have to be," she argued.

"I'm sure." He smirked, and instead of finding it irritating, she found it attractive. So attractive that she felt her face flush.

Or maybe that was the result of one too many fireball pie pumpkin, err, pumpkin fireball pie, whatever they were called, shots. "Is it warm in here?"

"A little. You okay?"

A wave of nausea overwhelmed her. She covered her mouth with her hand and carefully shook her head. "I think I'm going to be sick. Be right back."

She hurried to the bathroom, not bothering to lock the door behind her. "Occupied!" she said into the toilet when she heard the door open a minute later.

"It's me," Hunter, the sexy cowboy and flirt master—who should have knocked first—said.

"Please go away." She shooed him.

He didn't budge. He stayed and handed her a wet paper towel. Rubbed her back. Left for a quick minute to check on Nova. When he returned, he took her under his arm and got them both safely home via the town trolleys working that night. She felt like shit, and the only thing she wanted to do was crawl under a blanket and sleep away the pain and misery. He sat on the foot of his bed while she got herself into the bathroom to put on her pajamas, brush her teeth, and down a couple of aspirin.

"Let's get you tucked in," he said softly when she exited.

Sleep blessedly came quickly. Before she completely dozed off, she heard him leave the bunkhouse, returning to the crawl, no doubt. And all the Brittanys hoping for a chance to be his cowgirl now that she was Wilma'd out.

• • •

Hunter caught the trolly working overtime tonight and went back to Sutter's. With Callie safely asleep on his couch, he hurried in answer to the SOS text from Nova.

He walked into the restaurant to find Brett folded into a corner booth with a bottle of whiskey and a shit-ton too many shot glasses. Why he needed more than one when he was drinking alone, Hunter didn't know. What he did know was his friend needed to get his ass home before he drank himself to the point of no return.

Glad he'd eaten enough to combat much of the drinking he'd done himself, Hunter slid into the booth across from the heartbroken man. According to Nova, Brett and Janey had had another one of their public blowouts, only this time they'd yelled words they couldn't take back.

Hunter lifted the bottle of booze and handed it discreetly over to Nova as she walked by the table. Brett turned into The Hulk when drunk and upset and had apparently put on quite the show twenty minutes ago. Thankfully, Janey had left a minute later, and Nova and a couple of other friends had managed to plant Brett here.

"Hey," Hunter said.

"Don't." Brett's bloodshot eyes held little steam to go along with the one firm word.

"I hear I missed all the excitement." Hunter held up two fingers and mouthed *two waters* to a passing server.

"It's over for good this time," Brett slurred. "She accused me of being a rude slacker and letting my business degree go to waste."

To Hunter's mind, Brett just hadn't found his calling yet. The boot camp seemed to fulfill him at the moment, and with their plans to grow it, who knew what might happen? "I'm sorry, man."

"I need another drink."

The server put down two glasses of water. Perfect timing.

"There you go," Hunter said. "Drink up."

"Not what I meant, asshole."

"Too bad."

"Where's my bottle?" he sloppily shouted. With boisterous conversations all around them, no one noticed. Or if they did, they decided to ignore him.

"I'm not letting you poison yourself anymore. Let's get you home."

"I don't need you or anyone else telling me what to do," he snarled with a slur. "I'm good right here."

"Let's agree to disagree on that."

"Hey." Bella stopped at their table dressed in a sexy nurse's costume. She wore the outfit well; anyone would say so. "How's he doing?" she asked under her breath.

"Hey! My nurse is here!" Brett bellowed.

Bella handed him his glass of water. "Drink this."

He did, downed the entire eight ounces.

"Looks like you're my lucky charm to help get him out of here," Hunter said.

"Let's do it," she agreed.

With Bella's assistance, they got Brett home without incident. Getting him out of his cow costume proved futile, so they left him as is on top of his bed. "Think he'll be okay?" Hunter asked.

"Yes, but to be sure, I'll stay a while. If he gets sick, I don't want him to choke on his own vomit."

"I'll stay, too, then." Brett had a good six inches on Bella and at least fifty pounds. She'd have a tough time maneuvering him, if need be.

They took to the couch, talking quietly so they'd hear any signs of distress from Brett's room.

"You're a good friend," Bella said.

"He is, too. He's saved my ass a time or two when I've messed up." Hunter ran a hand through his hair. "I think he's better off without Janey."

"That's what your sister said, too. Breaking up then getting back together more than once seems like a good sign there's a problem with the relationship that can't be fixed."

"Yeah." He stared down at the carpeted floor, thinking about his brothers' relationships. His parents. They'd all set great examples for love. Commitment. Respect. Hunter had spent his twenties sowing his wild oats while waiting for something to happen between him and Callie. And tonight, if she'd hadn't gotten drunk, they may have given in to the chemistry between them. Eventually, no matter how hard they fought it, the heat that crackled when they were close to each other had to go somewhere.

He hoped it didn't go south.

"Chad was telling me about your ranch. You have a mule named George who is whip smart and likes to get into trouble?"

Hunter lifted his gaze. Their ranch hand gave good publicity.

"He does." The conversation continued to flow with ease. Bella shared freely. She showed interest in more than the ranch and asked about him. Her long, bare legs were nice to look at.

But the entire time they were together, he couldn't stop thinking about Callie and getting back to the bunkhouse.

CHAPTER NINETEEN

Callie tied her hair up in a bandana. She wiped her hands down her denim overalls. Pulled down the sleeves of her shirt to cover her chilled hands. The corn maze in front of her shone through the dusk with a slight sway to the stalks.

"Team One, ready?" Margo Brand asked from the entrance to the popular maze on her family's ranch.

Callie, Hunter, Bella, and Kennedy all answered, "Yes!"

"Team Two, ready?" Margo asked.

Nova, Maverick, Chad, and Brett all answered, "Yep!"

"Flag holder for Team One?" Margo held out a red flag, taller than the cornstalks, so the watchperson in the tower could help if anyone got lost and couldn't find their way out of the maze. Dusk definitely made this more of a challenge.

Callie's team had nominated Kennedy flag holder for no other reason than she was the shortest among them. She'd taken Hunter's teasing like a champ when he'd shared that. "Thank you," she said now, accepting the flagpole.

"Team Two?" Margo held out a blue flag.

"That would be me," Maverick said, clearly ready to take his team to the finish line first. Then he placed all his attention on Kennedy and said, "Good luck, Shortcake."

"Right back at you, Cowboy."

"On my count of three," Margo said. "One. Two. Three!"

Callie's team took off through the left entrance while Maverick and his team went right. The distance to the exit being equal, they'd done an official coin toss to decide who took which route.

"This way," Hunter said. They'd designated him leader earlier, counting on his good sense of direction to lead them to victory.

Looking up over the tops of the corn, Callie counted four other flags in action. Besides those groups, kids raced by them kicking up dirt, and single adults went this way and that with smiles on their faces. Hunter stopped at a fork in the maze.

"What do you think?"

"Left," Bella said at the same time Callie said, "Right."

"Let's try left." He and Bella walked side-by-side to lead the way. They made a cute couple. They'd joked with each other before the teams were made and high fived when both were chosen by Kennedy. Their easy camaraderie hurt more than Callie wanted to admit so she focused on the dirt ground and putting one foot in front of the other, ignoring the ache in her chest.

"What do you think?" Kennedy asked her.

"I think this is going to loop around and take us back the way we came."

"I meant about the two of them." She gestured toward Hunter and Bella.

"Oh, uh…I like Bella, and she seems to really like Hunter." Callie's stomach knotted. Bella was exactly the kind of person she'd wish for him. Kind, smart, and marriage minded. Nova had mentioned she'd been engaged once before, but that her fiancé lived in London and Bella wanted to stay here.

Hunter glanced over his shoulder, and their eyes connected. With one little look, he made her feel like the most important person in the corn maze. Did Bella get the same jolt of electricity?

"Watch…!" Too late. Hunter ran into a scarecrow. "Out," she finished, trying not to laugh.

The scarecrow wobbled before Hunter stilled it. "Is this the same—"

"Yes," Callie interrupted. "We've been here before."

"Damn it. I'm all turned around."

"Callie, you lead," Kennedy ordered good-naturedly. "We need to hurry if we're going to beat Mav." The friendly competitions between the couple were common knowledge. Also, the losers had to hold a sign with the words "I'm corny and I know it" and walk up and down Main Street.

Callie stepped forward, and Bella stepped back to allow room for Callie beside Hunter. "Girl power," she whispered, making Callie like her even more.

"Keep an eye out for those figures made out of straw," Callie teased, setting out at a brisk pace.

"I can't help it if I was distracted," Hunter said.

Her. She distracted him.

Torn between leaving it at that or asking about Bella, she didn't say anything. Couldn't. For fear he'd give her answers she didn't want to hear.

"By the way," he added, for her ears only, "I went

Bella's way so she wouldn't feel left out."

"Left out?" Callie's brows knit in confusion.

"I invited her to join us and then spent most of the time we were in the petting zoo with you."

That's true. He had.

"She's really nice. I like her." Callie made a hard right, her intuition helping to lead the way.

"I do, too."

Yep. Wrong answer. His easy admission magnified the knot in her stomach. She let out a short breath and focused her attention on the path before them.

They wove through the maze, the setting sun stealing more and more natural light. Kennedy and Bella talked nonstop about the office and Kennedy's upcoming wedding. Callie listened intently, soaking up the solidarity and hoping to learn more about Bella. Despite her heart's protests, she truly wanted the perfect match for Hunter.

Suddenly, he turned and backward jogged. "Triple C, you did it." He twisted around and ran for the exit. She followed on his heels. The deal was the entire team had to cross the finish line to be declared the winner. Bella and Kennedy ran toward them, their red flag waving. And aligned almost evenly was Maverick's blue flag, moving closer to the other exit. Nova ran through first.

"Hurry!" Callie shouted, jumping up and down.

"We're neck and neck!" Nova called out, doing her own jumping.

The rest of both teams spilled out...at the same time.

"We win!" Hunter declared. "Since Callie and I

were out before anyone on your team."

"Doesn't matter," Maverick countered. "This was a group competition." He wrapped an arm around Kennedy. "Am I right?"

"He's right. Nice job, everyone."

"Come on," Maverick said, taking Kennedy's flag and turning it in along with his team's. "I'm buying the drinks."

"Actually," Kennedy said, reading a text on her phone. "I need to make a house call."

"Need any help?" Bella asked.

"I might. Do you mind?"

"Not at all. I can drive us."

"I'm gonna head home," Brett said. "And hope this headache goes away." Poor guy still felt the effects of his hangover.

If not for Hunter waking her in the middle of the night with another dose of aspirin, Callie might be feeling the same. She glanced at him and caught him looking at her.

"I've got to go, too," Chad said.

"Me, three," Nova piped in. "I promised Jenna I'd be home in time to tell her about the maze and bring her a treat."

Maverick was Nova's ride, so that left her and Hunter.

Just the two of them.

Alone under a dusky sky, soft sounds of music spilling out from the barn nearby and the scent of pumpkin spice in the air.

"You want to stick around?" he asked.

"Sure."

"Grab a spot at that picnic table and I'll be right

back." He could have said *roll around in the dirt and oink* and she would have. Something about the way his eyes sparkled with mischief and his lips moved to form words had her under his spell more than usual.

"Okay."

He returned with one of those huge caramel apples covered in additional treats. He sat across from her, placing the gourmet goodie between them, already sliced for easy eating. She reached for a piece.

"This looks amazing. What's on it?" she asked.

"Crushed ginger snaps drizzled with white chocolate and a pinch of cinnamon."

"Oh my God, it's so good," she said around a crunchy, sticky, delicious bite.

Hunter watched her.

She licked the tips of her fingers. "What?"

"Nothing." He picked up his own piece. "You're right. This is tasty. I remember being a kid and making plain ones with my mom." He leaned his elbows on the wooden table as a devilish smile played across his face. "This one time, I was really mad at Cole about chores or something, so when my mom left the kitchen for a minute, I grabbed an onion out of the fridge and covered it in caramel before she got back. I put the stick in and told her it was for him."

"That's terrible!"

"I'm pretty sure he deserved it."

"Did you see him take a bite of it?" She took another wedge of their apple.

"What kind of prankster would I be if I didn't? It was one of the funniest things I've ever seen. He took this huge bite, and his eyes bugged out of his head like a cartoon character." Hunter started to laugh. "He spit it out and…" He laughed harder. His amusement contagious, Callie joined in, laughing even harder when he finally said, "He spit it out and it hit Maverick in the eye."

Callie's whole body shook as the two of them cracked up. She couldn't remember ever laughing like this with anyone other than Nova. Now that they'd gotten to know each other better, and Hunter seemed much more relaxed around her, his personality shined through.

"Hey, you two."

She and Hunter tore their eyes from each other to look up at Vivian. The pretty reporter smiled down at them. "Sorry to interrupt, but I wanted to say hello."

Vivian's attention settled on Hunter. No surprise there. "Hey," he said.

"Do you want to join us?" Callie asked.

"That's okay. I'm here on official *Gazette* business."

Callie had read a couple of her human-interest stories. Her strong, friendly voice sucked the reader in.

"Since I did run into you, though, can I ask you a follow-up question from the other day?"

"Go ahead," Callie said.

"Have you ever thought about sewing the applique into a dress for yourself? I mean, wouldn't you want to bring that magic to your own love life?"

The question surprised her, and her natural tendency to keep her deepest beliefs private had her at a loss for words. Nervous, her vision slithered out of focus.

"I'd probably sew it into all my clothes," Vivian joked, thankfully appearing not to notice Callie's unease.

"Callie is selfless and single-minded when it comes to her designs," Hunter said, drawing Vivian's attention. It gave Callie time to let out the breath she'd been holding. "I've never known anyone more focused on building a business where the people she helps find the most important success and happiness."

Vivian looked back and forth between Hunter and her. "Interesting," she said, like she could read Callie's mind and see "anti-marriage" in big, bold neon letters. It shouldn't matter if Callie shared that about herself, but she didn't want it printed in a newspaper. "I'm in further awe of you, Callie. And I'm clearly more selfish."

"I don't think that's it," Callie said, finding her voice. "I'd call you hopeful, which is a great quality to have. If I recall correctly, the maids of honor I've dressed have all been optimistic about love."

"And Hunter?" Vivian asked, her gaze flicking between them before settling firmly on Hunter.

"I have a feeling he's already met his match," Callie said. If not Bella, Vivian might be the one to steal his heart.

Because it couldn't be her.

CHAPTER TWENTY

Callie opened the bunkhouse door and found Hunter and Jenna dancing to "Good Feeling" with their arms in the air and big smiles on their faces. They didn't notice her, so she stood in the doorway to watch them in total joy and abandon. Nothing on their minds but having fun right this minute.

They sang along at the top of their lungs. Jumped up and down. Punched their fists toward the sky. The adorable bond between uncle and niece melted her insides. Safe to say, Hunter had completely recovered from his BW bite. He'd also make a great dad one day.

Her phone pinged once, twice. She pulled it from her pocket and stepped back onto the porch to find a group text.

Brooke: *Hey. We're going to Florida to help there. Not sure when we'll be home now.*

Mom: *Good luck with your shop and we'll see you soon. Love you.*

A sudden, sharp pain of disappointment overwhelmed her, and the usual ache in her heart flared to life before she pushed it away. She missed her family. This was the longest stretch she'd gone without seeing them. They'd barely texted since her return from Africa. She rubbed her chest to rid the dull pain of feeling like an afterthought.

Callie: *Thanks for letting me know. Be safe. Love you.*

She tucked her phone back in her pocket, wishing she could tuck her feelings away as easily as that.

During her parents' divorces, it had been her mom who fled, claiming to need time alone. Liane Carmichael hated constraints, and she hated talking about her emotions. She hated feeling too much, and Blake Carmichael made her feel all kinds of things. Love. Hate. Resentment. They argued about holding each other back. Made up. Argued some more. They didn't fight for their marriage. And they couldn't live without each other for long. Their complicated relationship put Callie on edge more times than she could count. Their lack of harmony had left an indelible mark.

"Hey. Is there a reason you're standing out here and not inside dancing with us?" Hunter asked in her periphery.

"Hey. I'm not really in a dancing mood." *Anymore*.

"What do you mean?" He stepped closer. "Today's the day you get your own place and leave my good-looking ass behind." He smiled in that humble way of his that made his smugness cute. "'Good Feeling' might be Jenna's favorite song, but I figured it was perfect for you, too."

He stood near enough for her to smell his scent and feel the heat radiating off his body. She'd miss both.

"Callie," he said softly. "What's wrong?"

He'd gotten good at reading her moods, his notice and comfort something she'd grown to appreciate over the past several weeks. And something that enabled her to let down her defenses.

"It's nothing." Okay, so she still had one shield up.

His hand squeezed her shoulder, bringing with it a rush of warmth that both soothed and unsettled her. "Talk to me. Just because we won't be roomies anymore doesn't mean I'm not here for you."

The music stopped inside the bunkhouse, and Jenna stepped outside. "Uncle Hunt, I gotta go. Catch you later. Hi, Callie! Bye, Callie!" She skipped away, her ponytail swaying.

Two seconds later, Hunter pulled her into his arms, sending an electric current through her entire body. Affection and strength radiated off him. They'd never touched like this before. "Okay, Miss Nothing. I know it's something. Talk to me."

And that was it. She lost the battle with herself and relaxed. He held her tighter, her back to his front. The last day of their cohabitation and he does this—splinters the last remains of her defenses. "It's my parents and Brooke. They're not coming home for a while."

"That sucks. I'm sorry."

"I should be used to it."

He squeezed her closer and canted his head so his lips brushed her ear. "Whatever you feel, it's okay. Don't ever think it's not. And if you ever want to talk about it, I'm here."

She spun around to face him. "Thanks. That means a lot." She fought the urge to kiss his cheek. Because if her lips got too close to his, she'd want to see how they fit against her own. Which meant she needed to change the subject. And quickly. "Okay, enough about that. It's moving day!" She stepped beside him.

He slung his arm over her shoulders and walked

them through the bunkhouse door. "It is. And as luck would have it, I'm free the rest of the day, so put me to work."

"I'm not sure that makes me lucky."

"Such a teaser."

She leaned her head on his shoulder and in all seriousness said, "Thanks for everything."

They worked together to gather her stuff. There wasn't much besides her sewing supplies so it didn't take very long.

"What's this?" He held up the bag she'd left tucked beside the toaster for him.

"A small gift for letting me stay here."

"I didn't *let* you anything. I should have a gift of thanks for you. You made my recovery a lot easier." He pulled the glass spider out of the bag. Grinned. His dimples were her thanks. "I love it. Thanks, Triple C."

"You're welcome."

A couple of hours later, they had everything in the cottage, including her stuff from her parents' house, thanks to his pickup truck. He gloated, proud to be of service and teasing her about being her lucky charm today. He'd also talked nonstop, sharing more stories about himself. She committed each one to memory so when she laid in bed at night alone, she could replay them and pretend he was on the other side of a sliding barn door.

"Then there was Cole's bachelor party. He was drunk as a skunk, and Maverick put him in bed before going to grab a small bucket to put by him. Mav was bending over to put the bucket on the floor beside the bed when Cole rolled over and threw up on his head." He chuckled at the memory.

"Oh no."

"Oh yes. So, after Mav cleaned up, he grabbed me, and we shaved one of Cole's legs while he was passed out."

"Oh my God. You didn't."

"We did."

"His whole leg?"

"Actually, we made stripes." He grinned. "He was so pissed."

"What about Bethany?"

"She thought it was hysterical and just made him shave both legs completely before their honeymoon to Hawaii."

Callie shook her head. "Brothers."

"They're the best and the worst."

"What's the worst?" Birdy asked, walking into the cottage with a pizza box in her hands.

"Boys." Callie took the box from her. "Thank you for picking up lunch."

Hunter crossed his arms over his chest. "All boys?"

"Definitely," Birdy said. "The male species is excellent at disturbing the peace. My husband, rest his soul, drove me crazy every day." She took a seat in the cream-colored velvet armchair Callie had bought this week. The rest of the store space looked a mess with moving boxes, fabrics, luggage, and new furniture that needed to be put together.

"And yet you were married for how many years?" Hunter asked.

"Fifty-six," she said fondly.

Callie sat on the floor, opened the pizza box, and

pulled a slice out to eat right away.

"So, what I'm hearing is you couldn't live without his annoying self?" Hunter sat down beside her, grabbed his own piece.

Birdy laughed. "You got that right. Neither of us was perfect, but we refused to give up on each other, even at our worst."

Hunter's eyes connected with Callie's. Their upbringings were very different. Mary Rose and John were still committed to each other while her parents had set a very different example.

"I need to run." Birdy got to her feet. "Not literally, of course." She winked. "Let me know if you need me for anything else." She put a motherly hand on Callie's head, then left.

"Everyone should have a Birdy in their life," Hunter said, reaching for another piece of pizza.

Callie nodded, suddenly overcome with emotions she didn't want to deal with. The nice words that came out of his mouth were too much sometimes. Birdy meant the world to her, and the fact that he recognized Birdy's importance added another reason to like Hunter more than she should.

"Hey." He took her chin gently between his warm fingers and tilted her face toward his. "Did you know it's illegal to be unhappy while eating pizza?"

She shook her head out of his hold. *"Really?"*

"Yes, it's in section two point three of the Life Is Better manual."

How on Earth was she supposed to think him anything but charming? And when he added that bone-melting smile of his, she once again understood why so many instantly fell for him.

"You've got this manual memorized?"

"Most of it."

"What else should I know?" Finished eating, she reached for the stray pillow that had been separated from her bedding and laid down on her back, her head on the pillow. From this angle, she could comfortably stare up at his handsome face.

His eyes roamed over her body. In her leggings and hoodie, she looked sloppy at best, but appreciation clearly sparkled in his gaze. A little shiver shot through her.

"Section one point seven states that business owners are not allowed to mope on their first day in their new shop. It's bad for future business."

"I'm not moping."

He raised his eyebrows.

"Anymore," she amended. Then she gave him a big smile. "What else?"

"Section three point five states that fake smiles are not allowed and grounds for tickling." He dropped his third slice of pizza in the box, moved to his knees, and tickled her. She didn't have time to scurry back or push his arms away before his hands were on her sides making her wiggle and laugh.

She retaliated, his stomach muscles flexing as she tickled him back. There wasn't an ounce of fat on him, his lean body hard yet pliant. Unfortunately, he wasn't nearly as ticklish as she was. Her hoodie rose, and his fingers slipped underneath, making contact with her skin. His hands roamed higher as she tried to wriggle out of his grasp.

Eyes locked on one another, they laughed and

didn't let up, an unspoken challenge between them to see who begged the other to stop first. He definitely had the advantage, but she didn't mind. She didn't mind his hands on her. Not one bit.

But then his knuckle brushed the underside of her breast, and he froze, as if realizing just now that he'd slipped under her sweatshirt. She stilled her hands on his waist. The air crackled between them. No longer laughing, they were both breathing hard.

Her body ached for him to continue his exploration. To cup her breasts, play with her nipples, rip her clothes off so he could add his mouth to the mix.

Oh no, no, no. Crapola in a crayon box.

She scrambled away at the same time he pulled back. "Sorry," he said. He didn't look sorry, though. He looked like he wanted to pounce. She wondered if she looked like that would be okay.

"Don't be silly." She waved off his apology. "You have nothing to be sorry for."

"It's just hearing you laugh is a really amazing sound," he said.

"Shut up." She nervously looked around the cottage. She needed to get back to work, but she also wanted to stay right where she was and see what else he might say.

"I got carried away, but it won't happen again." He stood. "What do you need done next?"

"Umm…" She'd like him to do her. Head to toe. Then repeat. "I should get my room set up first. Would you mind putting together the bed frame?" She rose to her feet with the pillow in her arms.

"You do realize me putting together your bed isn't helping the situation."

"The situation?"

He narrowed his eyes. Her feigned innocence wasn't fooling him, yet he gave her the benefit of the doubt when he said, "Tell me I'm not the only one feeling the gravity between us."

It wouldn't be easy, but she could tell him he was. She *had* to tell him that. Because she couldn't give him what he was looking for.

And because Hunter Owens had the potential to hurt her more deeply than any other person if she gave him even a sliver of her heart.

"You're the only one," she lied.

CHAPTER TWENTY-ONE

When the ranch had given up cattle, they'd planted pine trees, hundreds of them, and now they had a lucrative business of selling Christmas trees. They also had OFO, Owens Family Organics, and were killing it with the safe pesticide Maverick had developed last year. Hunter couldn't be prouder of his brother, but it was yet another reason why he wanted to stand out on his own. Why he wanted the ambassador position so badly.

The warm sun made his shirt stick to his back as he rode Rebel up and down the neat rows of trees. This late in the season, he and Maverick made sure disease hadn't infected any of the trunks or branches and that small animals hadn't chewed through the irrigation. Uncle Tim and their groundskeeper Jerry rode along the northern slopes. The rest of their team picked up any slack along the borders.

"I forgot to ask, is it cool if we add one more to the bachelor party?" Maverick said from atop his horse, Magnolia.

"Yeah, that's fine." Although "bachelor party" wasn't exactly correct given the girls were doing the same thing, at the same time. They'd rented two cabins in Big Sur for the weekend after Thanksgiving. Massages, gourmet food, and poker for the guys. Massages, gourmet food, and wedding romcoms for the girls.

"Andrew is coming with Ava for Thanksgiving

now, so he'll be joining us."

"He doesn't want to hang with the girls?" He was Kennedy's best friend and her man of honor, along with her sister, Ava, as maid of honor.

"No."

"Okay, cool."

"He's a little upset that Callie isn't making his suit for the wedding but is making yours, which by the way, do we need to talk about that?"

"I liked you better before you met Kennedy and didn't want to talk."

Maverick laughed. "I take it that means you're in over your head again."

"Nope. Not even a little." Rebel gave a little neigh and shake of her mane, like she was calling *bullshit*.

"You've been grumpy as hell since Callie left the bunkhouse."

"I've had a toothache," he lied.

"More like heartache." His brother's accurate assessment made him grumpier. The past three days had felt like three months.

"It's not that exactly. I miss her, yes, but I know the score. It doesn't mean I like it, but I will respect it. She…"

"She?" Mav prodded, rather than let it go like he was supposed to.

"She's focused on her business, and that's enough for her." He couldn't stop his mind from traveling down the road of What-If. What if one day she changed her mind about marriage?

"Make it enough for you, too."

Hunter grumbled. "I am."

"Maybe. But I see your mind still working over-time."

"You're damn annoying, you know that?"

Maverick smirked. "I think you mean 'right.'"

"Whatever. Are we done here? I've got a date."

"Yeah, go have fun with *your date*," he said like he knew exactly who Hunter had plans with. Damn his astute brother.

• • •

"I'm almost certain it's here," Jenna said a little while later, a shovel taller than her in her hands.

"What makes you *almost* certain?" Hunter asked, fighting a smile. They'd been hunting for treasure ever since she'd gotten home from school. If they didn't settle on a spot to try their luck soon, they'd require flashlights. What made this spot especially funny was they'd circled back to where they'd start-ed, near the barn and under a giant oak tree.

"Papa said the ranchero would hide his chests near a landmark so he'd know where to look when he came back."

"What makes this tree special?" There were hundreds of trees, not counting the pines, on the property.

"It's the biggest one, so that means it's the old-est." She examined the tree's thick trunk then craned her neck to look up. "For sure this beauty is over a hundred years old so it was here back then."

"You are one smart cookie," he told her, full of pride and inwardly smiling at her word choice.

"I know." She grinned. "I'm not sure all six chests

are here, though."

"No?" He leaned against his own shovel, enjoying everything that came out of her mouth and in no hurry to start digging.

"Uh-uh. If someone else found the spot before he came back, he wouldn't want them to find all his silver, right? So he probably buried them in different places."

"Good thinking."

She stood a little taller. "My brain is always working."

He kicked at the hard ground with his boot. She followed suit and kicked it with her yellow rain boot. "Should I get us started?" he asked, not feeling very optimistic but faking it. If Jenna believed there was treasure buried here, then he would, too.

"Hey."

At the sound of Callie's voice, he immediately turned in happy surprise. "Hey."

"Hi, Callie. We're digging for the silver treasure that is buried here. Want to help?" Jenna said.

"The treasure from the story your grandpa told us?"

"Yep. Me and Uncle Hunt have deducted it could be right here."

"Nice work with the spelling word," Hunter said, putting out his hand so he and Jenna could do their newest secret handshake: touch pinkies, lock hands, swipe through each other's arms, then slap palms, front and back.

"Wow, that's exciting. I'd love to help, but I'm here to tell you it's time for your piano lesson."

Jenna dropped the shovel like a hot potato. "I

almost forgot. Good thing the treasure will still be here tomorrow. Love you, Uncle Hunt! Bye!" She skipped off, on to the next thing in her busy life.

Hunter picked up her shovel and leaned it along with his against the tree.

"I was with Nova and your mom when Cole said he needed Jenna for her lesson. I volunteered to come get her because I had a dream last night…" She looked toward the barn with uncertainty.

"About the barn?" he asked.

"More like who's in the barn." She let out a breath, blowing air through her mouth, then twisting her lips in a very distracting manner. "I have a feeling my next ambassador assignment is going to be horseback riding. So I thought maybe you could help me…"

"You want to see the horses up close?" he supplied, more than happy to help. They will get their next assignments tomorrow.

"Please."

"Let's do it."

They walked into the barn and he headed straight to Rebel. Callie walked a few tentative steps behind him, her hesitancy palpable. While he waited patiently for her to reach his side, he racked his brain for the best words to help alleviate her fears. He understood what a huge step this was for her and felt a responsibility to do right by her. Rebel's gentle eyes whispered friendliness while he rubbed down her mane.

"Hey, girl. We've got a visitor who needs some extra TLC. Her name is Callie, and she's important to me, so I know you'll treat her right. Today is just an introduction so she can see how good-natured you are. She had a bad experience the last time she was on a horse, so she's a little nervous."

"You do always talk to your horse." Callie stood a foot behind his left shoulder.

"Yep. She's a great listener."

Callie very slowly stepped forward, her side pressing against his. The closeness tied him in knots at the same time it put butterflies in his stomach. Freaking butterflies. He didn't get flutters like that, not from anyone or anything else. Unable to stop himself, he put his arm around her. He'd gladly be the person for her to lean on, no matter the situation.

"I know it's ridiculous and I should be over my fear by now, but I can't get that day out of my head. And how scared I was."

"It's not ridiculous. Certain things stay with us forever. What are you feeling right now?"

"Let's see." She raised her hand. "Fear. Embarrassment. Anxiety. Anger. Doubt." She ticked off each one with a finger.

He squeezed her tightly against him, feeling her quiver, before reluctantly letting go. "Do you trust me?"

"It depends. What are you going to do?"

"Give me your hand?" He voiced it as a question so she held all the decision-making power.

She looked from him to the horse and back to him before doing as he asked. He palmed her hand inside his so that together they could pet Rebel. So Callie would hopefully feel a sense of protection. Not that she couldn't take care of herself, but this situation required teamwork and guidance.

He gently tugged her closer so they could rub Rebel in her favorite spot. "It's always best to approach a horse from the side," he said, bringing their hands to Rebel's neck. "And pet her here and then down to her shoulder. She'll stand here all night and let us pet her if we want to. She likes long strokes best." Hunter guided their hands along her mane.

Callie's clammy hand did nothing to take away from the intimacy of the moment. In the quiet barn with sunlight fading, he felt a closeness that went far beyond anything else up to this point. That Callie did trust him meant everything.

"How old is she?" Callie asked, a slight shake in her voice. How did she not know how strong she was?

"Sixteen."

"How old will she get?"

"Horses generally live twenty-five to thirty years. Not nearly long enough for my liking."

Rebel lowered her head, indicating she wanted a scratch on the forehead. At the sudden movement, Callie whipped her arm back.

"It's okay," he said, "she just wants us to scratch here." He rubbed her forehead as Rebel stood perfectly still and let out a big sigh. "Hear that? She likes what we're doing."

Callie cautiously reached out to pet his horse again, their hands touching and overlapping. "She seems friendly."

"She is. Horses are known to help calm people. They're great at reading human emotions and are often used for therapy."

"I did know all that. I've done some research hoping it would help with my anxiety, but the knowing still doesn't make me want to ride again."

Hunter took her hand in his and brought their arms down. Rebel gave him the *two more minutes?* look, making him smile. "Not this time, girl," he told her, then turned to Callie. "I think that's enough for your first day. You should be proud of yourself. You did great."

"Thanks to you." She looked up into his eyes with more emotion than ever before. Affection. Awe. Appreciation. The connection between them grew more intense by the second, and he wanted to kiss her so badly, he swayed. Swallowed the thick lump in the back of his throat.

They stared at each other, caught in something that felt so right it bordered on painful. At least for him.

He bent his head slowly, giving her time to back away or shake her head or speak her objection. One kiss. He needed to brush his lips against hers just once to seal this moment in their memories.

The closer he got to her mouth, the mouth he'd dreamed about for years, the faster his heart beat. She'd been reluctant the last time he'd gotten too close, and he'd stop the second she gave any sign of hesitation.

But she didn't.

Her long, dark eyelashes swept down. She tilted her chin up. Thank the heavens he had her agreement. He might have died right there on the spot otherwise.

"You sure?" he whispered, needing to hear her

permission, too.

"Yes."

Tingles—actual tingles—broke out on his arms as he inched closer. The sounds and smells of the barn vanished, and the only thing he was aware of was Callie.

His lips brushed hers. Softly. Tenderly. With complete and utter worship.

His eyes closed, the touch of their mouths filling him with heat and lust. No, not lust. Yes, he wanted to take this further, learn every dip and curve of her body with his hands and tongue, bury himself deep inside her. But more than that, he wanted her to feel like she was the most important person in the world to him.

Because she was. No matter how hard he fought it.

He continued to kiss her with light, gentle strokes as feel-good sensations dazed him. *Finally*. He was finally kissing the woman he couldn't get out of his head.

The unforgettable moment shattered, though, when she abruptly pulled back. Without a word, she turned and ran out of the barn.

Shit! He'd just ruined everything.

CHAPTER TWENTY-TWO

Callie's horseback riding inkling came true. Maybe she *did* have more than a little magic in her.

Faking bravery, she went back to the ranch the next day. Not that she wouldn't have gone back anyway. She owed Hunter an explanation for running away like a coward.

She found him outside the barn in worn denim jeans that fit him to perfection, a cowboy hat on his head and a look of relief on his handsome face when their eyes met.

"Hey," he said with caution. She hated his carefulness and needed it to end immediately.

"Hey. I'm sorry about yesterday."

"I'm sorry if I—"

She shushed him with a finger to his lips. "You have nothing to be sorry for. You didn't do anything wrong."

He took her wrist and guided her hand down. A slow, sexy slight turn of his lips followed. "I know that," he drawled. "A kiss that good isn't wrong. I was going to say I'm sorry if I took you by surprise."

"You didn't."

"So, I…" He trailed off, eyebrows raised. Eyes colored with confidence. The man who'd given her The Kiss That Changed Everything knew he kissed well.

"Let me help you out," he offered when she didn't say anything. "The earth shifted and you felt like we were the only two people who existed in the entire world. Oh, wait, that was how I felt. Now it's your turn."

Her heart skipped a beat at his easy confession. As far as compliments went, that was a great one. No one had ever said as much to her before. She appreciated his candor—and owed him the same in return. "There was a definite shift, and I felt your kiss everywhere. It was too much."

"So you ran."

She nodded.

"And you're here now because…"

"I wanted to apologize and also tell you my premonition came true."

"The horseback riding?"

Again, she nodded. If presented with riding a horse or kissing Hunter a second time, she wasn't sure which scared her more.

He lifted his cowboy hat off his head, ran his fingers through his golden locks, then put the hat back on. "I was just about to check on something out by the Christmas trees, but if you can wait twenty minutes or so, I'll be back and we can pet Rebel again."

"Sounds good. Thanks."

While she waited, she walked around the perimeter of the barn to enjoy the mid-day sunshine and give herself a pep talk. If she really wanted to come out from underneath the shadow of her sister, she needed to ride Rebel. The ambassador assignment wouldn't get done otherwise. She wouldn't win the job without facing her biggest fear.

Logically, she knew her accident was a fluke. Logic didn't always take into account fear and emotions, though. And common sense didn't always factor into reasons for wanting something. Callie believed being ambassador would set her free from the comparisons to Brooke and bring her a sense of peace. But what if it didn't?

The clatter of hoofs drew her attention. Her heart sped up when she saw Hunter riding Rebel toward the barn where she stood outside the open doors. He made riding look so easy and effortless. *He* looked sexy and strong, and her dirty mind immediately went to riding him. She shook that thought right out of her head.

Rebel slowed the closer she got to the barn and came to a stop a few feet away. Hunter dismounted with one fluid, graceful motion, and she couldn't take her eyes off him. He smiled at her, and her nipples stiffened. Then he had the nerve to take off his cowboy hat and wipe the back of his hand across his forehead. That, combined with his long, jean-clad legs, boots, and well-fitted shirt, resuscitated the dirty thoughts she was trying to file away for later. It would be nice if this brand-new issue of thinking him sexy all the time died a quick death.

"Hey." He slid the hat back on, shading his bright blue eyes, but not detracting in the least from their appeal. "You done with the pep talk and ready for another session with Rebel?"

"How did you know I was doing that?" Some people loved it when their significant other read their mind, but she'd prefer Hunter to knock it off. Besides, he wasn't her significant anything.

"Lucky guess." He stopped in front of her. He might be sweaty, but he still smelled good.

Cedarwood and man and if she weren't anxious to get on a horse, she might run away again to avoid her body's response to him.

He leaned his head toward Rebel. "You cool like this? Without a gate between us."

With her feet on the ground, yes, she could be cool. Or at least try. "I think so."

Like he'd done yesterday, Hunter held her hand to get her started rubbing down Rebel's mane. The horse seemed much bigger outside her stall, causing goose bumps to spread up Callie's arms.

And as always, Rebel remained calm and sweet.

"Smile, Triple C," Hunter reminded her.

Callie unclenched her jaw and did as he said.

"Horses are very observant and in-tune to their surroundings. If you seem like you're having fun and relaxed, then Rebel will be at ease, too. And the more you assure her that everything is fine, the more you'll start to believe it, too," he added softly.

Easy for him to say. He'd been riding forever. And clearly, he and Rebel had a special relationship.

"I sort of know how you feel," he said. "My situation was different, but the fear was there."

Her breath hitched. "What do you mean?"

"I was driving to San Francisco and a moving van lost control and fishtailed across two lanes. It slammed into the front end of my truck and my car flipped. Miraculously, I didn't hit anyone else, but the car was totaled. The fire department had to pry me out."

"Oh my God. How did I not know about this?"

"It happened when you and Nova were studying abroad."

"Were you hurt?" She would have heard if he'd been seriously injured.

"A lot of bruises and whiplash, but otherwise I was okay. Mentally, though, I took a beating. It took me a few weeks before I got back behind the wheel. I was freaked out. Scared and worried someone would hit me again. I still flinch sometimes if another car swerves or makes a bad lane change. It's not even close to what happened to you, but I do understand your worry and panic." A faraway look crossed his face before he visibly shook his shoulders. "I hate thinking about it."

She squeezed his arm, in support and gratitude. "Thank you for sharing that with me. It means a lot."

"You're not alone in your feelings, Cal. We all have memories we don't like thinking about. And you. You came back so positive and strong; I was in awe."

Was it admiration he remembered now instead of pity? God, if that was the case, she'd wasted years feeling humiliated whenever she saw him. She sighed in profound relief.

"You okay?" he asked.

"I'm great." Even standing next to her biggest fear. Because with Hunter there, too, she had nothing to worry about.

He scratched behind Rebel's ear. The horse lowered her head and pushed against his chest. The move startled Callie, and she jumped back.

"She's just letting me know she likes the scratches," Hunter quickly said.

Apparently, Callie's flight-or-fight response still held power, because despite the reassurance from

Hunter, the thought of getting on a horse made her lightheaded and sick to her stomach. She rolled her lips together to stave off the tears of disappointment threatening to fall. She still couldn't do this.

"Hey." Hunter stepped between her and Rebel. His hands settled on her shoulders in comfort as his gaze touched on hers with warmth and patience. "I won't let anything happen to you." He brushed a wayward curl away from her face. "I… You're important to me, Cal, and I like you too much."

She blinked up at him. The way he said "like you" sounded so affectionately sincere she wondered if he truly did *like her,* like her. That their kiss meant more than a physical desire. The trouble with that was he wanted to walk down the aisle sooner rather than later, and she had no plans to get married. Ever.

Not next year. Not in five years. Not if a magical spell was cast that promised her the forever kind of love.

"Thanks, but right now I can't do this," she whispered, eager to get away and be anywhere but here for more reasons than one. Suddenly, standing here with him was too much.

"I could put you on George instead."

"George is a mule, not a horse."

"I won't tell if you don't tell."

George might be closer to the ground than Rebel and a beginner's perfect match, but it was more than that. She didn't want to get on any four-legged animal. And she didn't want Hunter to say another sweet thing to her. Her defenses were only so strong.

Jenna's dog, Rumi, chose that moment to run

toward them, barking in playful excitement. Rebel's hooves kicked up dirt.

The horse's response made Callie's pulse jump back into panic mode. She took a big step back, ready to flee. Hunter moved with ease to pick up Rumi with one hand while his other grabbed Rebel's reins. Callie scooted further back to give him plenty of space, then watched as Rumi and Rebel went nose-to-nose, obviously friendly with one another.

"Okay, you got to say hello, now go on." Hunter put Rumi down. She scampered away just as Nova came jogging over.

"How did it go?" Nova asked.

"It didn't." Callie hung her head, shame and fear not so easy to get rid of, even with Hunter's support and kind words.

"Stop it." Nova wrapped her in a hug. "You are still all kinds of awesome and so what if it takes more time?"

"I don't have much of that." At the moment, she doubted she'd ever get on a horse during her entire lifetime.

"Well," Nova said, stepping back and planting a pleased-as-punch smile on her face. "I have some news for you that I think you're going to love."

CHAPTER TWENTY-THREE

"They're calling you the Marry Matchmaker!" Nova's elation successfully wiped out any lingering distress over Rebel. *And* the confusing tenderness Hunter sparked.

"Who is?" Callie asked, intrigued.

"That reporter from the *Gazette*? Vivian something. She's dubbed you the Marry Matchmaker, writing about how your maid of honor dresses lead the wearer to their perfect match. Did you know it's happened six times? I hadn't realized that."

"Birdy's kept track," Callie said, nodding.

"My best friend is the Marry Matchmaker! You need to start using that in your marketing."

"I totally will." Holy ceremony. With a moniker like that, she'd get more business for sure. Guaranteed if Hunter and Kennedy's sister met their perfect matches. She took a second to put positive vibes out into the world.

"There's sure to be more weddings next year," Nova announced with enthusiasm, her eyes zeroed in on Hunter, like she expected him to reach groom status or else. "Speaking of weddings, we're all set for the bachelor-bachelorette party, right?"

"Yes," Hunter said, seeming unaffected by his sister's expression or Callie's new nickname. He turned to her. "You should come. I'm sure Kennedy would approve."

"Already beat you to it, big brother. Kennedy

said you are totally invited, Cal. There's plenty of room in our cabin and we really want you there. Will you come?"

Hunter put his arm around her shoulders. "You deserve a weekend away. Come with us."

Callie blinked back tears *again*. These people were more her family than her own, and being included meant more than she could say. Nova had mentioned the Big Sur weekend last week, hinting she wanted Callie to tag along, but now that it was official, she couldn't say no.

She didn't want to say no. These were her feel-good people. Especially Hunter. *No. Not Hunter.*

"Sounds good. Thank you."

"Now how about I treat you two girls to some funch," Hunter said, dropping his arm.

"Funch?" she and Nova said simultaneously.

"Fun at lunch." He grinned, and *gah*, she couldn't resist him when he did that.

She and Nova exchanged a look. "Burgers at Sutter's?" they asked.

"Where else?"

The three of them did lunch, and it was just what Callie needed to get over the horseback-riding fail. On the solo walk back to the cottage afterward, she couldn't stop thinking about the ambassador opportunity. She loved Windsong with every beat of her heart. She carried small-town pride and values with her every day. Somehow, she'd get on that horse and share much more than the activity in her article. She'd write about overcoming fears.

Feeling better about the future, she picked up her pace. The sun disappeared behind a big, puffy cloud.

Wind rustled lightly through the trees lining the sidewalk.

"Callie, wait up!"

At the sound of Hunter's voice, she turned to find him jogging toward her. He'd ditched his cowboy hat at the ranch, and as he came to a stop in front of her, he ran his fingers through his light brown hair. "Hey," he said.

"Is everything okay?" she asked.

"Yeah, I just wanted to let you know when you're ready to do the horse thing again, come find me."

She twisted around and resumed walking with him at her side. Her shop didn't officially open for appointments until Monday, but there were still a few things left to do. And okay, maybe she didn't really want to get into a long conversation about horses.

"I will." Probably. "It's a good thing I've got a couple of weeks."

"That leaves us plenty of time."

"Thanks for making it an 'us' when you didn't have to. We are still competing for the job."

"Hey, when I win, it's going to be fair and square."

"And when I win, I'll thank you in my acceptance speech."

"Feeling pretty confident, are we?"

"Honestly? I don't know." She blew a wayward curl off her face. "Today, you said some things that rearranged what I thought about that day, but deep down, I'm still terrified of getting on a horse again."

"Like I said, everything you're feeling is justified. I was there that day, too, and scared out of my mind."

Callie made a conscious effort to swallow her

pride. He'd seen her at her very worst but seemed to remember her at her strongest, and that's what she should carry with her.

They were quiet for a few steps before she asked, "Why were you scared?" She'd never imagined him afraid that day. She only remembered a look of pity in his piercing blue eyes.

When he didn't answer, she stole a peek at him. He appeared to be deep in thought.

"Sit for a minute?" he asked when they arrived at her front stoop. She sat beside him, close enough to touch each other. Over the past month, she'd grown so comfortable being near him that his strength, his scent, his warmth enveloped her in a way she'd never been wrapped up in before.

"I remember that day vividly," he said softly. "The second I laid eyes on you, I thought you were the prettiest thing I'd ever seen. I was too young to lead you and your sister on a ride, but I lingered nearby. When you got hurt, I was terrified and worried you wouldn't be okay."

Callie could barely believe her ears. He'd been scared? "Your face was the last thing I saw for three weeks."

"I wanted to visit you so badly, but I didn't want to go against your wishes."

She turned to face him. "What are you talking about?"

"Before you went unconscious, you whispered, 'Don't,' and so I stayed away."

"I don't remember that. The last thing I remember is you looking at me with pity, and I was so embarrassed that I must have said that to mean don't feel sorry for me."

Anguish crossed his face. "The last thing I felt for you was pity, Callie." He gently cupped the side of her face.

Her heart galloped at his tenderness, at his further confessions.

"I had a crush on you at first sight. I didn't know your name, so in my mind, I called you Red."

"Why didn't you call me that after we met again?"

"Practically every redhead is nicknamed Red. It wasn't good enough for you."

She pressed her cheek into his hand. "I don't know what to say." All their awkward interactions *were* because he'd liked her, and she'd used their differences as a tool to keep her distance because of her shame.

"You don't have to say anything, just kiss me." This time there was no cocky megawatt grin. This time he gave her a small, closed-mouth smile that almost seemed shy. Hopeful. It extinguished any doubts about kissing him again.

The gravitational pull was too strong to fight. She knew it a bad idea, knew she'd hurt him or he'd hurt her. Right here, right now, though, she didn't care. She leaned forward and pressed her mouth to his.

His lips were warm, inviting. The hand on her cheek moved to the back of her head. His other hand wrapped around her waist. He wasted no time taking control of the kiss, slanting his mouth over hers with mastery, coaxing her lips apart with one touch of his tongue.

She scooted closer and melted against him. He

tightened his hold, pressed his mouth to hers like he couldn't get enough. Kissing Hunter ranked high on her list of Best Things Ever. She never wanted to stop. He eased up a little, brushed her lips like he savored them. Their tongues advanced, retreated. He nibbled, sucked, caressed.

She'd never been so thoroughly kissed.

A delicious ache built between her legs. Her skin tingled. When he groaned in enjoyment, she smiled. Feeling the corners of her mouth lift, he broke the kiss.

Staring deep into her eyes, he said, "I like making you smile."

"You should keep doing it, then."

He quickly claimed her mouth again, tempering the steely touch with softer strokes. He'd shaved this morning, and his smooth jawline felt better than any material she'd held against her skin. They kissed and kissed until…

"*Ahem*."

Callie recognized that *ahem*. She pulled away from Hunter, not embarrassed to be caught with him, but disappointed that their encounter was interrupted.

Birdy stood on the sidewalk with a far-too-amused expression on her face. "Did you forget we had an Insta meeting? I'd come back later if I could, but I have a thing."

"I didn't forget," she fibbed. She couldn't even think of her own name at the moment.

Hunter crossed his arms over his lap, making no move to leave yet. "Hey, Birdy. I'm not staying."

"*You* could come back later," Birdy offered. She

had on her favorite yellow tracksuit with a white stripe down the sides and apparently thought herself a matchmaker.

"I—"

"He can't," Callie piped up, cutting Hunter off. He couldn't because Callie needed time to think about The Second Kiss That Rocked Her World. Plus, she had dresses to sew and a best man suit to finish. She also had pictures to hang on her walls. With her brain still scrambled from kissing him, though, she blurted out, "I have to wash my hair."

It's true with all her long curls, it did take at least five minutes.

Rather than call her out, Hunter busted up laughing.

She couldn't help it, she laughed, too.

"You're funny, Triple C." He stood, looked down at her with his back to Birdy, then whispered, "Trust me when I say it won't feel anywhere near as good as me coming back."

"I don't know," she retorted. "I can stand under the hot water for a very long time."

He bent over and brushed his mouth against her ear. "But I can go all night."

Her lips parted on a sigh. Or maybe it was a pant. Whatever it was, he walked away leaving her wanting more.

CHAPTER TWENTY-FOUR

"Try not to move," Callie said for the third time, slowly backing away from a shirtless Caleb McNeal. The firefighter, clad only in jeans and who knew what underneath, stood with one bare foot on a stack of hay, one elbow on his knee, and a bouquet of red roses in his hands.

Her job as production assistant to Nova and their photographer friend, Sarah, did not suck.

Once out of the way, Sarah started snapping away with her fancy Nikon camera. "That's it! Now don't smile, and give me a smoldering look. Yes!"

Callie and Nova exchanged a look and laughed.

"What's so funny?" Sarah asked.

"You said smolder and Caleb is our final firefighter," Nova said.

"Oh, right! Caleb, you don't by any chance have your firefighter's helmet, do you?" Sarah called out.

"Sorry, no."

Sarah shrugged and got back to work. They'd shot most of the months for the Botanical Society calendar fundraiser, each volunteer being a good sport.

"Hey, Nova. Callie," Maverick said, coming to stand beside his sister. "I can't believe I'm doing this."

Nova gave him a quick hug. "You're doing it because you love me."

"That's exactly right."

"And because Kennedy wants to plaster you on her wall at work."

He chuckled. "That, too."

"Where's Hunter?" Nova asked.

"He's right behind—"

"Here I am," he said, jogging to Callie's side. Their last two models were here.

Here being a beautiful spot on the edge of Owens Ranch with green grass, trees, and an ocean view in the distance. The weather gods were with them this afternoon, and the sun had command of the sky. Not a leaf rustled in the still air. They'd used a couple of all-terrain golf carts to transport several bales of hay to the site, as well as buckets filled with water and twelve different kinds of flowers. This *was* supposed to be a calendar showing off pretty blooms.

Glancing over her shoulder, Callie saw the guys' horses tied to a tree.

"Hi," Hunter said to her.

"Hi." They hadn't seen each other in a week. Before that, she'd tried two more times to ride Rebel. Both had been failures on her part. An invisible yet undeniable barrier kept her from swinging her leg up and over Rebel to take a seat. She'd given up to save her sanity. Hunter had done his best to ease her mind and body with a helping hand and words of encouragement, but it just wasn't meant to be.

"How did your article turn out?" he asked.

Refusing to concede, she'd put her own spin on horseback riding, writing it from the perspective of a spectator rather than a participant. Hunter and Chad had graciously ridden inside the paddock while she sat on the fence to watch, and the words had flowed. She wrote about her accident, the aftermath, and her struggle to "get back on the horse." Wanting the essay to end on a funny note, she shared how she'd been at the barn, talking to the horses, when a huge fly started buzzing around her head and wouldn't let her be. She ran out of the barn and stepped right in horse poop. She'd titled the article, "Another Shitty Day in Windsong Paradise."

"I think it turned out well. How about yours?"

He scrunched up his nose. "Fine. How anyone drinks tea, I don't know, but I feel like I did it justice."

"It's too bad we couldn't switch." Not that she liked tea, but she could chamomile over cowgirling any day of the week.

"My thoughts exactly."

Caleb strode toward them with his shirt in his free hand. She stared at his sculpted abs and muscled chest with her lips pressed together, lest she accidentally drool. Glancing at Nova out of the corner of her eye, her bestie was in the same boat. Hunter made a grumbling noise.

"Thank you so much, Caleb," Nova said. "I appreciate you being here and for gathering up a few of the other station guys."

"I'm sure we'll hear about it, but we're always happy to help with a good cause." He handed the flowers back to Nova. "I hope the calendar is a success. Hey, Maverick. Hunter." He shook hands with both men. "Looks like I'm in further good company."

"It's hard to say no to your baby sister."

Maverick rustled the top of Nova's hair, a move that always annoyed her. On the flip side, the act filled Callie with warmth. Nova's three older brothers teased her because they loved her.

"Stop it," Nova said, batting his arm away.

Caleb's eyes landed on Callie. "You free later to grab some dinner?"

"Umm…" She sensed Hunter tense to her left and Nova bubble with excitement to her right. When Caleb arrived for the shoot, he'd flirted. Asked about her trip to Africa. Complimented her appearance. So why was it so hard for her to say *yes*?

Dumb question. She knew why.

"Can I text you when we're done here?"

"Sure. Have fun with Double Trouble."

Hunter reached over and fist bumped Maverick behind her and Nova's backs. "We haven't been called that in a long time," Maverick said.

"Not since that thing at the bonfire years ago," Hunter added.

"What thing?" Nova asked. "Why don't I know about this thing?"

"There's a lot you don't know about." Hunter gave Caleb a lift of his chin. "See you around, man."

"Maverick!" Sarah called out, glancing up from the clipboard in her hands. "You're next." Sarah *did* have a hot date tonight and didn't want to run late.

Nova walked with her brother to help get him positioned for his shot. She'd saved a magnolia flower for him—the name of his horse.

"So, Caleb, huh?" Hunter said.

Callie shrugged. "I don't know. Maybe."

"Sounds like you'd be open to a better offer." His

side brushed hers, and just like that, she hoped he offered.

"I don't—"

He shut her up by pressing his finger to her mouth. His electric blue eyes zeroed in on her with THA—typical Hunter affection. "There is no more 'don'ts' only 'dos'. There's something going on between you and me and we can leave it at that. This doesn't have to be anything serious." Arms at their sides, he discreetly linked his pointer finger around hers. "Just two consenting adults who like to spend time together. Unless I'm wrong about that."

"You're not wrong."

"What are you guys so deep in conversation about?" Nova asked. She eyed them back and forth. "Never mind." She waved her hand in the air and turned around. "Continue on."

"Duty calls," Callie whispered to Hunter before jogging over to her best friend. "Hunt and I can talk later. I'm here for you."

"Great, because my brother is being a pain in the ass."

Callie noted the pained expression on Maverick's face and bit her lip to keep from laughing. "He really doesn't want to be here."

"Bro!" Hunter said, stepping into the action. "Can you lighten up? You look constipated."

"No, I don't," Maverick argued.

"I'm pretty sure if we looked it up in the dictionary, we'd see your face. Imagine this is for Kennedy and you want her to get turned on when she looks at you."

"Eww," Nova said.

"Just wait until it's your turn," Maverick grumbled.

"I will definitely look better than you." Hunter puffed out his chest.

The statement struck her as funny given the two of them could pass for twins, Hunter almost an identical version of his older brother. Looking at a shirtless Maverick, Callie could agree he was very attractive. Hunter, though, was a hundred times sexier.

"Forget it, mini-me, we both know who the better-looking one is." Maverick grinned.

And Sarah's camera *click, click, clicked.* "That's it! Give me another one of those smiles."

Hunter gave his brother a dirty look. He hated the mini-me moniker.

Maverick was all smiles after that.

"I'm doing this for his benefit," Hunter said out of the side of his mouth. "He loves riling me up."

"You're not upset?"

"Nah. I'm over it, and besides, I'm stronger, faster, funnier, and don't have any love handles."

Callie studied Maverick. "I don't see any love handles."

"That little bit of fat above his jeans? I have none of that." He patted his stomach. She could attest to his lean-and-muscled body. Not to mention his naked butt was permanently etched in her memory.

"He doesn't, either," Callie whispered.

"Shush. Don't ruin my mental picture."

"Okay, I think we've got enough shots." Sarah lowered her camera.

Nova tossed Maverick his shirt. "You owe me,"

he said to her with fondness, then rustled her hair again just as Nova's phone rang from the rear pocket of her jeans. "Hey, Mom. Oh no. Okay, I'll be right there." She tucked the phone back in her pocket. "There's a flower emergency for tomorrow's wedding, and I need to get to the inn asap. Cal, can you finish up with Hunter?"

"Sure."

"Sarah, thank you so, so much for everything." Nova hugged her. "Let me know when I can come review the proofs."

"Will do," Sarah said.

Maverick pulled his phone out and looked at the screen. "Looks like I have an emergency, too." By the sound of his voice, he was fibbing.

"What? You don't want to stay and see how bad I'm going to make you look?"

"Give it your best shot and tell me about it later."

"All right, let's get this done," Sarah said with a clap of her hands.

Hunter took his shirt off, and yep, he looked a thousand times yummier than his brother. Smooth skin, muscles, a trail of light brown hair that disappeared behind the button of his jeans. He put his cowboy hat back on his head. "Where would you like me?"

Oh, there were many places Callie would like him.

Sarah asked him to stack one hay bale on top of another and then another so he could lean his back against it. Callie pulled a large sunflower out of the bucket and carried it over to him.

"Let's put the flower in your pocket and have

you cross your arms over your chest so we show off your biceps," Sarah said.

Hunt crossed his arms, then raised his eyebrows at Callie. He wanted her to place the flower. Okay, no problem. She definitely didn't want Sarah doing it.

The flower wilted because of the stem length, so Callie grabbed the scissors they'd brought and cut it shorter.

Chin down, Hunter watched her pull his pocket open and slide the thick stem inside. Being this close to his bare torso and the zipper of his jeans, she licked her lips. Having her hands in his pants sparked flutters. The soft, well-worn denim fit him lovingly. His stomach muscles jumped when she grazed them with the back of her hand.

She stepped back. With a shorter stem, the flower's bloom stood tall. "Stay still."

"You talking to me or the flower, Triple C?"

"Both."

"Callie," Sarah said, "can you tilt his hat up just a bit?"

Eyes locked, she moved closer to lift the front of his cowboy hat. He smelled amazing, and masculinity rolled off him in warm waves. This man was a protector. Someone trustworthy. Generous.

She glanced at his mouth. The corners lifted before she looked back up at his eyes. *Caught.*

"Perfect," Sarah called out, breaking the magnetism Callie had fallen under.

No filter required, Callie thought, watching Sarah take pictures. The sun loved Hunter. As if this time of day was dedicated to him. With his chin down, his hat just so, and his body perfectly rugged, she'd bet his month a favorite with buyers.

"Let's have you lift one arm, like you're about to take off your hat."

Hunt followed Sarah's directions.

"No, that doesn't work," she said. "Let's put the flower between your teeth and have you put both hands in your pockets. Then cross one ankle over the other."

He placed the flower stem between his teeth and pocketed his hands, leaving his thumbs out. The move slid his jeans down low enough to show off the *V* on his hips. Callie swallowed. She heard Sarah sigh. Then he smiled and his gorgeous dimples appeared on his cheeks.

This was the money shot, the one that would sell the calendar. Callie made a mental note to suggest Hunter for the cover.

Sarah snapped away, then had him do one more pose. When finished, Sarah apologized for having to rush off and left.

Hunter unstacked the hay. Callie watched him rather than clean up the waters and snacks Nova had provided for their models. He'd yet to put his shirt back on, and she enjoyed the way his muscles flexed in his back and arms. The way his strong, capable hands gripped the hay bales like they weighed nothing.

He turned around to catch her staring at him. The lazy spread of his mouth, corners lifted, did her in. She marched toward him with one thing on her mind: putting his lips to better use.

CHAPTER TWENTY-FIVE

Callie stopped in front of him, a burst of courage and desire weaving through her.

"I think I'm going to like this," Hunter said. His drawl in combination with his sheer ruggedness were undeniably sexy. So much so, if she weren't standing before him, she'd think him photoshopped.

She pushed his shoulder to knock him off-balance so he'd sit down on the bale of hay behind him. He got the hint, taking a seat with an ease that said, *I'm all yours.* Then he looked up at her with eyebrows raised and lips pressed together in a smirk that further fed her determination. With her hair piled in a bun on top of her head, the sun warmed the back of her neck. Blowing a loose tendril off her face, she straddled his lap.

Her soft knit joggers rubbed against his jeans, and they both let out a soft sigh of satisfaction. "Hello, cowboy."

"Hello, gorgeous." His hands remained at his side, like a full-access pass to do as she pleased.

She loved that he seemed to know her thoughts, know that she needed to be in control of the situation. She placed her hands on his broad shoulders, doing her best to build up the anticipation. They stayed like that, gazing into each other's eyes, their chests moving up and down.

Slowly, she slid her hands down, over his collarbone, down to his pecs. She took her time caressing his chest, closed her eyes, and committed the shape and feel to memory. Feathering her fingers out, she delicately rubbed up and away from his breastbone. He shivered when she rubbed her thumbs over his flat nipples.

Reconnecting with his heated gaze, she took a steadying breath. Being outside like this added a hint of danger to an already dangerous man. She'd never acted so out of character before. Reckless felt good. Powerful.

"I love your hands on me," he said, voice husky.

"Me, too," she answered, a little breathless. Then she continued her exploration, down his sides, to his stomach, where the muscle there once again quivered from her touch. "You're beautiful."

"No one's ever called me that before."

"What have they called you?"

"Stud. Hot. Sexy. Handsomer than my brothers." The corners of his eyes crinkled. "I might be the only one to use that last one."

"All true," she agreed. She slid her hands up his torso, resting them back on his shoulders. Lifting one hand, she flicked his cowboy hat off his head. Her fingers found their way to his messy, light brown hair. The strands soft, she relaxed her arms atop his shoulders and combed the longish locks, eliciting a contented groan from him.

His eyes closed, giving her unfettered access to study every inch of his face. High cheekbones. Slightly crooked nose. Long eyelashes. Full mouth. Each part came together to make a gorgeous whole.

"It's taking all my strength to keep my hands off you," he said, eyes opening.

"Thanks for giving me time to touch you."

"I've heard about sweet torture but never experienced it until now."

"Torture, huh?" She wiggled in his lap, feeling how she affected him. She was equally afflicted but didn't let on.

"*Callie*," he warned. "A man can only take so much."

She crossed her arms behind his neck and pressed closer, her breasts grazing his chest. Her sweatshirt, providing only a thin barrier, was a relief and a hindrance. She thought about taking it off. Unlatching her bra and tossing it aside.

Hunter interrupted her musing by making some sort of growly sound and looking so intensely into her eyes that she knew they'd reached his breaking point.

Okay, time to end this slow burn.

She smashed her mouth to his with zero control now. His lips parted on a moan, and she slipped her tongue inside. He kissed her back with eagerness and passion that swept over her entire body. And when his hands moved—one to the nape of her neck and the other to her lower back—she lost herself in the kiss. He tasted like pumpkin spice and everything nice and filled her with the kind of luck she felt looking at a picture-perfect rainbow after a cold, rainy day.

Heat spread to between her legs. Her boobs grew heavy. Every kiss with Hunter was better than the last.

"Callie," he murmured, pulling back just enough to catch his breath.

"Hunter," she mumbled, feeling too much to say anything else.

He dove back in, kissing her with fierceness one moment and tenderness the next. His grip on her tightened, eliminating any hint of space between them. She held on for the ride, hoping he never stopped kissing her. She'd die if he did, for sure.

They kissed.

And kissed.

And kissed.

She loved that he didn't rush to take it further. His hands roamed her body, yet he seemed to enjoy the intimacy of their mouths fused together as much as she did. He seemed to know she wasn't quite ready to take it any further. He *knew* her. The heady thought had her easing back.

"That kiss should have set this hay on fire," Hunter said.

She grinned, happy he felt the kiss as deeply as she had.

He touched her cheek, then slid a fingertip down the column of her neck, making her shiver. "You do things to me. Insanely good things." He took her hand and brought it to his chest, over his heart. "Things I feel here."

His heart pounded under her palm.

Fear suddenly squeezed *her* heart. His words flattered her. Mattered to her. She could feel herself falling hard for him. But they wanted different things. Not to mention, his perfect match awaited him at the same time her lucky matchmaking reputation counted on it.

"I feel the same," she gave him before getting to

her feet and handing him his shirt. "We should get going before it's dark."

He took the clothing and pulled it over his head. "Are you going to meet Caleb?"

"You know I'm not." She couldn't, not with Hunter's taste in her mouth and scent on her skin. Not that she'd really planned to before the kiss, either. "I've got some sewing and paperwork to do."

"Can I stop by with food?"

"That's nice of you to ask, but not tonight." She really did need to focus on her job and not a certain cowboy.

"Another time, then," he said with an upbeat attitude.

She nodded. She could do that. She was the girl who had a good time and didn't count on tomorrow. Today had been great. Beyond great.

She turned away and touched her bottom lip. Not everyone got kissed like she just had. *Lucky girl.*

CHAPTER TWENTY-SIX

"Three…two…one!"

The hundred-foot-tall Christmas tree standing in the middle of the roundabout on Main Street lit up, casting a spectacular glow over the crowd assembled on the sidewalk. Everyone oohed and ahhed. Jenna, sitting atop Hunter's shoulders, whistled. Pride filled him. He'd taught her to whistle the other day. He'd also been the guy to pick the tree making everyone smile.

"You did good," Maverick said from beside him. Every year his family donated the giant evergreen to celebrate the start of the holiday season. Usually, Mav did the picking, but when Hunter told him he could do it, his brother had said, "Okay." Just like that. Then he'd added, "You want more responsibility around here, so that's what we'll do."

"Thanks," Hunter said now, a yawn slipping out. He'd worked his ass off the past two days, arranging to have the tree cut down, then helping with the transfer and setup.

"Who wants hot chocolate?" Hunter's mom asked.

"I do!" Jenna said.

"I thought so." His mom put out her arms to help retrieve Jenna from his shoulders.

"We'll join you," Cole said, a sleeping Gia tucked against his chest inside a baby carrier. Bethany nodded in agreement.

"Any other takers?" Hunter's dad asked.

Kennedy looked at her phone. "Ava and Andrew are almost here, so we should head home. They're sorry they missed the tree lighting."

"No worries," his mom said. "You guys go do your thing, and we'll see everyone tomorrow for dinner."

"It's you and me and the turkey trot bright and early tomorrow morning, right, Jenna Wenna?" Nova asked their niece.

"Right! I'll be ready."

They said their goodbyes, and then Hunter and Nova caught a ride with Maverick and Kennedy back to their place for tonight's pre-Thanksgiving pizza party.

"I thought Callie was going to be here," Hunter said to his sister on the way to Maverick's truck.

"She's going to meet us at Mav's. She was Zooming with her parents and sister tonight since they're still out of town, and I guess they won't be available tomorrow."

His stomach sank at that. Callie didn't complain about her family's indifference, she lived with it, and that had to be especially hard around the holidays. "What's she doing for Thanksgiving?"

"She's spending it with Birdy since Birdy's two boys will be here for Christmas this year instead. I invited her to our house for a second dessert, though."

He nodded, lost in thought. Their kiss last weekend had left a permanent mark on him. That she initiated it made it even better. If all they did was kiss, he'd take it. He'd take whatever she wanted to give him before he put on his best man suit.

They arrived at Maverick and Kennedy's cabin a few minutes later. Barley greeted them at the door with her tail wagging. "Hey girl," Hunter said to the golden shepherd mix. He lavished her with pets and let her lick his chin.

Kennedy got right to work setting up the kitchen with all the fixings to make their own pizzas. Maverick set out plates, napkins, and utensils. Hunter opened the fridge to grab a beer. "Anyone else want one?" He raised the bottle in the air.

Maverick snagged it out of his hand. "Thanks, man."

Hunter was about to grumble until he noticed his brother give the beer to his fiancée. "Here you go, shortcake."

"Thanks, honeybun."

Hunt pulled out two more bottles, handing one to Maverick. He then joined Nova in the family room. She had her nose buried in her phone so didn't even notice him sit down on the couch beside her. He leaned over for a peek at what had her riveted. She whipped the phone away so fast she fell onto her side. Then she rolled off the couch and jumped to her feet. *Impressive.*

"That wasn't obvious or anything," he said.

"What are you talking about?" She hid the phone in her pocket.

"You're texting someone you don't want me to know about. Why don't you want me to know about it? Who is he?"

"It's no one."

"Liar." From the way her cheeks were flushed,

she had something—or someone—she wanted to keep under wraps.

"I'm entitled to my privacy, so just forget about it."

"No can do, baby sister. Spill."

The doorbell rang.

"I'll get it!" Nova called out, hurrying around the couch. Saved by a literal bell.

He'd get to the bottom of it eventually.

She opened the door. "Hi, guys!"

Squeals of delight rang out that pierced the air and sent Barley scrambling over to him. "It's okay. It's just Ava and Andrew." Barley hopped onto the couch and laid her head on his lap.

Kennedy appeared in the entryway, happiness shining on her face at the arrival of her sister and best friend. Maverick welcomed them, too. Before the door closed, Callie stepped inside and was caught up in the welcome.

Hunter watched with gratitude. Family meant everything to him. It was exactly a year ago that Maverick returned from a three-month trip and re-united with Kennedy. And from that day on, they'd been inseparable.

Callie's gaze slid over to his. He'd been staring at her hard, hoping she'd look his way, and she did. That meant something, right? He made Barley comfortable on the couch, then stood and walked over to say hello to the new arrivals, too.

The pizza-making started right after that. Everyone stood around the kitchen island talking and laughing while assembling various pizzas. He'd made sure to stand next to Callie. Andrew was on the other side of him, regaling them with stories from Hollywood, per usual.

"So, the casting director asks me to read from *Pride and Prejudice*, even though I'm auditioning for a role as a villain. I had no idea if it was a test or what, so I decided to go with a Darth Vader voice while reading lines."

"You didn't," Kennedy said, sprinkling cheese on her pizza.

"I did, and everyone laughed so hard they didn't hear my reading, which, if I do say so myself, was epic." Andrew continued dropping olives on his pizza to make a happy face.

"Did you get the role?" Callie asked.

"No. *But* the casting director said she'd keep me in mind for future comedic projects."

"Tell them about the audition for the role you *did* get," Ava said proudly. Kennedy's younger sister stood on the other side of Andrew and gave him a nudge with her elbow.

"Okay, so I *really* wanted this role. It's a small part in *The Mandalorian*."

"Oh my God!" Callie and Nova shrieked at the same time. "We love Mando and Baby Yoda."

"Right?" Andrew grinned. "I knew the audition was a big deal, and I wanted the part badly, so after the audition I told them I'd do anything for the role. *Any-thing*. They said if I wanted to stand out from the others, I could do a dance. Two seconds later, I broke out in a half-robot half–funky chicken dance that ended in applause. Needless to say, it worked."

"You have to do the dance at the wedding," Ava said.

"Of course." Andrew popped an olive into his mouth.

"You're obviously a big Star Wars fan," Hunter said.

Andrew gasped and brought his hand to his chest. "Please don't tell me you're not. It'll ruin the fantasies I have about you."

"Andrew," Kennedy admonished. "Leave him alone."

"It's okay," Hunter said. From the first time they'd met at Sutter's, when Andrew and Kennedy had come to town to crash a wedding on the ranch, Andrew had made no secret of his attraction to Hunter. Hunter rolled with it. He liked Andrew. He couldn't help it if he charmed everyone without even trying.

"Speaking of the wedding," Kennedy said from across the countertop. "While you're here Ava, Callie needs to do a fitting."

"Yes," Callie said. "Your dress is ready for you to try on."

"I can come by tomorrow morning if that works," Ava said.

"Sounds good."

"I hope you're ready to be the next one to walk down the aisle," Nova said.

Ava giggled. "So you say, but what about Hunter? He's older and more ready to settle down than I am. Are you hoping for a trip down the aisle?" she asked him.

"I'm definitely not opposed."

Nova, Maverick, and Kennedy all stopped and stared at him liked he'd said the most outlandish thing they'd ever heard.

"*What?*" Hunter said. "I wouldn't have asked Callie to make my suit if I wasn't serious about settling down."

"It's just the first time we've heard you say it out loud," Nova said.

He shrugged. "Mav knows."

"I know certain feelings you have on the issue, but it's good to hear you're not wavering."

"I am one hundred percent yours if you decide to switch teams," Andrew said. "I would treat you *so* well."

"Thanks, man. Whenever you do find that someone, they'll be lucky to have you."

"Aw," Kennedy said. "This is why you're going to make some girl very happy."

Maverick leaned over and kissed Kennedy.

"What was that for?" she asked dreamily, gazing up at him.

"No reason. I'm just damn happy I'm marrying you."

"Right back at you, cowboy."

"*Ugh,*" Andrew groaned. "Would you two stop being so cute? My singledom is bad enough without my bestie drooling all over her hot fiancé."

Kennedy gave him a cheeky smile, then put a few pizzas in the oven.

"Callie, is it weird that your dresses have had this magical effect?" Ava asked.

"My best friend is becoming a total celebrity." Nova tossed a piece of pepperoni at Callie. "I'm your date when you're invited to some famous wedding, right?"

Callie added the pepperoni to her mostly vege-tarian pizza. "You are," she said to Nova before directing her attention to Ava. "And to answer your question, it is weird, but I'm getting used to it. It makes me happy that my maid of honor dress has had such a positive impact."

Hunter bumped her arm with his. "Just wait till I walk down the aisle."

"I hope to ride this wave for as long as possible," she said optimistically.

"You've got a long career ahead of you," he said. He wished her the best. He also wished she'd realize she could be part of the equation.

His equation to be exact.

It didn't matter how many times he tried to talk himself into being open to love with someone else, until he wore that best man suit and surrendered to the luck that came with it, he'd keep hoping Callie would see him differently.

Even though he knew it was doubtful.

CHAPTER TWENTY-SEVEN

"Let's play SDS," Ava suggested, breaking into Hunter's rumination. He had no idea what she was talking about, but if it got his mind off Callie, he was all in.

"What's that?" Nova asked.

"It's like Screw-Marry-Kill, only it's Stakeout-Deserted Island-Sext. So, who would you want to be on a stakeout with, a deserted island with, and sext with? At least one of them has to be with someone in this room. The other two can be whoever you want, real or fictional."

Maverick gazed at their younger sister.

"What's that look for?" she asked him.

"I like that you can't say the *F* word out loud."

"I *can*. I just choose not to," she argued.

Hunter mentally picked Callie for all three scenarios. He could picture them on a stakeout in his truck, passing binoculars back and forth and eating peanut butter pretzels (her favorite snack, he'd learned, during one of their late night talks before falling asleep). He could picture them on a deserted island, her hair a wild mass of curls, her skin tanned, her body pressed against his every night under the stars. And he could picture sexting her, telling her what he wanted to do to her when he finally got her naked.

"Let's do it!" Nova said.

"We definitely need a drink first. I'll play

bartender," Andrew said, stepping around the kitchen island and opening the cupboard with the alcohol and bar glasses.

"I may need two or three," Maverick mumbled under his breath.

Andrew assembled a few different liquor bottles, a mixing glass, and shot glasses on the counter in front of him. He filled a bowl with ice and pulled pineapple and cranberry juice out of the fridge. "It's like you knew I was coming," he said to Kennedy.

Hunter noticed that Callie watched everyone. She'd been observing the whole time they'd been standing here, taking it all in. He could tell from her relaxed posture and small curve of her lips that she enjoyed the conversation and busy space. She didn't get this with her own family, which made this group special.

"Having fun?" he whispered to her.

"I am," she whispered back, her soft voice sliding down his spine better than any drink would.

"Okay, what's your poison, people? First up is vodka, pineapple juice, and Midori." He stirred the ingredients and poured the drink into four shot glasses. "Next we've got vodka, cranberry juice, and a splash of grenadine." He stirred and poured that mixture into another four shot glasses. "And yes, I know there are eight shots and seven of us. I'm double fisting it tonight."

"Which one do you want?" Hunter asked Callie.

"The one with pineapple juice."

He grabbed two of them and slid one in front of her. When everyone had a shot, Andrew counted down from three, and they all tossed one back.

"That is really good," Callie said. She licked her bottom lip, and Hunter had to stifle a groan. "Let's do another."

"That's the spirit!" Andrew poured seconds.

"Okay, back to the game. I'll go first," Nova said. "I would go on a stakeout with Maverick." She smiled at him, and he smiled back, his eyes cutting to Hunter's. *She picked me*, they said. *Fine with me*, Hunter's eyes said back. Hunter knew she picked Mav because then she could do all the talking. "I'd like to be stuck on a deserted island with this guy I met at a bar and that's all I'm going to say about it. And I'd like to sext with The Rock. I feel like he'd have a lot to say."

"What guy?" he, Maverick, Callie, and Kennedy all said at the same time.

"Who's next?" Nova lifted her chin with an air of smugness. She would not be elaborating. Hunter wondered if the guy was who she'd secretly been texting with earlier on the couch. Weird, though, that Callie apparently didn't know about him, either. The two of them shared everything.

The timer on the oven dinged. Kennedy pulled out the pizzas and put another batch in. Looked like they were group sharing. Maverick placed some ready-made salads within reach.

"Callie, you go next," Nova said.

"Okay. I'd go on a stakeout with Vera Wang. Be stranded on a desert island with Baby Yoda. And sext with…oh crap, can I backtrack? I have to pick one of you now."

"No backtracking," Ava said.

Hunter forced himself not to look at Callie. No

way would she pick Maverick. And he didn't think she'd pick any of the girls. That left him and Andrew, and if she picked Andrew, he'd be supremely disappointed.

"Fine. Hunter." She said it like she was settling and never in a million years would it happen. *Huh.* Sounded a little too nonchalant and convenient to him. Maybe she wanted everyone to believe she'd messed up so when she did say his name with sexting, no one would give it a second thought. The other, more obvious clue that she'd planned to pick him? The blush to her cheeks she tried to hide by taking a bite of pizza.

"Ow," she said, followed by a string of words he couldn't understand because it seemed her tongue had grown five sizes too big for her mouth. "Hawwt."

Kennedy quickly handed her a bottle of water.

"I'll go next," Hunter said, waiting until Callie appeared okay. "I'd go on a stakeout with James Bond because he is the greatest secret agent of all time. Be stuck on a desert island with Dolly Parton so I could listen to her sing. Get your minds out of the gutter, people. And for sexting, I can't leave Callie partnerless so will sext with her." That sounded casual enough. He hoped.

"Is this a love connection happening right before my eyes?" Andrew asked, looking between him and Callie with interest.

Maverick raised his eyebrows.

Hunter put his arm playfully around Callie. "I should be so lucky, but we're just playing the game."

Callie giggled. From nerves or relief, he didn't

know. What he did know was whenever he and Callie were near each other, he had trouble forgetting how much he wanted her and not whoever waited for him after the wedding.

CHAPTER TWENTY-EIGHT

Nova: *I'm coming over.*

   Callie: *You're not. You have to leave in a few minutes with everyone.*

   Nova: *I'll drive up with you instead.*

   Callie: *You can't. You're in the wedding party and have to stick together. The drive there is part of the fun, and I'm not sure how long I'll be.*

   Nova: *I hate the idea of you driving by yourself. There's a huge rainstorm coming.*

Callie hated the idea, too. *Achoo! Achoo! Achoo!* She sat on her porch wearing her heaviest hoodie and watched the dark clouds roll in. A crack of thunder sounded in the distance. A gust of wind blew the empty brown box at the bottom of the stairs onto the small patch of grass.

   Callie: *I know. I might stay home.*

   Nova: *I have a better idea. Come now and bring the kitten with you.*

Callie looked down at the tiny gray-and-white furball curled up in her lap. *Achoo!* Why did kittens have to be so cute? She couldn't resist holding the abandoned animal while she waited for Chandler to come pick it up.

Callie had called the animal shelter for help when the scared kitten scratched the backs of Callie's hands in fear. Chandler walked Callie through how to calm the kitten, and then said she'd be over as soon as possible.

Achoo!

Callie: *You know I can't do that. I'm already a mess.*

Itchy, watery eyes. Runny nose. Wheeze in her chest.

Nova: *I can't believe someone left her in a box.*

Callie: *Me, either.*

Nova: *Hey! Why don't you call Birdy to keep her until Chandler shows up?*

Callie: *Birdy is in SF visiting her cousin.*

Nova: *Darn it. Any neighbors around?*

Callie: *I don't know, but even if they were, she's finally sleeping, so I don't want to disturb her.*

Good thing they were texting, otherwise Nova would insist on rescuing Callie from her allergies. *Achoo!*

Nova: *Don't think I don't know you're texting me so I won't hear all your sneezing.*

Callie: *I hate when you read my mind.*

Nova: *Bestie brains.*

Callie: *Sister senses.*

The fun labels started in high school. Their unspoken communications filled the void left by the weak connection Callie had with her own sister, and she was forever grateful for it. *Achoo!* After her horseback-riding accident when no one else wanted to be around her or knew what to say, Nova had done and said everything. She had *tried*. And that meant everything.

Nova: *Where the hell is Chandler?*

Callie: *It's not Chandler's fault.*

Nova: *I know. It's the terrible person who left a kitten in a box. Shoot, I have to go. Kennedy is* *calling for me. Hey, did you see the cute doctor covering for her while we're gone?*

Callie: *I didn't.*

Nova: *I may have to fake an illness as soon as we get back.*

Callie: *Of course you will.*

Nova: *Right? I hope you make it down to be with us, but I understand if you don't.*

Callie: *I'll let you know. Say hi to everyone for me.*

Nova: *Bye! Love you!*

Callie: *Love you!*

Callie rubbed the kitten's back without thought. *Achoo!* The tiny feline's soft fur and delicate size made it easier to ignore feeling like crap. How someone could abandon this precious animal, she had no idea. *Achoo!* Sniffling, Callie reached up and rubbed her nose. She blinked repeatedly, trying to rid the itchiness all around her eyes.

The sky darkened further. Another clap of thunder boomed. She had thought it best to wait outside given her strong allergy to cats, but if Chandler didn't get here in the next five minutes, she'd live with the consequences of moving inside.

"You are so sweet," she said softly. "If I wasn't allergic, I'd keep you."

Fluffy lifted her little face and looked at Callie like she understood and wished the same thing. Sometime during the conversation with Nova, Callie had given the kitten the name Fluffy. If she'd had a furry pet as a child, that's the name she would have given it.

Fluffy dropped her head. She curled into a tighter ball.

Callie let out a regretful sigh as Chandler's pickup pulled up to the curb. She hopped out and rounded the hood. "Hi!" she called out. "I'm here." Dressed in worn jeans, work boots, and a pink, long-sleeve T-shirt with the words I LOVE ANIMALS printed underneath a heart comprised of pawprints, she looked every bit the animal lover.

Chandler stopped at the bottom of the three stairs. She looked from Callie to the kitten, the kitten to Callie. "I can't believe you've held her this whole time. You look terrible."

"I feel it, too." *Achoo!* "Here you go." Callie lifted Fluffy toward Chandler.

"She is so cute," Chandler said, cuddling the kitten to her chest. "I'll have no trouble finding her a home. Thanks for keeping her safe until I got here."

"I'd say it was no hardship…" Callie stood and walked down the steps.

"But we both know it was. Coffee next week?"

"Sounds good." A flash of lightning lit up the darkening sky just as a big fat raindrop landed on Callie's cheek.

"I hope you feel better. Take an antihistamine ASAP." Chandler jogged back to her truck. As she pulled away, another recognizable truck pulled up. Hunter jumped out, the sight of him in light blue jeans and a white Henley underneath a denim jacket making her forget about her allergies. After the other night, she'd half expected him to actually sext her. When he hadn't, she didn't know whether to be relieved or disappointed.

"Hey, what are you doing here? Shouldn't you be with everyone else on their way to Big Sur?" She turned to walk into the cottage before she got more wet from the rain.

"I'm here to drive you." He fell in step beside her, smelling better than any man had a right to smell. He'd obviously showered and shaved this morning.

He closed the cottage door behind them and took a good look at her. "Although I'm wondering if you should see a doctor first."

"Give me a minute." She hurried back to her living quarters. Flipping on the light in the bathroom, she almost gasped at herself in the mirror. Puffy, watering eyes, red nose, rash on her chin and neck, and frizzy hair. (The hair wasn't the kitten's fault, but the weather's.) She took two antihistamines, two puffs from her inhaler, and pressed a warm washcloth to her eyes.

"Are you okay?" Hunter called out. "It's been longer than a minute."

She pulled the cooled washcloth away from her face.

If she said "no," would he stay here with her for the weekend? Could they pretend the outside world didn't exist and do all the things she'd imagined him doing to her? She had a feeling he might, but she couldn't keep him from his brother's bachelor party.

"I like—" He stopped talking when she opened the bathroom door. He'd made himself comfortable sitting on the edge of her bed. "Feeling better?"

"I am." She remained in the doorway. Seeing him so at ease in her bedroom unnerved her.

"I like what you've done with the place."

"Thanks." *I like the way you look in my place.*

"I see you're packed." He nodded toward her small suitcase. "Ready to go?"

No. Yes. No.

"Yes." Being selfish didn't come naturally, so feeling like she wanted to keep Hunter to herself left her a little on edge.

"You'll be okay, right? Your allergies will keep decreasing?"

"They should. Luckily, Kennedy's a doctor should I need one." At Hunter's pained expression, she quickly added, "I'm kidding. I really will be fine." She took his hand to squeeze it in thanks and help him to his feet. "Come on, let's go. Thank you for coming to get me. I'm sorry you didn't get to be with everyone else."

He grabbed her suitcase before she could. "Are you kidding? This is the best chauffeur gig ever. I'm not at all sorry I'm missing being stuck with everyone in a Hulk-size van."

"Good point."

The rain pummeled the truck's windshield as they made their way out of Windsong. The drive to Big Sur normally took about three hours, but with the storm, it would probably take longer.

A shiver slithered through her. Even with the heat on in the car, she couldn't shake a chill that had seeped into her bones. Hunter glanced at her, then pulled over to a safe spot on the side of the road.

"What are you doing?"

He undid his seat belt and took of his fur-lined denim jacket. "Put this on. It'll keep you warm."

She swallowed the lump in her throat while he waited for her to undo her seat belt so he could help her quickly don the coat. He never hesitated to make sure she was comfortable. Never put his own needs before hers. He may be confident, and cocky on occasion, but there wasn't an egoistic bone in his body.

His smell immediately surrounded her. Within seconds, her body relaxed. Warmed up. She settled into her seat content to drive for hours now.

"Want to play a game?" he asked once they'd resumed driving.

"What did you have in mind?" She slipped the hair tie off her wrist and gathered her curly hair into a bun on top of her head.

"How about Two Truths and a Lie? I'll go first." He kept his attention on the road in front of them, for which she was grateful.

"I can juggle.

"I have never broken a bone.

"If I could, I would pay to fly to the moon."

She knew the answer without a second thought. "The lie is you've never broken a bone." She crossed her arms over her chest, 100 percent satisfied with her answer.

"You didn't even need to think about it?" he asked surprised.

"Nope."

"How did you know?"

"Your nose is a little bit crooked, and I've always assumed it's because it was once broken."

He nodded. "That's exactly right. Brett punched me years ago when he caught me kissing Janey."

"Hunter!"

"It was fake! He and Janey were broken up and

both miserable so she asked for my help to make him jealous. We were at a party and pretending to make out. I barely touched her mouth, but it did the trick. He punched me, and they got back together. I'm genuinely a very selfless person."

He really was. She'd learned so much about him—and changed her opinions about him—over the past several weeks.

"Okay, my turn," she said.

"I've always wanted to try paragliding.

"I've eaten worms.

"I went to prom wearing a designer dress that cost one thousand dollars."

"Hmm…"

She loved that he had to think about it.

"I'm going to guess eating worms is the lie."

"Sorry, that one's true. I ate Mopane worms in Africa. They're boiled with garlic and tomatoes and eaten straight out of the pot."

"Do they taste like chicken?" he teased.

"They do, actually!" She took in his handsome profile as he navigated a two-lane road. "The lie is the dress. I made my own prom dress."

"I almost said that one."

Her phone chirped with a text. She pulled it out of her purse. "It's Nova. She says Andrew is singing Broadway show tunes and telling stories about Kennedy with an Australian accent."

"He's a talented guy. And funny."

"I'm sorry you're missing it." She double tapped the text to give it a heart.

"I'm not, so please stop apologizing. We'll have all weekend with them. Tell me another Two Truths and a Lie."

She watched the windshield wipers work extra hard as the rain continued to pour, and she thought about what to tell him. He turned on the defrost to help stop the windows from fogging up. A branch fell off a tree and hit the hood. Thankfully, there weren't many cars on the road.

"I can blow a gigantic bubble with bubblegum.

"I hate the color red.

"I have a birthmark that looks like a heart."

"Okay, you are way too good at this game," Hunter said, slowing down as they took a curve through the mountains.

"You have ten seconds to guess," she said, sitting taller in her seat.

"I'm going to guess the lie is you hate the color red."

"You got it." Her posture deflated. "What made you pick that?"

"You're a redhead. No way could you hate the color. It's one of my favorite things about you."

One of. How many things did he like?

"And I'm tucking the birthmark away for later."

Oh boy.

They played a few more guessing games and listened to the radio until they lost reception.

"I've been meaning to ask what your last ambassador assignment is?" Callie asked.

"Bike riding. What about you?"

"Community theater. I'm going to see *Mamma Mia!* next week. Have you gone on a bike ride yet?"

"I went on two." He glanced over at her. "Bella joined me on one ride around town. We rented a tandem bike, which I'd never been on before."

"Sounds fun." She ignored the stab of jealousy jabbing her in the middle of the chest. "And the second ride?"

"Was with Vivian. We just happened to be at the same trailhead at the same time. She likes to mountain bike in her spare time."

Stab to the heart take two. Coincidence or not.

"Both gave me good content to write about. It's all about the ambassador gig, Triple C."

"Not finding your soul mate?" she couldn't help but ask. Both women were viable options. New to town. Smart. Pretty. Interested in him.

He shrugged. "You said it, not me."

She wished she could read his mind, but since she couldn't, she made the decision to drop any references to his best man suit and impending love connection.

The radio sputtered back to life. "Love on the Brain" by Rihanna. She glanced at Hunter. He glanced at her. And they both fought a smile. The next song to play was "If I Ain't Got You" by Alicia Keyes. The music fairies were having some fun.

They fell into companionable listening until Hunter slammed on the brakes and his arm shot out in front of her like her seat belt wasn't enough to keep her safe. Swirling red lights blurred through the windshield as they came to a stop. Hunter rolled down his window.

"The bridge is flooded ahead," a highway patrolman wearing a bright yellow raincoat said. "You'll need to turn around."

"How long until we can pass?" Hunter asked.

"Hard to say. There's no sign of the storm letting up."

"Thanks. Be safe." Hunter made a U-turn. "Will you—"

"Already on it." Callie tried calling Nova. When it went right to voicemail, she texted. *Where are you guys?*

Three dancing dots immediately appeared. *Just got here. The cabins are gorgeous! Be careful out there. It's raining even harder here.*

We're not going to make it tonight. There's a bridge out. Will call you soon.

"They got there safe and sound," she told Hunter.

"That's good. What do you want to do? We're at least three hours from home now with traffic, or we could try and find somewhere nearby to stay the night and hope that tomorrow we can pass through."

"Let's do that. I feel terrible that you might miss everything."

"Hey." He darted a glance at her. "None of this is your fault, so you have nothing to feel bad about, okay? When I heard you saved a kitten, I...,"

"You what?"

"Nothing. I think I saw a motel a few miles back." He drove them through a massive puddle, splashing water high into the air. Callie decided it best to let Hunter concentrate on the road rather than talk further.

A few minutes later, they crossed a small stream into a dirt parking lot for a "motel." It looked more like a string of rundown cabins. As long as the roof didn't leak and the room was clean, she'd be a happy camper.

"Why don't you wait here and I'll run in?"

"Okay."

She watched him disappear inside a cabin labeled *Office*. Lighted windows shone through the murkiness, the rain falling in sheets. Christmas lights hung down from trees and blew in the wind. The inside of the cab cooled quickly with the engine shut off. She gathered Hunter's jacket tighter around herself, inhaling his masculine scent. The sharp tapping of raindrops filled her ears, sending a small jolt of worry through her. *Hurry up, Hunt.*

A minute later, he jumped back into the truck, soaking wet. "Damn, it's raining hard." He gave her an appreciative look.

"What?"

"Just like seeing you in my jacket. It looks a lot better on you."

She ignored his compliment because she knew the blush on her cheeks said enough. "Did they have a cabin available?"

"They did." He turned the key in the ignition. Something about his quick answer and hurried movements told her he was keeping information from her.

He parked in front of a cabin set away from the others. "I'll grab our stuff. You make a run for the door."

When she got to the door, the placard read LOVE NEST. *Um, what?*

Hand on her hip, she turned around. Hunter shook his wet hair out when he met her under the awning. For a second, she forgot to be mad at him. Droplets clung to his long, dark eyelashes. His shirt molded to his body.

She managed a glare at him.

"It was the only cabin they had left," he said. "I swear. I asked for one with two beds and the guy behind the counter told me this was all they had. I guess the day after Thanksgiving isn't big on romantic getaways."

She let out a breath.

"Look at it as an adventure," he said. "Plus, I hear there's a fireplace and a waterfall shower." His sincere smile, warm and sexy, did her in. Who was she kidding? She'd go anywhere with him.

He unlocked the door for her. She stepped inside, and her jaw dropped.

"Wow," Hunter said.

Yeah, wow.

CHAPTER TWENTY-NINE

Hunter hadn't been the least bit disappointed when the motel manager told him he only had the Love Nest cabin available.

He didn't mind paying the two-night minimum.

And if it was wrong that he silently prayed for the storm to continue until Sunday, then he was the worst kind of wrong. Because having Callie all to himself, remembering their nights in the bunkhouse when they talked before falling asleep, made this the best bachelor party weekend ever.

Sorry, Maverick.

Laying eyes on the inside of the cabin now made it even better. "Wow," he repeated. A room that looked like this deserved a second accolade.

"I will never judge a cabin by its outside ever again," Callie said, equally awed. "It's like we've opened a door to a different world. Caveman meets Parisian boudoir."

Picture a rustic room of solid rock, pink, gold, and black animal prints, French-style furnishings, a gold chandelier, and a massive fireplace.

The walls, ceiling, and floor were literally natural stone. A large, amoeba-shaped fur rug rested between a king bed, the fireplace, and an armchair and ottoman.

Callie skipped further into the room. "I love it."

Hunter did, too. He didn't want to think prematurely, but this might be the best weekend of his life.

"The bathroom is the same!" Callie called out over her shoulder. "It feels like a cavern, only there's small white lights and fluffy pink towels."

"Should I start a fire?"

"Yes, please." She slipped off his jacket and placed it over the arm of the chair. She took a good look around the room—there was a gift basket filled with items for lovers that he pretended not to notice—before kicking off her shoes and sitting on the bed with her legs crossed. "I'll sleep on the chair and ottoman."

"No, you won't. I'll take the chair and you'll sleep in the bed. You slept on my couch for weeks, and there's no way you're sleeping anywhere but where you are right now."

"You're much bigger than I am, Hunt. There's no way you'll be comfortable."

"I'll be fine." As the first flames of the fire crackled, he wished the sleeping arrangements included them wrapped in each other's arms.

"Fine. But please let me know how much I owe you for the room."

"You don't owe me anything."

"Yes, I do. I want to pay my half."

He took a seat in the armchair. Her serious expression told him he'd waste his breath arguing with her. "Okay."

It was easy to keep eye contact with her, open his emotions to her. He hoped she saw how much he enjoyed being stuck with her. How much she made a rainstorm feel fun. This was already a thousand times better than the bike rides he'd taken with Bella and Vivian, trying to put Callie out of his mind.

"Do you think they have room service?" she asked, glancing around for a menu, he assumed. "I'm starving." She didn't wait for an answer. She crawled over to the phone next to the head of the bed, giving him a nice view of her spectacular ass in her leggings.

"Hello, this is the Love Nest." She giggled. "Sorry. We were wondering if there's room service available? Oh, okay. Two orders of chicken nuggets and fries would be great, then." She covered the receiver with her hand and looked at him. "What would you like to drink?"

"Coke is fine."

"And two Cokes please. Great. Thank you." She hung up. "Their chef couldn't make it in because of the rain, so the only hot food available was chicken nuggets and fries."

"Perfect."

She fluffed up three pillows behind her back and leaned against the wall. "It kind of is," she agreed. "Comfort food goes great with being stranded. Although we're not really stranded."

"I'm pretty happy with where we are."

"Me, too." She picked up her phone. "I'll text Nova to let her know we're here."

"I'll text Maverick." He didn't think his brother would be too upset with their absence. After all, there wasn't anything they could do about it. Sure enough, when Mav texted back, he told them to stay safe and touch base in the morning.

"Nova wants pictures." Callie moved to her knees and took some pictures of the room. "I'm pretty sure our cabin wins over theirs." She paused, mid-type on her phone, and looked up at him. "Maybe I shouldn't have said anything. I don't want to take away from where they're staying."

"I made the arrangements. The two villas I booked are a different kind of amazing than this, so I think you're good to share." While this was fun and imaginative, the other was sophisticated and classic.

"Okay. Thanks." She finished texting, then watched the fire.

Outside, the storm continued to rage. Inside, warmth and contentment filled the space.

As much as he wanted all of Callie, just being close to her like this relieved the ache in his chest. He took a slow, deep breath as the fire crackled.

"How are you feeling?" he asked. "You look all better."

"I am."

"That's good. Can I ask you a question?"

"Only if you promise never to ask that before asking me a question."

He liked that. It meant she didn't mind his unrelenting interest. "Promise." This particular inquiry had been on his mind for some time, and now that they were stuck in this cabin together, he finally decided to ask it. "This is a serious question," he prefaced. "The answer will determine if we can still be friends after this weekend."

She chuckled. "Uh-oh. Are you sure you want to ask it, then?"

"Are you implying that I need you more than you need me?" He totally did.

"You said it, not me." Her teasing, closed-mouth smile did his heart good. He'd said the same thing to her.

"Did you check out my butt the first night you stayed with me?" Okay, so it wasn't exactly serious or important.

Her eyes widened. "What kind of question is that?"

"I'll answer that if you promise never to answer my questions with a question."

"You're ridiculous." Her gaze darted around the room, telling him her answer.

He grinned. "You did."

"Not on purpose." She crossed her arms over her chest.

"How was it an accident?" he prodded, enjoying her blush. Not from embarrassment, he sussed out. Rather, she'd been found out.

"It was right there in front of me as I was walking to the bathroom."

"So was my back, my shoulders, the back of my head…" he said playfully.

She grumbled at the same time her eyes twinkled with humor. "Your butt was paler, so it stuck out."

He laughed. "I thought I was dreaming when I looked at you. It wasn't until the morning that I realized you were really there."

"I thought you were just being cocky."

"So that's what you really think of me." He wasn't bothered by it. Sometimes he was cocky. Not that night, but she knew that now.

"No," she said adamantly. "Well, at least not anymore. And for the record, any woman in my position would have checked out your butt."

"So, on a scale of one to ten—"

"Oh my God." She rolled her eyes.

"I'm kidding." Nova had told him in high school that her friends only went to football games to see his butt in his football pants. His sister thought it gross that they talked about him like that. He, on the other hand, had found it awesome.

A knock on the door had them both jumping to their feet.

The same guy who had checked them in delivered their food. Hunter tipped him, then joined Callie on the rug to eat. She'd waited for him before starting.

She held up her can of Coke. "Cheers."

"Cheers."

"From the time I was five or six until ten, I think, this is all I would eat." She dunked a nugget into ketchup. "My mom hated it."

"I was one of those weird kids who ate everything."

"*Everything?*" she asked with skepticism.

"Pretty much. Speaking of your mom, will your family be home soon?"

"According to my sister's last text, not until January. They really like the nomadic lifestyle."

She didn't say it, but Hunter heard it: they chose that way of life over being a part of hers. It pained him. He put his hand on her knee. "I'm sorry, Cal. I know you miss them."

"I admire their humanitarian work, but it hurts having them gone so long." She straightened her legs, effectively dislodging his hand.

"Have you ever thought about joining them?"

"All the time."

"But?" He grabbed a few fries.

"Since my parents' relationship is complicated, it's not always easy for me to be around them. Plus, they rely on Brooke for a lot and when I'm there, I just tend to get in the way." She took a slow, deep breath. "Let's talk about something else," she urged, her voice stronger, her posture straighter as she dug back into the food. "These chicken tenders are really good." She took a big bite of one. "And so are the fries," she added with her mouth full. "What should we get for dessert?"

This amazing woman. She had no idea how strong she was. "Whatever you want."

"I like that answer."

He ran a few of his fries through her ketchup. She stole his last chicken nugget. Then she once again crawled over to the phone, making his jeans tight behind his zipper.

"Hello again. Can you tell me if you have anything for dessert?" She nodded silently as she listened. "Okay, we'll take that. Can you make it a double?" She smiled into the phone. "Thank you."

"What are we having?"

"The Love Nest special," she said with a gleam in her green eyes.

He had to refrain from leaning over and kissing her senseless. When she looked at him like that—with mischief and affection—he felt like he'd won a prize. He had a small collection of them committed to memory. He wanted a million more.

"Everything I do with you is special," he said.

"Shut up."

"What?"

"You don't need to feed me cheesy lines to…"

She busied herself by gathering their plates onto the room service tray.

"To what? And I'm being serious. You're someone special whether you believe it or not. Now let's circle back to you finishing that sentence. To...kiss you again?" he ventured, hoping like hell it was true.

She lifted her eyes to his, and time stopped.

Her eyes said so much, and without a word, he knew she felt the same constant pull he did. And the only way to take the edge off would be to jump off that edge with both feet. He swore to himself he'd catch her. Make this the best night of her life and tomorrow morning tell her again how special she was no matter what happened next.

He wanted her to be his only *next*.

He'd take whatever she offered.

Slowly, their faces moved closer. Inch by inch, her mouth came within reach. The sweet torture revved his desire for her. Almost there.

Knock! Knock! "Room service."

She pulled back with a coy smile playing at her perfectly pink lips. "Dessert is here!" She jumped to her feet.

He moved quicker. Grabbed her wrist and tugged her to his chest. He couldn't let the moment go without getting a small taste of her. She placed her palm over his heart. Tilted her head back to look up at him. Blinked her agreement.

One quick kiss to get them through dessert.

He'd miscalculated, though, because the second their mouths met, he didn't want to stop.

Another knock, louder this time, broke their connection. "Room service!"

"We have to get that," Callie said, a little breathless. A lot sexy. "Our special is melting." She hurried to the door.

He picked up the dinner tray to do an exchange.

The dessert tray contained the biggest ice cream sundae he'd ever seen, piled high and wide with numerous scoops and toppings. He laughed. "Good thing you asked for a double."

"I know. Right?"

Shaking his head in amusement, he joined her back on the rug. She handed him a spoon, then picked up her own. Chocolate and vanilla ice cream. Chocolate syrup. Chocolate hearts. Red candy hearts. Mini chocolate chip cookie hearts. Topped off with a dollop of whipped cream and two cherries.

"Mmm. It's delish," she said.

He dug in, discovered the chocolate hearts were filled with caramel, and angled his spoon for more of the same.

"Hey, no hogging those." She cut off his spoon with her own, their silverware clinking.

"A chocolate-and-caramel girl, huh?" He scooped up a bite with the cookie pieces.

"It's my favorite."

"Mine, too." He ran his spoon through some chocolate ice cream and syrup. The rest of the chocolate hearts were hers.

Callie loaded her spoon with a bit of everything. "What do you think is happening at the bachelor-bachelorette party right now?"

"We had reservations for dinner on the property. After that, the guys were going to play poker. Not sure what the girls had planned. A romcom, I think."

A part of him did wish they'd made it. Maverick wasn't just his brother, but his best friend. Missing out on the first night of the pre-wedding celebration suddenly hurt. He rubbed the ache in his chest with two fingers, then grabbed his phone and fired off a text telling Mav he missed him and to not rub behind his ear during poker. Mav immediately texted back, asking what that meant. *It's your tell, dude.*

"Everything okay?" Callie asked.

"Yeah." Hunter put the phone down. "Just wanted to check in with Maverick."

She planted her spoon upright in the middle of the sundae. For two people, they'd made a respectable dent in the huge dessert and yet a lot remained. "You miss him," she said softly.

"I do. Which is ridiculous. I saw his annoying ass earlier today." He glanced at the fire, staring unfocused for a moment before reconnecting with Callie. "You've been looking at me differently."

"Have I?"

"Yes."

She wiggled her mouth back and forth, thinking about what to say. "The love you have for your family is insanely attractive. It's one of the things I admire most about you." Rather than give further explanation, she pushed their dessert aside and climbed into his lap, her legs and arms wrapped around him like she had no plans of letting go anytime soon.

Hallelujah.

CHAPTER THIRTY

Hunter Owens held far more magic than Callie did. When she was with him, everyday life seemed brighter. More significant. Her worries slipped away, and she found herself smiling without thought. He had this infectious charisma that snuck under her skin and warmed her from the inside out. Even when he got contemplative, like right now, his drawing power didn't diminish.

If anything, it made him more attractive. He was human like the rest of us.

She *was* looking at him differently. She'd kissed him. Seen his glorious backside naked. Watched him interact with his family and his horse. Every little thing added more and more to his appeal. And she got it now. Why every single person in Windsong wanted him to pick them.

"Howdy," he said, wrapping his arms around her waist.

"Howdy." She tried to keep a straight face. It lasted all of two seconds before she laughed. "Sorry. But who says 'howdy'?"

"Apparently I do when a beautiful woman sits on my lap and scrambles my brain cells."

Moments like this, when his confidence dipped below 100 percent, were her favorite. "You scramble mine, too."

"Good to know." He took a long curl that had escaped her bun and twirled it around his finger.

"I'm assuming this new position is a signal."

"What kind of signal do you think it is?" She wiggled just a tiny bit to help him with his answer. Not that she had any doubt he could figure out her intentions on his own.

"The kind that starts with my mouth here." He reached behind him to take her hand, then gently kissed each of her knuckles. "Your hands are a huge part of who you are, Cal. They're soft yet strong." She could say the same about his lips. "Capable and some say magical." Yep, his lips were those things, too. With each kiss to her fingers, she fell further under his spell.

"I want these hands all over my body." His voice deepened to a husky sound that sent a shiver down her spine.

"I'd like that," she managed to whisper. His deliberate focus and flattering words made it difficult to breathe, let alone speak.

"What do think about me putting *my* hands all over *your* body?" He opened her hand and held it between them. There wasn't much space between their chests, but he made good use of it. Especially when he traced his fingertip along the lines on her palm. It tickled in the best possible way.

"I think the sooner the better." Honest to God, if he didn't get on with it soon, she might combust.

He blessed her with his dimples. The sight of the sexy indentations in combination with his body heat, scent, and gentle ministrations made her achy and in desperate need of relief. She wiggled with more effort.

"Is that a yes, Cal? To anything and everything I

want to do to you? I need you tell me you want this as much as I do. Because I am so into you, it hurts."

His words wiped away any lingering doubt she had about crossing the line with him.

Tonight, it was just the two of them with an equal desire to make each other feel good. "Yes, Hunter. Yes. Yes. Yes."

He cupped the side of her neck, stared so deeply into her eyes, she was sure he touched her soul. He waited a beat, then crashed his mouth to hers. This kiss wasn't sweet or gentle. It was unrestrained fire. With his lips, tongue, and teeth, he kissed her with skill, tenacity, and passion. She felt it everywhere.

If she thought she'd wake up tomorrow morning the same person she was right now, she was wrong.

He broke the kiss only long enough to get them both on the bed. When his mouth returned to hers, she took control this time. She kissed *him* with authority and eagerness, loving the growly sound he made when her hands found their way underneath his shirt.

She rocked against him, her hips moving—no *seeking*—more. "God, Callie." He nuzzled her neck. Kissed behind her ear as his hand slid between her legs. He rubbed her over her leggings, lifted his head to look at her. She closed her eyes and let her knees fall open.

"I've dreamed about this moment for a long time," he said with affection.

Grateful she had her eyes closed so he couldn't see what his words did to her, she said, "Please no more talking. Just doing."

"Yes, ma'am." His hand did really good things,

then slipped inside her leggings. He stroked her with perfect pressure. Kissed her jaw, her neck, her collarbone. When his fingers slid underneath her panties and then inside her, she pressed her heels into the mattress. He touched her with skill, bringing her to the edge, then retreating. The wet sound of her arousal excited her further.

"You are so fucking sexy," he whispered, prolonging the intense pleasure until she couldn't take it anymore and begged him to make her come. It took all of five more seconds for her to orgasm.

"Step one done," he said, slowly withdrawing his hand.

He gave her a quick kiss on the lips—too quick for her liking—before moving down her body and taking her clothes with him. Leggings, panties, shoes, and socks, *gone*.

"Umm…" She looked down at him, his shoulders spreading her knees wide. With a devilish glint in his eye, he buried his face between her legs. *Oh, God*. Her head fell back. She gripped the comforter. Sensations stormed through her already sensitive body.

He licked and sucked, seeming determined to make her come for a second time. Unhurriedly determined, by the leisurely way his tongue worked her. Which was okay with her. His mouth felt so good, she wanted to make it last for as long as possible.

Not an easy task with his face attached to her most intimate spot. He palmed her thighs, his hold gentle yet firm. She bucked against his mouth. Her hands moved to the back of his head to press him tighter. She knew what she liked and had no problem helping him out.

She once again dug her heels into the bed. Her moans grew louder with every sweet-tortured swipe from his tongue. "You taste so fucking good," he rasped.

Emotion flooded her. Happiness and joy. Gratification. A sensual high she didn't want to come down from. In the back of her mind, she'd hoped they'd end up here. She'd dreamed about it, going as far back as the first night she'd stayed with him. His perfect, naked ass was to blame.

"Oh, God," she murmured, so turned on, and *so* close to climax number two. Add his tongue to his list of magical body parts.

Her breathing ragged, she let go of his head and yanked her sweatshirt over her head. She was hot. And bothered. Her bra came off next.

Without lifting his head, Hunter's gaze slid over her stomach to her boobs. One peek from him and her nipples were hard as a rock. He released her right thigh and brought his hand up to cup her breast. He caressed and squeezed. Rubbed his thumb over her nipple.

She pushed down on the bed, arched her back, and let go. Sounds she'd never made before tumbled out of her mouth. She came hard. Tingled everywhere.

He brought her back slowly, drawing every bit of orgasmic bliss out of her. "Step two done," he said with a satisfied smile.

"I'm dead." She lay there completely naked and satiated, her limbs wet noodles.

"I hope not. I'm not through with you yet. God, you're gorgeous." He stood at the side of the bed, staring down at her. Tracing her skin with his eyes like he was committing every inch of her to memory. His undivided attention thrilled her.

"I think it's my turn to touch you."

He lifted his shirt over his head with one hand, tossed it aside. In the firelight, he looked ethereal, a one-of-a-kind human made just for her. "You can touch all you want while I'm inside you."

He quickly took off the rest of his clothes, pulling a condom out of his wallet and tossing it on the bed beside her. He was hard and thick and bigger than any other man she'd been with.

"Ready for step three?" he asked, crawling onto the bed between her legs. He sat on his haunches and stroked himself.

Holy hell. The sight made her salivate. She gulped. Watching him touch himself made everything inside her tight and needy all over again. "I'm ready."

"I've imagined this a million times." He ripped open the condom and rolled the protection on.

"Steps one to three?" she teased, a sexy, playful side she didn't know she had coming out to play.

"Mostly step three." He kissed her stomach. Her chest. Her neck. Lined his body up with hers. His fingers found her center. "Are you ready for me?"

Rather than answer with words, she reached between them, wrapped her hand around his length, and guided him to her entrance. He didn't need any further assurance. With one swift thrust, he filled her.

She moaned in pleasure.

He groaned before claiming her mouth and kissing her like he'd been waiting his whole life to be in this position. Being connected like this, with his scent on her skin and their bodies moving as one, she'd swear the world stopped.

Alone in this cabin made for lovers, with a storm raging outside, and nothing but heat and passion and affection blazing inside, she met his thrusts. She roamed her hands all over his body. She quivered. She burned.

For him.

With him.

The sounds of their lovemaking filled the room. Heavy breathing. Wet friction. The smell of sex filled her nose. He was about to do the impossible: make her come three times in a row.

"I'm close," he said against the shell of her ear, his voice gravelly. "I can't hold off much longer. You feel too good, Triple C."

Triple C.

She loved when he called her that. Loved it even more when he added, "The things you do to me…"

That was it. She tumbled over the edge calling his name, and he followed right behind.

He stayed inside her as their bodies relaxed, and then he gazed into her eyes, his weight on his elbows on either side of her shoulders. "Please tell me we can do that again."

It took her a minute. Not because she didn't want to. Because she did. Too much.

"Hey." He brushed a lock of hair off her forehead. "I mean while we're here. In this amazing bubble we've created. Once we leave, it's up to you what happens next."

Relief mixed with joy. She couldn't get attached. Didn't want him to, either. They were both adults and knew the score, though.

"I *suppose* we could do it again."

He rolled off her onto his side and laughed. "Okay, Miss Suppose. You let me know when." He propped his head in his hand, traced a finger over her hip. Goose bumps covered her skin.

She rolled over to face him with her hands tucked under her cheek. "I do owe you—"

"Nothing. You don't owe me a thing. I'm so damn happy right now." He traced a heart on her stomach. "Making you feel good and hearing you scream my name was incredible."

"I didn't scream." She totally did.

"Yeah, you did." He lightly trailed his finger along her bottom lip. "Be right back." He walked to the bathroom and closed the door.

She turned over onto her stomach and buried her face in the pillow to smother her ginormous smile. She'd just had sex with Hunter Owens. Correction: she'd just had the best sex of her life with Hunter Owens.

And he wasn't her boyfriend. Or someone she had a future with. She'd never slept with someone without being in a relationship, and it felt good exercising her independence like this.

Trevor hadn't exactly been her boyfriend, but they'd established a commitment to each other while they were both in Africa. She'd been drawn to him from the second they'd met. She'd dreamed for a split second that they could travel the world together—her teaching sewing to small villages while he helped those same villages develop new and improved growing methods for their crops. They could have been a powerful team helping those less fortunate.

Kennedy and Maverick's wedding flashed through her mind. The maid of honor dress that needed only a slight alteration after Ava's fitting yesterday morning. Nova and Bethany's dresses. Hunter's suit, hanging up and ready for him to try on.

Two fingers tiptoed up the back of her leg, over her bottom, and up her back, breaking into her musings. "Your body is incredible," Hunter said. "Your skin is so soft." He pressed his nose to the side of her neck. "And you smell like sunshine and my dirtiest dreams."

She turned her head to look at him. He had sex hair, and his electric blue eyes did things to her insides. Her insides were supposed to be sound asleep after what they'd just done.

"Also, my best dreams," he added.

"Do you remember all your dreams?" she asked, genuinely curious.

"Pretty much. Don't you?" He laid on his back and scooped her closer so she could lay her head on his chest.

"Sometimes." She crossed her leg over his, snuggled against him with a hand on his stomach. "After my accident, all I dreamt about was that day, so I made a conscious effort not to remember. More recently, though, some good ones have broken through my resolve."

He drew lazy circles up and down her arm. "Do

you think that means you've finally put the accident behind you?"

She hadn't thought of that. "Maybe."

"So, what kind of good dreams have you had, and more importantly, was I in them?" His teasing tone curled around her heart and gave it a squeeze. He seamlessly shifted from bad memories to good memories, and gratitude filled her.

"Possibly."

"That means yes," he said with a smug attitude.

"No. It means I'm not sure who the guy was. It was dark and mysterious, and I was focused on other parts of his body besides his face." She pressed her lips together, hoping he bought her lie. Her smooth-talking cowboy didn't need any more praise.

"You're a terrible liar, Triple C." He kissed the top of her head.

Grr. He knew her too well.

The idea actually made her happier than it should. He wasn't *her* cowboy. *For tonight, he is. And maybe tomorrow, too.* If it didn't make her feel so guilty, she'd wish for the storm to continue through Sunday. Instead, tonight had to be enough. Hunter deserved to be there for Maverick's bachelor party as soon as possible.

They laid there quietly, her hand lifting up and down atop his stomach with every breath he took. The fire roared. Rain pelted the window. She focused on this moment, committing everything about Hunter to memory. The feel of his skin, his warm breath, his scent, the way he moved with confidence, the deep, sexy sound of his voice. She pictured the way he looked at her with admiration. And she relished how he made her feel, like she'd won first place in his life.

She lifted her head to peek at him and found him fast asleep. She rested her cheek back down, cuddled even closer, and within minutes trailed him into dreamland.

CHAPTER THIRTY-ONE

Hunter woke with a start. Not a bad start, but an unbelievable twitch in his dick he was more than happy to accept. He looked down his naked body to see Callie on her knees between his legs, her mouth on his morning wood.

Best wake-up call ever.

They'd fallen asleep last night wrapped in each other's arms. Woken around midnight to have sex again, this time on the fur rug by the fireplace. Then climbed back into bed for the rest of the night and now here they were. Him getting the best blow job of his life.

Everything Callie did to him blew his mind.

Finally having her in the ways he'd fantasized about for years had exceeded his expectations. She'd been so responsive to his fingers, his mouth, and his cock, he'd almost confessed more than his crush on her.

"Morning," she said, licking him from base to tip.

He placed his hands behind his head. "Morning." He intended to enjoy this to the hilt. "You look exceptionally sexy this morning."

Her raised eyebrows did all the talking—she planned to torture him. Starting with sucking him deep.

Jesus.

She did some lips-tongue combo thing that had his hips jerking off the bed. He fought the urge to hold the back of her head in place so he could take charge and drive into her mouth. This was her show, and he was the lucky guy on the receiving end.

A boom of thunder startled her. She lifted and glanced toward the window. The storm hadn't let up yet.

As much as he liked her position, he took the opportunity to hook a finger under her chin and draw her attention back to him. "Hey, get up here."

She crawled up his body, resting her perfect nakedness against his. He kissed her because he couldn't wait any longer and he wanted her to feel safe with him. She sighed against his mouth like she'd needed this kiss as much as he did.

"Sounds like we aren't going anywhere," he said, kissing her cheekbone.

"No," she responded, a flirty twist to her lips. "Looks like we're stuck together a little longer."

"Lucky me."

"True." She smiled, and he smiled back.

He reached under his pillow for the condom—courtesy of the complimentary Love Nest Basket— he'd left for easy access in case of a middle-of-the-night sex emergency and handed it to her.

The most incredible shade of green sparkled at him under heavy-lidded eyes. She rolled the condom on him, then leaned over the side of the bed to pick up the bottle of lubricant they'd also received inside the gift basket. Kudos to The Love Nest concierge for thinking ahead.

She gave him the small bottle of lube and then touched herself. His dick got even harder at the sight of her fingers playing between her legs. He quickly put the lube to use. She watched.

"Ride me this morning, Callie," he told her when finished.

Two seconds later, he slid inside her with ease. Or rather, she slid over and around him, creating incredible friction between them. He put his hands on her waist while she rode him like a rodeo star. Her tits bounced, her back arched, and she set their rhythm, moving up and down at her desired pace. Her hair, a wild mass of soft curls, fell around her shoulders.

He'd loved Callie without a physical connection, but now that they'd crossed that line, he thought his heart might explode with the newfound affection and admiration he had for her.

The comfort they shared while being naked and vulnerable added another layer of attachment for him.

Focus on the sex. Not emotions. This does not end how you wish it would.

Easier said than done when she was finally returning his feelings. Some of them, at least.

Right now, for example. Her heavy breathing and lust-filled expression definitely matched his own. He hoped she was close because looking at her take what she needed from him was the hottest thing ever, and he struggled to wait his turn.

She continued to move up and down like an X-rated goddess, driving him wild. She swiveled her hips, and his eyes rolled to the back of his head. Christ, what she did to him. Thank God the same sensations seemed to overwhelm her because she put her hands on his shoulders and moaned in pleasurable release.

He thrust up once, twice, and grunted through his own climax. He held her close as their heart rates came down. And because he didn't want to slip out of her yet.

When she rolled off him and stared up at the ceiling with a satiated look, he removed the condom and wrapped it in a tissue. He reached for her hand, laced their fingers together. They stayed that way until he said, "I think we need to check out the waterfall shower." It looked awesome—roomy and built into the natural stone walls.

"*We* do?"

"I need someone to wash my back."

"Only your back?"

"Triple C, are you angling to touch more of this?" He gestured down his body with his free hand.

She jumped off the bed. "You'll just have to wait and see," she said over her shoulder. Her hips swayed on the way to the bathroom.

He followed her, and they made good use of the shower products.

• • •

Afterward, they wrapped themselves in the Love Nest's thick, terrycloth robes. Hunter started a new fire. Callie picked up the phone to order room service.

Knock. Knock. "Room service."

Callie looked at him quizzically as she hung up. He shrugged, then walked over to answer the door. A gust of cold air blew into the room. Rain fell in sheets behind the room service person.

"Good morning, Mr. Owens," a different employee from yesterday said.

"Morning."

"I've got your breakfast, and I'm sorry to say the roads are still flooded. For safety reasons, we're requesting everyone stay put."

Hunter accepted the oversize tray from *Brendan*, his badge said. "We didn't order—"

"It comes with the room. On your check-in form you checked no food allergies." He smiled. "Enjoy, and if you should need anything else, please ring the front desk."

"Thank you. We will." Hunter's stomach growled as he kicked the door closed with his foot. Whatever was under the warming lids smelled delicious. "What are you doing?" he asked Callie.

"Hiding." She lowered the pillow she held in front of her face. "I didn't want whoever it was to see me."

Cute. "Where do you want to eat?"

"Right here is good."

He set the tray down on the middle of the bed, lifted the two glasses of orange juice, then the coffees, and set them down on the bedside table so they wouldn't spill. Callie removed the lids from the three plates. French toast, croissants, bacon, and fresh fruit.

They talked while they ate, sharing their astrological signs, the first novel they ever read (*Harry Potter* for both of them), if they'd ever collected anything (seashells for her and baseball cards for him), and their favorite TV shows and movies. When finished, he took the tray and left it on the ground outside the door. As he sat back on the bed, their phones dinged with a text at the same time. At least the storm hadn't knocked out the power or internet service.

"It's Nova," Callie said. She'd texted them both.

He looked at the picture of the wedding party from dinner last night. *Miss you!* his sister wrote. With a heavy heart he texted back, *Miss you, too.*

A second later, his phone rang. "Hey, twerp. I've got you on speaker."

"Hi, Nova!" Callie said.

"Hi! Are you guys okay?"

"We're fine," Callie said.

"How's it going there?" he asked.

"It's going great. Mav and Kennedy are happy and laughing a lot."

"That's good," he said. "Everyone else having fun?" Cole and Bethany had taken Gia with them, so he hoped Beth was able to enjoy herself.

"Andrew is keeping us highly entertained. He should have his own comedy show. It sounds like it's still storming there."

"It is, but we're safe and dry. Is it still storming there?" Hunter asked, admiring Callie, comfortable in her robe and cozied up on the bed.

"Yeah. Luckily, we've got spa reservations today. Do you think you'll make it down here?"

"The roads are still closed, so not yet."

"Well, enjoy your room and time together, then! Love you!"

"Hey, tell Mav…" He got a little choked up. As much as he loved being cocooned with Callie, he hated missing this time with his brothers.

"I will," Nova said thoughtfully before disconnecting.

"I'm sorry you're not there," Callie said, dropping the phone beside her.

"I'm a little bummed *we're* not there, but like I already said, being here with you is the best thing to happen in a long time."

"Have you ever taken a girlfriend on a trip?" she asked, settling back against her pillow.

"Not just the two of us, but with a group of friends, yes. What about you? Any boyfriends whisk you away?" He didn't think so, given he paid close attention when Nova talked about her. And he'd shamefully eavesdropped on them more than once over the years.

"No. My college boyfriend and I were supposed to go to Hawaii after graduation, but things ended instead."

"Dick?"

"Sorry?"

"Your boyfriend, *Dick*. That's what I called him." She laughed. "Nova told me what a dick he was so that's the name I gave him."

"He *was* a dick." She smiled at him. "Thanks for that."

I wanted to punch him in the face for forgetting to pick you up for the airport and then leaving on the trip anyway so he didn't lose his money. What guy thinks he's meeting his girlfriend at the airport? A dick, that's who.

Hunter laid down with his hands on his stomach. "I can't remember the last time I had a day where I didn't have to do anything." He glanced up at her.

"Except you. You're on my to-do list. In the number one, two, and three spots."

"I like that list. I've got my iPad with me and thought I might read."

"More romance?"

"Yes." She walked over to her bag and rummaged through it. "Shoot," she said, climbing back onto the bed with the device in her hands. "The battery is almost dead, and I forgot to bring my charger."

"I've got one in the truck. I'll go grab it." He put on his jeans, boots, and jacket and grabbed his keys. "Be right back."

Shutting the cabin door behind him, he surveyed the scene before deciding on the best route. The wind had blown several large branches off the trees. Raindrops the size of nickels pelted his face as he ran a straight path to his truck. He opened the passenger side door and stepped up into the cab, reaching inside the glove box for the charger. He grabbed it, then backed down.

Unfortunately, his foot slipped, and instead of his boots landing solidly on the ground, he took a fall. His knee slammed into the door sill. He twisted his ankle on the other leg, wrenched his arm trying to catch himself, and knocked his chin on the railing before landing on his ass on the cold, wet ground.

He sat there stunned for a moment, trying to catch his breath. *Ow.* At least he still had the charger in his hand. Getting to his feet took effort. He limped back to the room.

Callie took one look at him and leaped off the bed. "What happened?"

Shivers, more from shock than the cold, racked him. "Got your charger." He held it up.

She took it and tossed it aside like it was meaningless. "I don't care about that. You're shaking like you can't stop. Tell me what happened." She pushed his jacket off his shoulders. "And you're bleeding!" His chin. It throbbed.

"I slipped getting out of the truck."

"Are you hurt anywhere else?" She proceeded to undress him—presumably because his pants were drenched and dirty—and check him for injuries. It was fucking hot. He loved when she played his nurse. "Your knee looks swollen." Leaving his wet clothes on the floor by the door, she helped him to the bathroom. "And you obviously twisted an ankle. Anything else?"

"Maybe." Wasn't that enough? He had to maintain some shred of dignity.

She positioned him against the sink—a smart move considering he wasn't sure he had the strength to stand on his own—then turned on the shower. She examined his face next. "It looks like you just scraped your chin."

He worked his jaw. It hurt, which meant a bruise probably wasn't far behind.

"Did you hit your head?"

"No."

"Are you sure?" Worry tinged her words, and he loved her more than he did an hour ago. *Play it cool, man.*

"Yes."

"Okay, get warmed up, and I'm going to call for some ice for your knee." He supposed he could stand under the water with a hand on the wall to help keep himself propped up.

"I probably need some for my ankle as well." He winced as he stepped into the shower.

"You got it."

The warm water helped. Five minutes later, he lay sprawled on the bed covered with a blanket, his feet propped up on pillows. Ice aided his knee and ankle. The rest of him ached.

Callie stoked the fire. She wore a sweatshirt that fell to the tops of her thighs, and occasionally he got a peek at the lace cheeky panties underneath. He had a primal urge to bite that fine ass of hers. Not hard. Just enough to leave his mark. She had no idea how sexy she was.

She moved to the chair. Tilted her head as she pondered him.

"You're too far away," he said.

"Is the ice helping?"

"Not as much as your nearness would."

She rolled her lips together, trying not to smile. He'd never run out of compliments for her, so she should just get used to it.

"I guess a pillow fight is out of the question now," he said. "Not that I wouldn't mind giving you the advantage."

"I don't need an advantage. I could take you down with one arm tied behind my back," she lobbed back. He enjoyed feisty Callie.

"You're experienced, then?" The pictures currently running through his mind lessened his aches and pains considerably.

"Whatever you're thinking"—she lifted her long

legs into the air, crossed them, and hung them over the arm of the chair in a move he labeled Flirtatious with a capital *F*—"I promise the reality is ten times better." The new position lifted her sweatshirt and gave him a nice view of her round bottom.

"I've no doubt." He wanted to continue this line of banter, he really did, but his eyelids suddenly grew heavy.

"Sleep," Callie said, appearing at his side just as suddenly and removing the ice packs. She tucked the blanket back around him. Kissed his forehead. "I've got you."

She did. More than she knew.

• • •

Callie watched Hunter sleep. Mussed hair. Lips slightly parted. His chest slowly rising and falling. She could stare at him all day and never grow bored. She *needed* to stare at him to make sure he was okay.

When he'd stumbled into the room after getting his charger, her heart had dropped. Pain clearly marred his face, and she couldn't get to him fast enough, leaping off the bed without a second thought.

He'd played the injury off with his usual charm and easy breezy attitude while her insides had tied themselves in knots. She'd flashed back to those first couple of nights after his spider bite, his body having to work extra hard to recover. She hated seeing him in any kind of distress. He gave so much of himself to others, and she hadn't given him enough credit for his care and consideration of the people around him.

After all these weeks together, she'd never make that mistake again.

She'd also never hold him back from having the life he deserved.

She forced her gaze elsewhere before she lost the battle to keep her distance and climbed onto the bed to cuddle next to him. Sex was one thing. Giving in to her emotions was something she tried hard to avoid. She could, though, do something nice for him from across the room. Pulling out her phone, she typed one long text to him.

You're super cute when you sleep.

Thank you for the multiple orgasms.

I love—delete, delete, delete, delete—*like your mouth and your eyes and your whole face, really.*

You make me smile even when you're not around.

Your family is lucky to have you, and so am I.

When you're naked, I want to jump you. Actually, I want to do that even when you're clothed.

Thank you for being kind.

Thank you for showing up.

That ought to do it for now. Her finger hovered over the send icon. Kept hovering...

She couldn't do it.

She couldn't risk exposing her heart any more than she already had. And she couldn't give him false hope about the two of them. Their affair had an end date: the day he wore his best man suit. Callie refused to interfere with the magic after that. Selfishly, she had her business to think about, too.

She deleted everything but the first line. *You're*

super cute when you sleep.

His phone dinged.

She looked up to find him awake, his cell already in his hand, and his eyes on her. "You looked so serious over there I was about to text you a puppy video." He glanced down at her text. "Thanks, Triple C, you are, too."

"Feeling better?" she asked, standing and walking to the bed. Her feet carried her closer to him without thought.

"Everything still hurts."

"Would more ice help?

"No, but you sitting on my face would."

Heat licked the back of her neck. She immediately felt his words between her legs. He could dirty talk her morning, noon, and night. "Such a giver."

"Trust me, the pleasure will be all mine. It's called sexual healing."

She cracked up. "Isn't that a song?"

"It is. Now please take off your clothes and get up here."

Excitement thrummed through her. "Since you said please." Her sweatshirt came off first. He stared at her breasts like they were too good to be true. She traced a finger between them, down her stomach, and then shimmied out of her panties.

Turned on from his gaze and invitation, she straddled his face, placing her palms on the stone wall. "Let the healing begin," she said.

"Hell yeah." The second he licked her, she was flooded with feels-so-good sensations. When he added a finger, it took no time at all for her to fly over the edge with his name on her lips. "Again," he told her, removing his finger but continuing to tongue her. She ground against his face, a minute later meeting his demand.

She fell to the side in a heap of exhausted bliss.

"I feel much better," he said smugly. "Thank you."

"Anytime."

"Really?" Had he meant to sound so hopeful?

"Umm…"

"Relax, Cal. There're no expectations once we leave this bubble. Remember, you're in control."

She appreciated that but was scared to death her control might slip.

CHAPTER THIRTY-TWO

"That boy has no idea," Birdy said, looking out the front window of Callie's shop.

Callie briefly wondered who Birdy was talking about but kept her focus on her best friend. "It's perfect," she said to Nova, eyeing her in her shimmery silver bridesmaid dress. "You look beautiful."

Nova did a little twirl on the round pedestal as she studied herself in the mirror. "You are giving bridesmaid dresses a new reputation, Cal."

"Agreed," Bethany said, stepping out of the second dressing room in her bridesmaid dress. "I feel prettier than I have in a long time and will definitely wear this again."

"You're gorgeous," Nova told her sister-in-law.

"She's right," Callie agreed. "Being a mom of two looks amazing on you." She stepped over to Bethany for a closer look at the sizing. With only three weeks to go until the wedding, this was the girls' final fitting unless something drastic happened. "Do the straps feel too tight?" She slipped a finger underneath the shoulder strap to check for flexibility.

"No, I think they're fine."

"Okay, good."

"He's going to cause an accident," Birdy voiced, her attention still out the paned window. "Someone is going to walk into the street because they're not looking where they're going and get hit by a car."

That grabbed Callie's undivided attention and

had her, Nova, and Bethany hurrying over to the window. "What are you talking about?" Callie asked.

"See for yourself." Birdy nodded toward the street.

Callie's eyes immediately zeroed in on Hunter, walking up and down the sidewalk wearing a front baby carrier with Gia inside. Her little arms and legs were sticking out, and her angelic face was nestled against his chest. He was talking to her and pointing at things.

And he looked insanely hot doing it.

Do not fall any more for him. Do not do it.

"Cole and Jenna are having a special father-daughter day, so he said he'd watch Gia for me while I was here," Bethany said.

He looked like a natural with her, enjoying himself completely. *Look away! And don't drool!* She failed at the first, succeeded at the latter.

Callie hadn't seen him since he'd dropped her off at home last Sunday. They'd made it to the tail end of the bachelor/bachelorette party, for which she was grateful. Seeing Hunter's face light up when he finally got to toast Maverick added to the intimate memories between the two of them that she would never forget.

Tingles prickled her skin every time she thought about it. About *him*. She rubbed her hands up and down her arms now to rid them. She'd missed him this week. Then reminded herself not to go there. They'd shared forty-eight hours of bliss. End of story.

"Hunt's going to make a great dad one day," Nova said.

Birdy cleared her throat and shot Callie a look.

"If those floozies have their way, it will be sooner rather than later," Birdy said good-naturedly.

As the four of them stood there staring out the window, three different women approached him. It was like the women were hiding behind trees waiting for a turn to say hello. And flirt. She'd seen enough people flirt with him over the years to know the signs: Playing with their hair. Touching his arm. Laughing and waving a hand in the air like he'd said the funniest thing ever.

It didn't bother her.

Much.

Hunter and flirting went hand in hand. Always had.

"I think Vivian's got a tracking device on him or something," Nova said. "She is always popping up wherever he is."

"She's definitely interested in him," Callie said, proud of herself for sounding neutral.

"She stopped by the inn the other day," Bethany said. "She's very nice."

"Got any popcorn?" Birdy asked. "This is better than Netflix."

"I'm not sure if I should be upset that Gia is in the middle of this or find it funny," Bethany said.

"Funny," Callie and Nova said at the same time.

"Jinx! You owe me a margarita," they mouthed off simultaneously.

"I'll make us all margaritas if someone makes popcorn." Birdy held up her phone in front of the window. She'd arrived a few minutes before Nova and Bethany to do a post for Instagram, then they'd convinced her to stay because having Birdy around was always a pleasure.

"Are you videoing this?" Nova leaned closer to Birdy to look through her phone.

"Nah. Just taking a few pictures."

"One of those women could be the future Mrs. Hunter Owens," Bethany said. "Did you hear there's some kind of pool going on?"

Callie placed a chair behind Birdy so she could sit down.

"I've seen it," Nova said. "It's ridiculous."

"What kind of pool is it?" Callie hadn't heard anything about it.

"People are guessing when Hunter will get engaged."

"And betting money on it?" Callie ignored the uncomfortable feeling in the pit of her stomach. The fact was the town loved Hunter and wanted to see him walk down the aisle. Thanks to her best man suit, the odds of it happening sooner rather than later had increased.

"The buy-in is a dollar a square, just for the fun of it. More important is going to be bragging rights," Nova said.

"I'm in for two bucks," Birdy said. "Halftime Show and Friday the thirteenth."

Nova gave Birdy a high five. "Nice. Friday the thirteenth gives you at least two chances next year, right?"

Birdy nodded and cleared her throat again. "First one's in February, so that's probably a long shot."

"Does Hunter know about this?" Callie asked.

"Probably, but you know him. He's used to the attention and won't let it affect him."

Callie only half heard what Nova said because Hunter hooked his fingers inside Gia's tiny hands and rocked side-to-side. His lips moved like he was singing a song, and the cuteness factor combined with his confident, masculine swagger made her lightheaded. And want to jump his bones.

Splat. I've fallen all the way now, damn him.

A car drove by and honked. Callie blinked herself back into focus. Nova was right. Hunter didn't let things affect him, and she did. He didn't play it safe, and she did. He wanted to get married and settle down. And she didn't.

"Uh-oh," Bethany said. "He's singing."

"It's a good thing we're inside and he's outside," Nova said.

And just like that, the street cleared and Hunter's female fans vanished back to where they came from. Callie rubbed her eyes to make sure she hadn't imagined the sudden retreat. "Is there something wrong with his singing?" she asked.

"It's worse than fingernails on a chalkboard," Nova said.

"Worse than a baby raccoon's crying chatter," Bethany said. At Callie's puzzled expression, she added, "A family of raccoons lives near the house, and the sound drives us crazy at night when we're trying to sleep."

"He sounds that bad?" Callie tried to recall if she'd ever heard him sing and came up blank.

"Yes," the three women said.

As if their affirmation pierced the air and gave away their location at the window, Hunter turned his head and looked right at them.

"Time to get changed!" Nova spun around and hurried toward the dressing rooms.

"Thank you again, Callie!" Bethany almost tripped darting back to her dressing room.

Callie raced away from the window right behind them. "Let me know if you need any help getting the dresses off."

Birdy stayed put. Waved out the window. "He's coming this way," she called over her shoulder.

Half a minute later, Hunter entered the shop. It was normal business hours, so anyone could walk in. "Hi," she said to him. "Bethany is getting changed."

"Great, thanks." Two words that felt like a lot more with his dreamy eyes locked on hers. Not to mention the second he'd walked inside, her chest fluttered. "Did you hear that, Gia? Your momma will be right out." He broke eye contact to kiss the top of her head.

"While you're here, do you want to try on your suit?" she asked. "It's ready to go."

"Great idea!" Nova shouted from behind the curtain of the dressing room.

"Oh, yes," Birdy said, getting to her feet. "Let's see this special best man suit."

"Looks like I'm putting on a fashion show." He flashed his dimples around the room, clueless to the power they yielded.

Bethany stepped out of the dressing room, the bridesmaid dress on a hanger in her hand.

"Let me get that," Callie said, taking the gown. "I'll slip it into a garment bag." While she did that, Bethany retrieved Gia. Hunter took off the baby carrier.

"How is my babylicious?" Nova cooed, reaching with grabby hands for her niece. "I left the dress hanging up. Is that okay?"

"That's fine." Callie bagged Nova's dress, too, then turned to find Hunter *right there*. Looking good. Smelling good.

"Hi," he said for her ears only. "I've missed you."

"I've missed you, too."

His entire face lit up. Happiness bombarded her. She did that to him. "Are you busy tomorrow night?" he asked.

"Are you asking me out on a date?" Her heart pounded *yes*. Her head, though, had reservations. Logically, a date didn't mean anything more than that, but they were way past that, weren't they?

"If I was, would you say yes?" When she didn't answer right away, he said, "I'll wait forever for you if that's what it takes."

Oh, God. This was really happening.

She didn't know what to do. Panic clawed its way up the back of her throat. She'd thought about this moment countless times over the past week. When he'd texted a picture of them in the Love Nest. When he'd called to ask if there was anything he could do to help fix her leaky faucet. (He recommended the plumber they used at the inn to her and the problem was fixed.)

She was in deep with him.

But if she let go of her fear of rejection and vow to never marry, who was she? Would she know how to act? Because she was certain that with Hunter, her life would be irrevocably changed.

"Hey." He hooked a finger around hers at her

waist. "Let me back up. Come to my place tomorrow night. No stress. No 'what happens after that'. Sound good?"

"Yes," she whispered, relieved.

"Ahem."

Hunter let go of her and took a step back. *Sorry*, he mouthed.

He didn't *look* sorry.

Nova, Birdy, and Bethany were lined up like a receiving line, ready to be provided with a detailed account of her and Hunter's conversation. Even Gia had an expectant look on her cute little face.

They could take their nosy noses home with them. "Hunt, your suit is right here." She spun around to grab it from the hanging rack. His dress shirt was also included. Ideally, he'd have his dress shoes with him, but no biggie.

"She's calling him Hunt now," Birdy said.

"It's been happening," Nova said.

"Ladies," Hunter said, addressing the line. "I realize three out of four of you are family, but prepare to be gobsmacked by my change of clothes." He took the suit from Callie and disappeared inside a dressing room.

She pressed her lips together to keep from smiling at his indirect compliment.

Nova raised her eyebrows, hinting that she wanted the full scoop later. It wasn't like her best friend didn't know they'd had sex last weekend. Callie had told her it was a one-off, but the tension in the air this afternoon indicated something else entirely.

"Ready or not," Hunter called out, sliding the curtain open and stepping out for his reveal.

She was not ready.

Not at all.

Birdy whistled. "You, young man, need to come with a warning label."

Does a suit make a man? Or does the man make the suit? Whatever the saying, Hunter looked like a million dollars. She raked her eyes over him from top to bottom and back up, reminding herself to look at him like a client, not the best-looking human on the planet.

Hunter tucked his hands into the front jacket pockets and struck a pose. He turned in a circle to give them the full three-sixty. Then he undid the button on the jacket in that sexy way men do. One flick and the coat parted. He lifted the left side to show off the inside panel and the small butterfly applique.

"That the magic touch?" he asked.

"Yes."

He let go so the jacket laid flat, and she couldn't help herself. She ran her hands over his shoulders and down his arms. "It fits perfectly. How does it feel?"

"Great. You are an amazing designer."

"She is." Nova put her arm around Callie.

Gia fussed, drawing everyone's attention. "She's getting hungry," Bethany said, "so we better get going. Nova, do you mind carrying my dress to the car?"

"Not at all."

"See you later, cutie pie." Hunter gave Gia a kiss on her chubby cheek. She kicked her legs and stopped fussing like she recognized his voice. Callie's insides melted.

"Cal, you're coming to the lantern lighting tonight, right?" Nova asked.

"Umm..." Mary Rose had started the family activity last year and decided to make it a yearly tradition on the first Saturday of December. With this new connection with Hunter, though, she didn't know if—

"I know my mom invited you, so we'll see you at seven." Nova carefully carried the dresses over her arm, refusing to let Callie back out. "Love you!"

"Wave goodbye to Callie." Bethany held Gia's hand and waved.

"Love you guys," Callie said.

"I love you, too," Hunter chimed in, sticking by Callie's side.

She turned to him once the front door shut. "Time to take off the suit."

His gaze jumped to Birdy before returning all his attention to her. "I'm not really into having an audience, but if you—"

"*Stop.*" She put her hands on his shoulders (because *reasons*), spun him around, and gave him a little push toward the dressing room. "In there, mister. Alone."

"Ah, gotcha." His playful expression got to her all right. Her stomach flipped.

"I missed something between the last time I saw you two and today." Birdy scanned Callie's face with grandmotherly interest and warmth. "Whatever that something was, I approve." She winked, then headed out.

"Bye," Callie said. She'd share a PG-rated version with Birdy when and if there was a reason to.

"Alone at last," Hunter said softly in her ear, his hands on her waist and his breath tickling the back of her neck.

Her head fell to the side. "Not for long. I have another appointment in a few minutes."

He kissed the sensitive spot behind her ear like she hoped he would. "I could make you come in two."

She appreciated that he kept his hands where they were, waiting for her to give him the go-ahead. He did know his way around her body. And being surrounded by him with his lips on her skin had her turned on. But...

"Sorry." He put space between them, taking his warmth, and making her immediately miss him. "I said I wasn't going to pressure you, and here I am doing it."

"It's okay." She gathered her strength and walked to the dressing room to get his suit. "I like this effect I have on you."

"I'm happy to hear that. So... ?" He waggled his eyebrows.

She chuckled. "So...I guess I wish we could be in a romantic bubble again. Just the two of us. Not caring about anything else." She fit his suit inside a garment bag and handed it to him. "You really did look incredible in this."

"Callie."

"Yes?"

He struggled with what he wanted to say, which made her think it was probably best if he didn't say it.

"I'll see you tonight," she said to save them both.

"For the lantern lighting."

"See you tonight," he echoed.

She watched him go, then straightened the room up for her next client. Business had started to pick up, thank goodness. Not nearly enough to guarantee she could buy the cottage in five months, though. And so, with that sobering thought, she pushed a certain cowboy out of her head.

CHAPTER THIRTY-THREE

Stars and a smiling moon filled the night sky as Callie stood with the entire Owens family along the bank of Boone Lake. The manmade lake was named after Hunter's grandfather and offered guests of the ranch the opportunity to canoe and paddle board.

Tonight, it provided the chance to manifest good luck for the year ahead. Mary Rose had given each person a lantern made from eco-friendly rice paper and wood to decorate. Nova had drawn flowers on hers. Jenna's had horses and dogs and their mule, George. Hunter's had stars, and he'd written, *Whatever is good for the soul, do that.* Callie had drawn butterflies and hearts on hers.

She stole a peek at Hunter. They'd been stealing glances all night, each time ramping up the anticipation between them. When he'd not-so-innocently brushed his side against hers, a flash of heat had sparked under her skin. Her body still tingled, twenty minutes later.

"It makes us so happy to be here with all of you," Mary Rose said on behalf of herself and John. "You know how much I love traditions, and this one started thanks to our soon-to-be daughter-in-law, Kennedy." Kennedy's face lit up with joy as she looked at Mary Rose. Maverick held his future wife's hand and smiled down at her with pride.

"In fact, it really should be you, Kennedy, speaking and leading us in releasing our lanterns."

"I second that," Maverick said.

Jenna quickly moved from her grandmother's side to Kennedy's. "I can be your assistant."

Kennedy blinked, overcome with emotion. She wasn't close to her own mother and had formed a close bond with Mary Rose.

Callie thought about her own relationship with the matriarch of the Owens family. Mary Rose treated Callie like family, giving her the same care and affection she did her own children. When Callie and Nova were thinking about becoming sexually active, it was Mary Rose they went to with questions and support. It was Mary Rose's texts that lit up her phone first on her birthdays, often just after midnight to guarantee she'd be the first one. And it was Mary Rose who was always there with open arms when she needed a "mom."

Family, Callie reminded herself, were the people she chose to be with. And how lucky was she to have family at large *and* right here in the hometown she adored?

"I just want to say I am so lucky to be part of this family and I love you all so much. I'm honored to be contributing to so many long-standing traditions, and as we collectively release our hopes, wishes, and dreams for the future, may we remember that family is the greatest gift of all."

"Hear! Hear!" Hunter shouted.

"Everyone ready?" Kennedy asked.

A resounding "Yes!" was the answer.

Callie kneeled with her lantern. LED candles lit up the inside of the lanterns and the glow along the lake's edge was beautiful.

"On three," Kennedy said. "One…two…three…"

Callie placed her lantern in the water, gave it a little push, and silently recited her hopes and dreams. She watched the soft light of everyone's lanterns reflected upon the water's surface.

Magical.

When her eyes met Hunter's, his warm gaze definitely cast a spell on her. He melted away feelings of fear and second-best. If only she could trust its permanency.

• • •

No way would Callie not love this.

Hunter gave the bunkhouse one last inspection before mentally patting himself on the back. He'd worked all afternoon to get it just right. Last weekend, they'd had a Parisian cave. Tonight, they had a Hawaiian bungalow. She hadn't gotten to take that graduation trip to Hawaii, so he hoped this created a better memory. Strings of tiny white lights. Blow-up palm trees and sea turtles. Real leis hanging from furniture. Throw blankets with sunsets on them. The sound of the ocean playing in the background.

If Callie needed a bubble in order to be with him, he'd deliver bubble after bubble until she realized their relationship was real and true and, damn it, that he *was* the forever kind and the man for her.

He wanted to love her for the rest of his life.

A knock sounded on the door. *Finally*. Never mind that she was five minutes early.

"Just a minute!" He opened the fridge and pulled out the pitcher of pina coladas he'd made earlier. He poured her a glass, added a pink umbrella.

Drink in hand, he opened the door. "Hi. Welcome to your tropical paradise." He ushered her inside and handed her the cocktail.

"*Hunter.*" Voice soft, enamored. She took the drink, her jaw slack, and looked around. "This is incredible."

"I'm glad you like it." He placed a lei over her head next. She sucked in a breath. "Aloha, Callie."

"Aloha. It smells just like I've imagined." She lifted the lei with her free hand to take a whiff.

"My mission is off to a good start, then."

"I can't believe you did all this for me." She moved further into the bunkhouse, took a seat on the couch. Having her back in his home made him feel like there wasn't anything they couldn't conquer together.

He poured himself a pina colada and joined her. "Cheers."

"Cheers." She clinked her glass with his, then resumed surveying the room, a look of pure delight on her gorgeous face. "There are even sea turtles! I love sea turtles."

I love you.

She leaned forward and kissed him. "I feel like we're on a Fantasy Island weekend again."

"I aim to make all your fantasies come true, Cal."

"I smell something else…"

"Oh, shit!" He put his drink down on the coffee table and jumped to his feet. "That would be dinner." Smoke billowed out of the oven when he opened it. "How do you feel about blackened salmon?"

"I will enjoy anything you've cooked." She stood

behind him. "Anything I can do to help?"

"No. I've got this." He plated the slightly burned fish, then added wild rice and steamed broccoli. They sat back on the couch to eat.

"And here I thought we'd be having pizza and beer." Callie dug into her food.

"We can do that next time."

"Next time?" She pointed her fork at him. "Next time I expect an Irish countryside or Egypt or Africa." Her eyes twinkled, making him very glad he'd done this.

"You're the expert on Africa. Maybe you should surprise me."

"Maybe I will."

He'd take that "maybe" given she fired it back with zero hesitation. He'd made strides in shutting down her reluctance to date him, every playful response from her further encouragement for him to keep going.

She took a sip of her pina colada. "This is my favorite tropical drink."

"I know."

"How do you know?" She made a face like she was trying to recall if she'd told him that or not.

She hadn't.

It was only a little embarrassing to tell her how he knew. "Your senior year of high school. You and Nova were getting ready for Homecoming and singing the pina colada song at the top of your lungs. When you got home from the dance, you guys made them and you said it was your favorite drink ever."

"You were spying on us?" Amusement tinged her accusation.

"I wouldn't exactly call it that." He was absolutely spying, home for the weekend from college and soaking up any sightings of Callie he could get. Her kindness and appreciation toward his family, especially Nova, had cemented his puppy love back then, and now, being with the woman she'd become, intensified that youthful longing and turned it into something much deeper.

"What would you call it?" Her raised eyebrows were not the least bit intimidating. Sexy? Yes.

He shrugged. "The point is, I have an excellent memory."

"Okay, I'll give you that. But you're also lucky. That was a long time ago, and I could have a new favorite."

"True, but you tend to stick with things."

She canted her head to the side, considering him.

"Throughout the years, I've studied you and listened to Nova talk about you. I've quietly kept up to date on you, Cal, and really hope that doesn't make me sound creepy."

"I didn't know," she said shyly.

"Now that you do, I'm thinking I should show you how much I appreciate you."

She put her plate on the coffee table, so he quickly followed suit. "I do like your showing methods."

He didn't need any further encouragement. He scooped her right up, enjoying her laughter, and carried her to his bed. He'd draped twinkle lights across the headboard and hung a lei on each post. She took them in, then stared into his eyes as he hovered over her body, his arms bent at the elbows, his thigh between her legs.

She ran her fingers through his hair. "What do you like so much about me?" she whispered.

It wasn't a question of doubt or uncertainty, but of pure curiosity. Had no man ever told her the things that made her special?

"I like that you're passionate about sewing. I like that you have your own style and are confident in your own skin. I like that you're a good friend. I like that you want to make other people feel good in what they wear. I like that you hang out with Birdy and post pictures with her on Instagram. I think you're funny and kind and smart. I like how loud you sneeze."

She made a face. "It's true," he assured her. "I like that you're honest and sincere. I don't think there's anything you can't do. And I especially like that when I'm near you, the world is brighter."

He touched his forehead to hers. "I like the way you taste and smell. I like the way you kiss me as if you need me for your next breath."

Her eyes shined with liquid emotion. He hadn't meant to make her tear up. With tenderness and care, he brushed his lip against hers. *I love you*. He kissed her cheek, her eyelid. *I love you*. He pressed his mouth to her hairline, breathed her in.

Loving her right now would be baring his soul, and because he didn't know if she was ready for that—or ever would be—he changed tactics. Pushing up, he stood on his knees. "First person to get naked wins a prize!"

Her competitive, adventurous side immediately came out to play. "Hey! You got a head start." She scrambled to her knees while trying to stay his arms so he couldn't take off his shirt.

They tussled and laughed as they each undressed and tried to stop the other person from getting their clothes off first. *Fun.* He also liked that she was fun.

Shoes went flying. The elastic on his boxer briefs snapped against his skin when she playfully tried to hang on to them and remove her bra at the same time.

"I win!" she shouted, naked and beautiful. "What's my prize?"

Technically, he'd call it a tie, but she'd always win with him. Besides, her nakedness was his prize.

"First, you need to put this back on." He placed the lei back around her neck. "Seeing you in nothing but a flower necklace is fucking sexy."

Taking it one step further, she laid back on the bed and struck a seductive pose. Legs bent to one side where he got a glimpse of her heart-shaped birthmark on her upper thigh. One arm raised above her head. Her other arm draped across her stomach. The lei covered her nipples, leaving the rest of her ample breasts to his perusal.

She rolled her tongue across her bottom lip. "Prize later, sex now."

Any control he had shattered. He spread her legs and buried his face between them. She writhed and moaned as he ate her out. She cupped the back of his head to bring his mouth tighter against her swollen flesh.

"Oh god! Yes! Just like that. Don't stop!" She ground against him. Callie was no delicate flower during oral sex, and he effing loved it.

He continued to tongue her. Suck her.

He added a finger inside her. Her muscles clenched. She released his head to take fistfuls of the comforter. "Ohhhh, yeeesss." She bucked. Stiffened. Yelled his name as she climaxed.

Rising, he found her cheeks pink and her green eyes glazed over in satisfaction. He grabbed a condom, rolled it on, and positioned himself at her opening.

She rose onto her elbows to watch him slowly slide inside her. She stared, her breath growing heavy again as they became one. When he was fully seated, she fell back, wrapped her legs around his hips, and met him thrust for thrust.

His dick had never been harder.

Their rhythm went from fast and furious to slow and sensual. Her nails raked down his back. His hand cupped and kneaded her breast. Her scent, her sounds, the feel of her wrapped so tight around him, were too much and yet not enough.

He pulled out and flipped her onto her hands and knees to take her from behind. Primal urges coursed through his blood. "This okay?" he asked.

"Yes," she panted.

The second after he got that green light, he sank into her. Stilled. Just for a moment. To relish the heavenly sensations throbbing through his body. She cried out in pleasure, and he kept those cries going as he drove into her.

Together they were wild. Passionate. Vocal.

Slick with sweat.

One hundred percent in the moment. Callie was all he could see, hear, feel. She rocked his world, and when she came, his own orgasm barreled through him.

She collapsed onto her stomach. He kissed her shoulder blade, then the constellation of freckles in the middle of her back.

"Be right back," he murmured in her ear.

He disposed of the condom, washed his hands. He walked to the kitchen to grab the shaved ices in the freezer. Maybe he'd spoon some on Callie's body and lick it off her.

"Ready for dessert?" he asked, rounding the barn door. He found her in the same position she was in when he'd gotten up. It was a fantastic position, one he didn't mind staring at for a while.

She flopped over, treating him to another incredible view.

"How would you feel about me chaining you to my bed, naked, for the next week or so?" He took a bite right off the top of one of the ices.

"What if I had to pee?"

"Good point." He handed her a cup of iced goodness. "Hawaiian ice for my hula girl."

"Does that make you my flame-throwing dancing guy?" She sat up, covering her lap with a sunset blanket.

"If I get to dance beside you, sure." He joined her on the bed, sharing the blanket. They'd worked up a sweat, and he kept the bunkhouse at a decent temperature, but the ices would cool them down fast.

"Mmm, this is good. Pineapple and watermelon."

"This one is kiwi and strawberry." He held it out for her to try.

She took a big spoonful. "Mmm."

They ate in easy silence, sharing the two desserts. When finished, he couldn't help but kiss her pink-stained lips. He took their trash to the kitchen, and when he returned found her in one of his T-shirts, looking hotter than he'd imagined. He pulled on some sweatpants before jumping onto the bed beside her.

"Ready for your prize now?"

"You're my prize."

"I think that's the nicest thing you've ever said to me."

Her happy, post-sex-and-Hawaiian-ice radiance dimmed as she seemed to absorb those words. Damn it. He hadn't meant to dampen the mood. "I meant—"

"Let me remedy that," she interrupted, taking his hand inside hers. "You're selfless. Loyal. Strong. I like that you love your family so much. I like your hands." She kissed his knuckles. "You're smart and funny. I like that you love animals and our small town. I think you can accomplish anything you set your mind to. And I like how serious you take your work."

Gratitude welled up inside him. He wasn't the kind of man who needed compliments or puffing up to boost his ego or make him feel valuable. He prided himself on being a good person. Hearing that she thought him serious, though, meant more than she could know.

"Thanks, Triple C, but I think you left something out." *Lighten the mood.* Because the way she looked at him, and the way he felt about her, he was two seconds away from telling her he loved her.

And despite her kind words, he couldn't risk it.

"Oh? And what might that be?"

"King of Orgasms." He smirked.

She burst into laughter. "You make it sound like you orgasm all the time. I think you mean King Orgasm-Giver? Or something like that."

"God, you're gorgeous." He kissed her soundly on the lips. Along with giving her what he hoped were the best orgasms of her life, he wanted to give her every kind of kiss. Then in keeping with the lighter mood, he said, "Now it's time for your prize."

He grinned at her, then leaned over the bed to pick up the ukulele he'd stashed away. He couldn't say those three little words yet, but he could sing them. He held the ukulele in his lap, strummed a few chords. Not that he had any idea what he was doing when it came to playing the instrument. He did, however, know the words to the song he planned to sing.

"My prize is…" Her brows knit in confusion.

"I'm going to sing you a song. And not just any song, but a Don Ho song." It 100 percent went with the theme of the evening *and* hinted at his feelings. A win-win.

"No!" She covered her mouth with her hand like she couldn't believe she'd shouted the word out. Her eyes, though, sparkled with mischief. No, not mischief…she had a secret.

"No? You have a thing against Don Ho?" He could sing something else, even though it wouldn't have the same effect. He sang to Gia all the time. Sang with Jenna. He mentally flipped through his current favorite playlist.

"Umm…"

"You're cute when you're tongue-tied." He continued to tap the ukulele's strings.

"I don't mind Don Ho. 'Tiny Bubbles,' right?" She took the ukulele out of his hands.

"That's exactly what I planned on singing. Great minds think alike."

She climbed into his lap, looped her arms around his neck. "I think I like my original assessment best. You're my prize, Hunt. Not that I'm not grateful you want to sing me a song."

"Why do I get the feeling there's more to it?" He wrapped his hands around her waist.

"I don't know. Maybe I've got an air of mystery about me you haven't discovered yet." She wiggled closer, his shirt rising up her thighs.

"If you're trying to distract me, it's working."

A seductive smile lifted the corners of her mouth.

"Before we take this any further, though, I have a question for you."

"Yes," she immediately answered.

"You don't want to know what the question is first?"

She shook her head. "No."

"You sure?"

"Positive. Now show me again whatcha got, Orgasm King."

He did. He showed her multiple times, keeping her in his bed all night. Come morning, she took the ukulele, a sea turtle, and his question with her.

CHAPTER THIRTY-FOUR

Overcome by orgasms. Or OBO, as Callie now referred to Hunter and his master delivery tactics. It was the only explanation for why she'd said "yes" to an official date with him. That and she'd answered before hearing the question. She'd been so bamboozled by his charm and his sex appeal and his *everything* that the question seemed irrelevant at the time.

Not that she wasn't looking forward to their date. She was.

So much that the Christmas music playing in Baked on Main had her dreaming of waking up Christmas morning wrapped in nothing but him. She glanced out the window to Main Street. A light rain fell that didn't require an umbrella or damper the festive spirit. Poinsettias filled flower boxes. Wreaths hung on shop doors. Christmas lights decorated trees and hung across the main intersection. And soon they'd know who won the ambassador position.

Her phone lit up with a text, drawing her attention back inside.

Nova: *Meet me at Wildflower in twenty?*
Callie: *That should work.*

"I'm sorry about that," Vivian said, hurrying back to their corner table in the bakery. "My brother and I are planning a surprise anniversary party for my mom and dad over Christmas and he called to confirm some things with me. Now where were we?"

She looked down at the handwritten notes she'd been taking.

"No worries. I could sit here all day with the delicious smells. What anniversary are your parents celebrating?"

"Forty."

"Wow. Congratulations to them."

"Thanks. They're still madly in love, too. They've had their share of ups and downs for sure, but my mom has always said marriage is about two imperfect people who refuse to give up on each other, and they've stuck to that."

Callie let those words of wisdom sink in. She'd heard similar ones from Birdy. What did it mean that her parents did give up on each other—twice?

"I hope to follow in their footsteps," Vivian continued. "They've been great role models." She took a sip of her coffee. "Enough about that, I've got two more questions for you."

"You want to get married and have kids?" Callie asked. The more she got to know Vivian, the more she thought her a perfect match for Hunter. *Unfortunately.*

"Absolutely. I think having a partner to do life with is important for a person's long-term health. Mental and physical. We need someone by our side. Friends fill that spot, but they can come and go. Once you make a commitment to love, honor, and cherish, I believe it's forever." She narrowed her eyes at Callie. "You keep getting me off track."

"It's more fun talking about you than myself."

"What if I told you there's a good chance the feature I'm writing on you is picked up by *Bride* magazine for their New Designers To Know write-up?"

Callie tucked her hands under her thighs to keep from jumping to her feet in excitement. *Omigod!* That would be ridiculously amazing. "I'd ask you what I need to do to make it happen." And then she'd do it to a *T*.

Vivian waved off Callie's offer. "I've got a good friend there, and your talent for dressmaking combined with the story behind the applique and the magic it brings makes for a great story. And I think Marry Matchmaker has a nice ring to it that will attract a lot of attention. Everyone dreams of getting married, and if they believe in a magical boost, then I think this could make you an exceptionally busy designer, my friend."

Her friend. She liked the sound of that. Appreciated Vivian's partnership in this. Vivian was more than a reporter in their small town. She seemed to want to put down roots.

Because of that, Callie dropped her guard a little. "Not everyone wants to get married."

"You're right. I shouldn't have said that. Bad reporter." She lightly slapped her forearm. "I think I'm getting a little caught up in it is all. I wish my bestie was getting married." She smiled warmly. If she'd figured out Callie didn't want to get married, she didn't let on.

"Well, when she does, I'm here for you. Thank you for taking an interest in my business and possibly elevating it to a whole other level. I do need more business and with your help…" She could buy the cottage *and* maybe even expand to other areas.

L.A. Chicago. New York.

"I don't know you well, Callie, but I think you deserve all the success the world has to offer. The people I've spoken to about you love you." She glanced at the time on her phone. "Shoot, I'm sorry, but I need to hurry. Okay, obviously the Owens wedding in two weeks is important, given you're dressing the maid of honor and best man. Kennedy has graciously invited me to be there so I can conclude my story that night. What are your instincts telling you?"

"I'm not sure yet. This is the first wedding where I have a personal relationship with the family, so it feels different."

"Hunter is the talk of the town right now. If the magic does work for him, do you think you'll continue to make suits for best men?"

"That's a good question, and I'm not sure of the answer yet, but I'm thinking probably not."

"How come?"

Callie's heart pounded. Because it would be hard to see Hunter get married. Give his smiles and care and undivided attention to someone else. "I've loved making dresses since I was a teen, and I see myself expanding on those designs."

"Well, if the suit matches Hunter with his soul mate, you may find demand requires it. Women wear suits, too, you know."

"You're right. Bottom line, I do want my business to grow, so I'll do whatever it takes."

"Well, I'll be rooting for you. And Hunter."

For a second, Callie thought she meant her and Hunter as a couple but then realized she meant separately. A rush of uneasiness laced its way through her back and shoulders. Deciding never to marry hadn't bothered her. Until now.

They stood. "Thank you so much for everything, Vivian."

"You're welcome. And please call me Vivi. Let's grab a coffee sometime and talk boys, not business."

"I'd like that."

On the walk down Main Street to meet Nova, Callie's thoughts strayed to Hunter for the millionth time. He'd made it clear he wanted to be with her. She wanted to be with him, too. It was as simple as that if she let it be.

But for how long? He wanted to get married. And that wish now directly had influence over her business.

She'd gotten herself into a big mess.

Coming toward her on the sidewalk were two women holding up the Botanical Society calendar Nova had put together as a fundraiser. Hunter graced the cover and the month of June, not that she'd purchased her own copy and stared at him a hundred times over the past few days.

"Hi, Callie," Bella said, having lowered the calendar so Callie could see her face. Kennedy's RN, Savannah, was the other woman.

"Hi. How are you guys?"

They giggled. "We're on a break and trying not to obsess over this calendar. Bella is particularly fond of the month of June," Savannah said. "Have you seen it yet?"

"No," she lied and immediately hated herself for doing so. It was just...Bella had feelings for Hunter.

She could see it written all over her face, and Callie didn't want to talk about him when her own feelings were probably just as easy to read. "But I'm on my way to Wildflower now to help Nova with some mailings. Have a great rest of the day." She stepped around them to hurry on her way. In truth, she didn't have a lot of time to talk with a fitting scheduled at the shop after she helped her best friend.

Nova practically tackle-hugged her when she walked into Wildflower. The catch-all store with high wood-beam ceilings and aisles of different offerings had volunteered to be the main seller of the calendar.

"The calendar is sold out!" Nova said.

"That's fantastic! What's going on back there?" Callie lifted her chin toward a crowd of people.

"Hunter is doing a signing. Come on." Nova led her toward the group.

The man of the hour wore a cowboy hat, jeans, and a short-sleeve blue T-shirt that made his baby blues even brighter and accentuated the muscles of his biceps. He handed the calendar back to a woman, his dimpled smile and gratitude causing her to fan herself. For real. She waved her hand in front of her face as she walked away.

Going unnoticed, Callie hung back to continue to watch him in action.

"Hey, Birdy." Hunter looked around at the few other women waiting alongside Birdy. "Mayor. *Mom.* Looks like half of the Baker's Dozen is here." At seeing the mayor, Callie's mind flitted to the ambassador position and whether Mayor Garnett had made a decision yet.

"We're here to support Nova and the Botanical Society," Mary Rose said.

"I'm here for you," Birdy announced. "And the other eleven hotties in the calendar. Where are they?" Birdy put a hand on her hip.

Hunter shrugged a shoulder. "Sorry, but it's just me here today. I'm sure if you head to the fire station, though, you could snag a few more signatures."

"That's an excellent idea."

"Actually, we're going to do one more signing at the Botanical Gardens this weekend with a few of the other guys," Nova said.

"See that? I'm already old news," Hunter said lightheartedly. He signed calendars, joked around, and gave his mom a kiss on the cheek that made everyone go, "Aww."

After things quieted down and he signed the final calendar, his gaze connected with hers like he knew she'd been standing there the whole time. She walked over to him. "Hi, cowboy."

"Hi, Triple C. Where's your calendar?"

"You guys are adorable," Nova piped in, appearing out of nowhere.

Hunter gave her a look that said, *My sister knows all about us?*

"She's my best friend," Callie said.

"And as her best friend, I know she already has a calendar and can't stop staring at your picture."

"Shh!" Callie swatted her away.

"No, no. Tell me more." Hunter leaned back in his chair and crossed him arms over his chest, thoroughly enjoying himself.

"There is nothing more to tell. I thought I was

here to help with mailings."

"I finished it," Nova said. "I just wanted to see your face." She grinned like the Cheshire Cat. "Hunter, is there anything Callie can help *you* with?" By her tone, it was clear Nova meant *in private*.

"Sorry, but I'm out of time," Callie said. "I have an appointment back at the cottage. See you guys later." She turned on her heels and marched away like the badass businesswoman she was.

Her phone sounded with a text when she reached outside.

Hunter: I liked seeing your face, too.

She texted back, *I liked seeing yours.* And for the rest of the day, she had a goofy smile on her face.

CHAPTER THIRTY-FIVE

The next night, Callie studied herself in the mirror. The cream-colored sweater dress flattered her figure and the asymmetric neckline left her right shoulder exposed and added a touch of sexy to the cozy material. Slip-on pumps donned her feet. She wore her curly hair in an updo with tendrils around her forehead.

When she'd left Hunter's last weekend, he'd told her he wanted to take her out for dinner in Rustic Creek. The next town over had just as many charming shops and restaurants as Windsong but without any nosy friends or family. Because, he'd said, he wanted to keep her to himself for as long as possible. She agreed it was a good idea. Nova and Birdy already had designs on her and Hunter living behind a white picket fence.

She turned off the light in her living quarters and moved to the front of the cottage to wait for him. Tonight, she'd ask him to stay with her. To mess up her sheets. Fall asleep under her covers. Eat breakfast in her bed.

She'd also tell him more things she liked about him. She owed him so many more nice words.

The decorative clock on the wall said six. She looked out the front window onto the dark street lit by tall lampposts, hoping to see Hunter's headlights any minute. Across the way, the windows of Kennedy's office were lit up. She often worked late, especially when walk-ins paid her a visit.

Wait. Was that Hunter's truck parked across the street? She leaned her face closer to the glass for a better look. It was. Confirmed when she realized he was also sitting in it. What was he doing?

Her feet carried her out the door and to his passenger-side door without thought. She gently knocked on the window, not wanting to startle him.

He turned his head to meet her eyes. His troubled expression worried her. She opened the door and hopped in.

"Hi. Is everything okay?" she asked.

He leaned over and kissed her squarely on the mouth. "You look beautiful."

"Thank you. You look very nice yourself." Dark pants. Collared shirt. Cleanly shaven and smelling amazing. Could they have their date right here inside his truck instead? Order food to be delivered curbside?

The glow from his phone sitting in the center console disappeared, cluing her in to his reason for sitting here. She turned to face him fully. "How long have you been here?"

"About twenty minutes." He reached into the back cab and produced a bouquet of red roses. "These are for you."

"Thank you. I love them." She took a sniff before placing them in her lap so they could talk. Hunter's normally cheerful demeanor felt off. "Did something happen?"

"Have you ever felt like you're juggling all these important things at once and you don't want to drop the ball on any of them but it's overwhelming trying to keep up?"

"I have. Life is hard, and sometimes you have to give yourself permission to fail. Or go out on a limb to ease some of the pressure."

His eyes warmed toward her. "That's a good way of putting it."

"I'm not just a pretty face," she teased.

That earned her a smile. "You're definitely more than that." He touched a tendril of her hair. "What prompted this mini existential crisis of mine was Brett just called to tell me he's moving to Seattle. A friend of his has a start-up there and has offered him a job. I'm really happy for him. It just reminded me of how much I want to be taken more seriously, professionally and personally. Before he called, I was sitting here debating whether to tell you how I feel about you." He turned to look directly into her eyes.

She gave him a soft smile. She felt things for him, too.

"I've been holding back because I didn't want to scare you away, but I'm going to go out on a limb now and tell you I think we can make this work, Callie. Scratch that, I know we can. Because there is nothing I will take more seriously than my commitment to you. I love you. I love you more than anything."

Oh, shit. She wasn't quite ready for *that.*

She blinked away the sudden, gut-wrenching feeling she was about to hurt him. Deep down, she thought she just might love him back, but she'd convinced herself she had to keep that a secret, buried somewhere deep inside her so that he'd follow through on his promise to find his soul mate after Maverick and Kennedy's wedding. How foolish, selfish, and mean of her.

"Hunter…" She put as much apology into his name as she could. And that's all it took for the hope and adoration in his baby blues to immediately turn to pain and sadness. Saying the *L* word changed everything between them. At least for her. She wished it wasn't so, but she couldn't just wish it away, either.

He shifted his attention out the windshield, shook his head. She felt the simple gesture like a punch in the throat. He was disappointed…and upset with her. "I should have known better than to voice that aloud."

"Hunt—"

"Save it, okay?" His clipped tone made the inside of the truck feel a thousand times smaller. "Sorry. I didn't mean to sound like a jerk."

"You're hurt. I get it. *I'm* sorry. But I…"

"You…?" Hope followed the one word.

"I wasn't expecting this. Not tonight."

He cut her a quick glance. "Meaning I haven't blown my chance?"

She silently counted to ten. That was a good idea, right? When the next words out of her mouth carried enough weight to brighten their world or drown them both.

Eight, nine, ten. She still had no good answer. Her heart pounded so loud in her ears she couldn't think straight.

"If it's taking you this long to decide, then I have my answer."

"Hunter."

"Please stop saying my name with so much pity. I get it. Your heart doesn't feel anything."

Ouch. That direct hit to her "unfeeling" heart stung deeply, considering it was currently beating harder than it ever had before. She gripped the flower stems in her lap. "That's not true. You know I'm not like that. But I told you from the beginning that I can't commit. And contrary to what you believe, it's because I feel too much."

Her parents' atypical relationship topped the list of influences. Add in the men who had disappointed her and made her feel like she didn't matter, and she'd had years to hone her skill to not get too attached. That way it didn't hurt as much when she found herself alone.

"You made me think…" His trailing off hurt more than if he'd come out and finished his thought because she had to fill in the blanks. And wonder.

"I'm sorry," she said again. She hated the misery etched around his eyes. Hated herself, too.

"Don't be." He suddenly sat taller. "Let's agree to forget this ever happened. I'll make good on my promise to try and find someone after Maverick's wedding. Your lucky wedding streak won't end with me."

The pulse at the base of her neck galloped. She hated that thought and how he said it like they hadn't meant anything to each other. If she didn't get out of the car immediately, she'd say things equally hurtful in return, and she'd already hurt him enough.

The roses slipped through her fingers onto the truck's floormat as she jumped out of the car and ran as fast as she could in her heels back inside the cottage. She locked the door, kicked off her shoes, and walked to her bedroom. She collapsed onto the bed where she stayed, motionless and lost in thought.

She refused to cry.

Hunter was better off without her.

CHAPTER THIRTY-SIX

Hunter pressed a hand to his knee to stop his leg from bouncing. Silence filled the banquet room as the mayor stood at a podium giving a speech about Windsong and the townspeople and the importance of small-town pride and values.

He and the other ambassador finalists were seated at a table in the front, Callie clear across from him, thank God. It was hard enough being in the same room with her. If she were next to him, he'd probably stop breathing from shame and guilt. Deservedly so.

He'd been awful to her the other night and owed her an apology. From her disregard of him so far this evening, he'd have some groveling to do, too. He hated to think the last thing she'd remember about him were the terrible words he'd spoken out of hurt.

His leg finally stopped moving. He didn't often get nervous, so tonight's string of shaking body parts bothered him. The question was, was he nervous because of the ambassador position or because Callie sat close by?

Up on stage, Mayor Garnett smiled like she'd pulled off a million-dollar heist. "As you know, we had an overwhelming number of applicants for Ambassador of Windsong. We narrowed it down to six, and when it came down to choosing just one, it wasn't easy." She directed her gaze at their table, touching on each of them with an appreciative smile.

"Many of you stepped outside your comfort zones, and one of you faced your biggest fear. Success is measured not only by accomplishment, but by personal growth, however that looks."

Hunter couldn't help himself; he watched Callie from across the table as she swiped at the corner of her eye. He wished she were next to him so he could take her hand and hold it dearly. Whisper in her ear how gutsy and impressive she was. This past week, the mayor's office made all the articles from the candidates available online, and the one she wrote about horseback riding had been particularly moving—and funny.

"My heartfelt thanks go out to each of you for wanting to help land Windsong on the list of Top Small Towns in America. And so, without further delay, Windsong's first ambassador is...Hunter Owens!"

Hunter took a minute, elation overwhelming him. He'd done it. He'd gotten the job. His gaze flew to Callie. She smiled warmly at him and mouthed, *Congratulations*.

A few tables over, his cheering section jumped to their feet and whooped for joy. The rest of the room applauded and cheered, too. As Hunter stood, so did his fellow finalists. They congratulated him before he made his way to the podium.

"Thank you, Mayor," he said, shaking her hand before she pulled him in for a hug.

"Way to go, Hunter!" he heard Nova yell.

He put his forearms on the podium, then looked out at the crowd. "First, I want to say what an honor it was to be grouped with the other finalists. I'm a big fan of all of yours." With the spotlight on him, it wasn't easy to make out individual faces, so he concentrated on the back of the room where the buffet tables were in better focus.

Swallowing the lump in his throat, he continued. "I love Windsong with my whole heart, and I promise to increase exposure to the unique and interesting features of our beloved town. I'll do my best to bring attention to our community events, festivals, and everything that makes our town great. I can't wait to showcase Windsong on a local, regional, and national scale and show off our Windsonger pride."

"Woot! Woot!" someone shouted.

Hunter grinned. A big-ass grin he couldn't contain, even with a tinge of sadness that he'd beaten Callie in order to be standing here.

"I'm up here today as the first ambassador to our amazing town, but I look at this as a team effort. Every resident is a vital contributor to our small town, and I'm excited to be the person to lead us to wider recognition.

"Thank you to the mayor's office for this incredible honor. And thank you to my family and friends. I'm afraid I'll forget someone if I start naming names."

"Jenna!" came the cutest voice from the middle of the room. The crowd laughed.

"Pipsqueak, let's eat cake first."

"Yes!" Jenna said.

"Have a great night, everyone." With that, Hunter stepped off the stage.

A cocktail reception followed. He mingled,

received kudos and slaps on the back, thanked the mayor again, had a drink with his parents, Maverick and Kennedy, cake with his niece, and threw back a shot of tequila with Brett. Across the room, Callie stood with Nova. Throughout the night, Callie drew him like a magnet to wherever she was. Besides her initial congrats from across the table, they'd not been within twenty feet of each other. What he wouldn't give to breathe in her scent, touch her, kiss her, one more time. He'd said some terrible things to her he wished he could take back.

Focusing back on Brett, he said, "The new job sounds great."

"Thanks. I definitely need the change of scenery." Brett lifted his chin toward the bar. "The reporter from the *Gazette* hasn't taken her eyes off you. You should go talk to her."

Hunter glanced in the direction of the bar to find Vivian looking at him with interest more intense than usual. "Not sure I'm feeling it tonight."

"Too bad. She's coming this way."

Vivian put her empty wineglass on a passing tray as she strode toward them. "Hello, gentlemen." She put out her hand to shake Brett's. "I'm Vivian. I don't think we've officially met yet."

"Brett."

"Nice to meet you, Brett," she said to him.

"You, too."

"Congratulations, Ambassador Hunter. I know what a big deal this is for you."

"Thanks." He'd shared how important this gig was to him on their bike ride. "But please call me Mr. Ambassador."

She laughed. "Brett, care to comment on Hunter's win? It had to sting a little, even though you took yourself out of the running."

"Not at all. The best person for the position won," his friend said. "Hunt is a fourth-generation Windsonger and will do a phenomenal job."

"Thanks, man." Hunter peered over Vivian's shoulder and locked eyes with Callie. He'd like to eliminate the distance between them and apologize, but tonight wasn't the time or place. Her gaze strayed to Vivian, then jumped to someone else.

He had royally fucked things up. He'd replayed the minutes in the car with her over and over again and hated himself for the things he'd said. The way he'd said them.

He focused back on the conversation at his table, listening to Brett and Vivian talk about Brett's move and his position at the start-up. "A friend is waving me over, so if you'll excuse me," Brett said.

Hunter searched out Callie again, hoping to catch another glimpse of her. No such luck.

"Would you like to go somewhere else and get a celebratory drink?" Vivian asked. "If you're ready to go, that is."

"Sounds good. Give me a minute to say goodbye to my family." The truth was, he was ready to escape. From the attention brought by his win. And from Callie and the way he felt about himself when she was near. He'd dreamed about being ambassador for months, but it wasn't as gratifying without her to celebrate with, too.

Vivian wrapped her arm around his, and they left the banquet room. At the coat check, he helped her into her jacket before slipping on his own.

He welcomed the cold night air on his face when they stepped outside. "It's a few minutes' walk to Main Street if you're good with that," he said.

"I'm good with anything you suggest." Her kittenish tone suggested they skip the drink and go right back to his place.

He ignored her flirtation and led her down the sidewalk toward Sutter's.

"Sorry," she said. "I can come on a little strong when I want something."

And she wanted him. The trouble was, he didn't want her. "It's okay."

Her high heels click-clacked on the concrete. "There's something going on with you tonight."

"Your reporter senses are damn annoying, you know that?" he said, teasing her.

She chuckled. "They're hard to turn off. Especially with people I care about." Sincerity replaced playfulness.

"It's been nice getting to know you," he said lightly.

"Uh-oh," she said. "This is where you tell me you can't be with me because your mind is elsewhere."

He put his hands in the pockets of his jacket and brought them to a stop under a streetlight. "If this reporting thing doesn't work out for you, you could be a fortune teller."

"Oh my God. You're the second person to tell me that this week. *Weird*. Anyway, I knew it was a long-shot when I asked you for a drink, but my momma taught me that if you don't go for what you want, you're giving up before you've even gotten started."

"She sounds like a smart woman."

"She is. My dad, too. *He* taught me if a man doesn't ask me out after"—she looked lost in thought as she ticked off one, two, three fingers—"three exchanges, then he isn't going to. I should have kept that in mind and not gone rogue tonight."

It was Hunter's turn to chuckle. "Please don't take it personally."

She raised sculpted eyebrows at him. "It's very much personal, but that's okay. I'm a big girl." She craned her neck to study him a little more closely. "Does she know?"

He gave her his best puzzled look, hoping she'd drop it. The woman could apparently sniff out anything.

"The woman you can't stop thinking about?" she prompted.

Silly him to think she'd let it go. He ran his fingers through his hair. "She knows."

"So, what are you going to do about it?"

I'm going to tell her I love her. She's going to freak out and break my heart into a million pieces, and I'm going to say hurtful things to her to get her back, and then I'm going to feel like shit even after getting my dream side job.

"Not sure yet. She doesn't see a future with me like I do with her."

"That got nothing to do with you, then. She's trying to figure out her own life." She gave him a friendly push in the shoulder. "Don't sell yourself short, stud. Besides, your brother's wedding is around the corner. She'll change her mind after you wear your best man suit. And if she doesn't, then it wasn't meant to be."

"Speaking of the wedding, I heard you dubbed Callie the Marry Matchmaker."

"Catchy, isn't it?"

"Very." There was more he wanted to say about Callie and her talents, but he worried Vivian would figure out it was Callie he was hung up on.

"How about we grab that drink and talk about the Forty-Niners?" she asked, steering them into friendship territory.

"You like football?" They resumed the walk toward Sutter's. A full moon helped light the way between streetlamps. The closer they got to Main Street, the livelier the streets grew with cars and pedestrians. In the distance, Friday Night Lights shined on the high school football field.

"Love it. My brother plays professionally."

"No way. For the Forty-Niners?" Maybe she could help him with some tickets for him and his brothers. They'd make for a great Christmas gift.

"Yeah."

Her last name was Fisher... Holy shit. "Your brother is Jonah Fisher?"

"You've heard of him?" she teased. The guy was a phenom. He'd taken over as quarterback after Nash Radcliffe was injured and forced to retire.

He opened the door to Sutter's, allowing her to enter first. They found a table and talked nonstop over drinks and potato skins. And for a minute, he forgot about the hurt he'd caused Callie.

Too bad it was only temporary.

CHAPTER THIRTY-SEVEN

Hunter tossed back another shot—correction, he tossed back his final shot. If he put one more ounce of alcohol in his body, the poison just might rival that of a certain black widow spider.

Thinking about the spider had him thinking about Callie. He missed her. Why wasn't she here with him?

His cousin Jace plopped an arm around his shoulders. The guy weighed a ton and needed to lean the other way before Hunter fell off his stool. "Aren't you glad you came out with us?" Jace Weighs-A-Ton asked.

Hunter picked up Jace's arm and flung it away.

"Ow!" his other cousin, Derrick, said when Jace's hand whacked him in the face.

All three of them cracked up.

"You boys need anything else?" Emma asked, stopping at their high-top table. That wasn't the waitress's actual name, but Hunter couldn't remember it, so he called her Emma in his head. She reminded him of Emma Stone, and that reminded him of his all-time favorite redhead: Callie. Where was she again?

"What are you offering?" Derrick slurred.

"How about another plate of sliders and a side of fries?"

"Can you give us an extra slider for me?"

"Sure." She smiled at Derrick, and tiny red hearts

floated out of his eyes.

Whoa. Hunter squinted to be sure he wasn't seeing things. The hearts were gone. But thinking about hearts made him think about Callie.

He'd misplaced Callie somewhere. He looked around Sutter's for her. Unless she was hiding under a table, he didn't see her. He laughed.

"What's so funny?" Jace asked.

"Callie under the table."

"She's under the table?" Jace investigated. "I don't see her," he called out before his head popped back up. "Besides, she doesn't love you, remember?"

Oh yeah. That's why she wasn't here. She hated him.

Everyone hated him, this last week one he wished he'd been on vacation for. Far, far away from the squinty eyes of his sister and the rest of his female relatives because they all knew now. At least he had Jace and Derrick. They'd decided to drive down from San Fran for a surprise visit and basically kidnapped him to come out with them. He'd said okay on the spot.

"Who doesn't love who again?" Derrick asked, scrolling through his phone.

Hunter picked up his own phone, thinking to text Callie, but the icons looked wiggly. Using his brain hurt, so he stopped.

"Hey, Kennedy's sister is hot," Derrick said, still on his phone. He liked to be on Instacram. Insta*gram*.

"Dude, I called dibs already," Jace said.

"You guys wanna get married?" Hunter asked them.

They shook their heads. "Not what we're talking

about," Jace said like Hunter needed correction.

He rolled his eyes. "I know that. But she's gonna be wearing a lucky dress and that's better than catching the bow-ket."

Derrick frowned. "What's a bow-ket?"

"I said bouquet."

"No, you said bow-ket." Jace always took his brother's side. As it should be. Hunter looked around for Maverick or Cole. Nope, they weren't here, either.

Plus, how come his cousins could drink him under the table? Oops. There he went under the table again. If Callie *was* there, he'd say he was sorry.

"Whatever." Hunter knew what he said. "The point is matchmaking."

"Huh?" Jace rubbed the side of his jaw.

"That makes no sense." Derrick polished off the last of his beer.

"I'll tell you tomorrow," he garbled, that last shot kicking in and scrambling his brain cells even more.

"Here you go," Emma said, reaching between him and Jace to leave their food on the table. "One extra slider on the side and the french fries are hot so be careful."

"She's into me," Derrick said as she walked away.

"How do you know?" Hunter asked, genuinely interested. He loved his cousin so much and wanted him to find love, too. Love made the world go 'round.

"She doesn't want me to burn my tongue." He grinned.

"So?" Jace questioned.

"*So.* She wants to kiss me when she gets off work."

Hunter and Jace exchanged a look before laughing their asses off. They laughed so hard Hunter's side hurt.

Derrick grumbled, then said, "Just watch. You'll see."

Hunter grabbed a slider and downed the delicious tiny burger in seconds. He ate a bunch of fries next. He hoped the food absorbed some of the alcohol clogging his mind and running free in his veins.

"Nova Scotia!" Jace shouted, also drunk as a skunk if he was shouting out random Canadian provinces.

Hey! Hunter had thought "Canadian provinces" with little difficulty. The food was working. He shoved another handful of fries into his mouth.

"Jace! Derrick! Hi," Nova said, arriving at their table. Now the outburst made sense. "I didn't know you guys were in town." She gave them each a hug, then turned to him. Her eyes widened like big flying saucers from outer space. "What are you doing?"

"What does it look like I'm doing? I'm hanging with my favorite cousins."

The saucers turned into evil slits. Uh-oh. She'd been abducted by aliens. "Are you drunk?" she demanded.

"Are you?" he countered.

"Hunt, you need to stop."

He paused with a french fry halfway to his mouth. "Eating?"

She grumbled. "Drinking like a fish."

"Fish do not drink booooze," he enunciated. He might be drunk, but he knew fish only drank water. Fresh and salty.

Nova put her hands on his shoulders. She looked at him funny, like she didn't know whether to punch him or hug him. "If you keep this up, you're going to ruin more than your relationship with Callie. You could lose the ambassador position."

His sister wouldn't lie to him. "Fuck," he said under his breath. Shame and nausea filled him. He kept screwing up. He jammed his fingers through his hair. Sucked to be him right now. "Thanks, Nova. I'm gonna walk home now. Clear my head." The mile's distance due north would do him some good. Or maybe it was due south? He'd figure it out once he got outside.

"I'll drive you home and then come back," Nova said. "You two"—she wagged a finger at Jace and Derrick—"stay put and drink plenty of water." She popped a french fry into her mouth. "And order the pie-eyed omelet. It's not on the menu but the best thing to soak up all the alcohol in your bloodstream."

"How do you know about the omelet?" Hunter knew of its healing properties. Maverick and Cole had introduced it to him. "Have you youtee... youtill...utilized it?"

"You don't know everything about me, big brother. Now come on."

"We'll be right here, eating pie when you get back," Derrick said.

Hunter just shook his head, pretty sure his cousin thought he was getting actual pie.

On the quick drive back to the bunkhouse, Nova stayed quiet. The silence spoke volumes. "Thanks for coming to my rescue," he said, opening the car door when she came to a stop.

"You've come to mine plenty of times over the years. I'm happy to come to yours now."

He trudged to his front door, let himself inside, and fell face-first onto his bed with his boots hanging off the edge. Despite the turmoil going on in his head, sleep pulled him under within seconds. In dreamland, he and Callie were madly in love and riding horses through a meadow. She wore a long white dress and her hair down. He wore a dark suit and his cowboy hat.

A piercing cry woke him with a jolt. He groaned and rolled over on to his back. They had a family of raccoons on the ranch, and the babies liked to make a screeching noise. He stared up at the ceiling and waited the screecher out. His throat felt drier than a desert. A killer headache throbbed behind his eyes.

He walked into the kitchen for a glass of water and a couple of aspirin, the events of the evening slowly coming back to him. The clock on the stove read 11:18. He'd slept for several hours.

The drink helped, and the two pain relievers he swallowed would hopefully kick in quickly because if he had any hope of getting back to normal, he needed to go over to Callie's right this minute and give her the apology he owed her. No more excuses. Because his sister was right. He was in jeopardy of letting *everyone* he cared about down.

He smelled like fried food and bad judgment, so he stripped out of his clothes and took a hot shower. He wished with every swipe of the soap he could wipe away the past few hours, not to mention the past week. He'd been short with everyone. Grumpy as hell. And drunk more than once.

He thought that might cure him of his love for Callie, drown his affection so it would stop bubbling to the surface, but drinking only made everything worse. He was so damn sorry. More than that, he wanted to laugh with her again, make her blush, listen to her talk about anything and everything.

Which was why he'd stayed away. To save himself more heartbreak.

He turned off the shower, dressed in clean clothes. He debated texting Callie a heads-up. Decided not to. She couldn't turn him away if he just showed up on her doorstep, right?

The drive to her house took no time at all at this late hour. He drove around the block a few times to think about what to say. This apology meant more than any other he'd ever given. She meant more to him than any other person ever had. *Used to.* Was there a twelve-step program for getting over a broken heart?

On the walk up to her front door, his heart hammered loud enough to wake the dead. Nerves took over the parts of his body that normally worked well—case in point, he tripped over his own feet, *and* when he lifted his arm to knock, the appendage fell right back to his side.

Don't wimp out now. You're here.

He gave three strong raps. Three was his lucky number. Then, so she didn't worry about who had knocked this late at night, he texted, *It's me at your door.*

The wait was excruciating. His leg shook with anticipation and dread.

Please open the door, Triple C.

When she did a few seconds later, relief and hope flooded him. She had on the same blue-and-white polka-dot pajamas she'd worn their first night together, when she'd watched over him, and the sight of her made him feel a thousand times better than the few hours of sleep and pain relievers had. Maybe he *could* salvage their relationship.

"Hi," he said, measuring her disposition before launching into a full-blown apology.

"Hi."

"Can I come in?" he asked. She opened the door to allow him entry. "Thanks. I've been meaning to stop by."

"And you decided midnight was the best time?" she said lightly, leading him to the back of the cottage and her living space. She sat at the small round dining table in the minimalist kitchen, elbows on the glass top, her fingers laced tightly together. He took the chair across from her.

"It's been a rough week."

"For me, too. I'm—"

He pressed two fingers to her mouth to stop her from saying she was sorry. She had nothing to be sorry for. He did. And if she even whispered the word before he did, he'd never be able to forgive himself.

The feel of her soft lips on the pads of his callused fingers sent a jolt of electricity through him. She seemed to feel it, too, because her soft, sleepy eyes widened, and she quickly scooted her chair back.

"I'm sorry," he said.

She gave a small nod, tucked her hands under her legs.

"I said some hurtful things to you that I wish I could take back. I'm so sorry for that."

"Apology accepted." Her acceptance and gracious tone eased the guilt and self-loathing churning in his stomach.

"I'm not sure where we go from here." He couldn't see her and not want her, so for a while, he'd continue to keep his distance.

"Me, either."

"It's going to take me a while to…"

Her head tilted to the side in consideration. "This isn't easy for me, either. I never meant for any of this to happen."

"I know you didn't."

She searched his eyes, looking for what, he wasn't sure. "You are an amazing man," she said softly. "And you deserve the best."

Did she not know that was her? That she was made for him and he would keep her heart safe and happy for as long as he lived? He understood her hesitations. Her apprehension. He truly did. But—

"And that's not me," she added.

He studied her. If he argued that wasn't true, he'd push her farther away than the million miles that already separated them. If he said okay, he'd be cementing her belief she wasn't enough. Both options sucked. His heart sank to the pit of his stomach. He silently considered what to do. She silently watched him.

"You can have any girl you want, Hunt."

Hunt. Knife to the chest right there.

He'd loved the few times she said it over the past couple of months. God damn her. In her mind, she already had him paired off with someone else.

"Okay. On that note, I should go. Let you get back to sleep."

She walked him to the door. "Thanks for stopping by."

"Thanks for opening the door." He dragged his feet to said door, not wanting to leave but knowing he had to.

"Bye," fell softly from her lips.

"Bye. Lock your door on my way out." He walked away without a glance back, letting his mind wander one last time to the days and nights they'd shared before locking the memories away for good.

CHAPTER THIRTY-EIGHT

"Ow!" For the second time today, Callie poked her finger with a sewing needle. Terrified of soiling the material in any way, she dropped it on the chair and went to the bathroom for a bandage.

First-aid supplies littered the countertop. She grabbed a tissue to stop the bleeding on her finger, held pressure for a minute, then bandaged it. She held up her hands, palms up, and shook her head.

She was getting careless, which meant she probably needed food. Glad she'd stocked the fridge yesterday, she pulled out hummus and sliced cucumbers. Pretzels sounded good, too, so she grabbed the bag out of the cupboard and poured some on her plate.

She took a seat in the armchair by the window. Cold and dreary outside, the holiday lights Kennedy had decorated the exterior of her office with cheered up the drab landscape. The lights had been on 24/7 this week, not that Callie couldn't sleep and spent more time in this chair or at her sewing machine than anywhere else lately.

And she most certainly wasn't hoping for a glimpse of a tall, handsome cowboy, yet there he was. She missed him so much it hurt.

Hunter strode down the sidewalk wearing jeans and a long-sleeve dark-gray Henley. No Stetson on his head. His hair was cut shorter, combed neatly. A little scruff on his jaw and around his mouth looked good.

He walked up the steps to Kennedy's office and disappeared inside. Callie's pulse did a little do-si-do. Was he sick? Should she go over and ask if he needed help?

Cool your jets, Callie. You don't get that privilege anymore.

She had her answer anyway when he walked back out with Bella at his side. *He's taking her to lunch.* Her heartbeat skittered to a stop.

She knew this would happen one day—that he'd move on with someone who wanted the same things he did. She'd practically pushed him into another person's arms with her "you can have any girl you want" comment. She obviously hadn't been thinking clearly, because seeing it up close—well, from across the street—took the wind right out of her sails.

Bella smiled at something he said. Was he commenting on her cute Christmas scrubs? Her perky ponytail? Asking about her holiday plans and could he meet her under the Christmas tree to listen to some *Spruce* Springsteen together. He had all sorts of corny sayings to make a person's heart flutter.

They paused at the bottom of the stairs to discuss something. Probably where to eat. Callie leaned forward to try to read their lips. The pretzels and cucumbers slid off her plate. She couldn't be bothered to pick them up, instead concentrating on Hunter's sensuous mouth and wishing her *magical* skills extended to lip reading or enhanced hearing.

She carefully lifted the lever on the window to unlock it. She should have thought to open it sooner. It's not like they were aware of her. Hunter hadn't even spared a glance in the direction of the cottage.

It didn't glide open easily, though, and the squeaky sound might draw attention. The last thing she wanted was to get caught.

"*Ahem.*"

Callie's entire plate clattered on the floor at the sound of Birdy's voice. "Jeez, you scared me."

"I've been standing here for a while. If that window was a portal, you would have fallen through it head first." *Ugh*. Birdy was right. "This is of your own making, you know."

"I know," she whined. She slouched back in her chair. Hunter and Bella were gone from view.

Birdy handed her a chocolate chip cookie from Baked on Main. "Eat this. It will make you feel better."

"I've been eating my feelings for almost two weeks, and it hasn't worked, but thank you." She took a bite of the cookie. Then another. "I do feel better seeing you." Birdy made a habit of stopping by more frequently since Callie had told her what happened with Hunter.

"I am a ray of sunshine." She gestured down her petite frame and yellow track suit.

Callie picked up the mess on the floor so Birdy could take the chair. She put the plate in the kitchen sink, then dragged another chair to the window for herself.

"What is happening to your hands?" Birdy asked with amusement and concern.

"There's been a disconnect between my brain and dexterity." She flipped her hands back and forth. Six fingers were wrapped in Band-Aids, four of the bandages crooked or barely staying on. She'd never been so clumsy with her sewing before.

"You're in trouble, missy."

"Tell me about it. I can't afford to waste any material because I get my own blood on it. Giorgio is especially expensive."

"That's not what I meant."

Callie closed her eyes to block out Birdy's wise, motherly expression. Unfortunately, every time she shut her eyes, Hunter appeared.

"It's not too late for you to change your mind." That's exactly what she wondered when accidentally pricking her fingers.

"From the looks of it, yes, it is."

"Love doesn't work that way, sweetie. You can't turn it off and on that easily. And that boy has been hopelessly devoted to you for years."

Tears pricked the back of Callie's eyes. "Some things just aren't meant to be."

Birdy rolled hers, and Callie tried not to laugh. "Don't you go spouting that excuse to me. You're the effing Marry Matchmaker."

Callie's jaw fell open at Birdy's use of "effing."

"Don't look at me like that. You should hear me yell at the crows in the morning."

"I don't want to get married." There. That ought to end this discussion.

"Tell me why that is again? Because it's hard? Because there is no perfect marriage? Because some men can be clueless, ridiculous human beings? Because your parents are still figuring it out? Or because you're scared you might have found the person who won't let you down?"

Okay, wow. Not one to mince words, Birdy had

also kept a lot of questions at the ready.

Both Birdy and Vivian had previously mentioned never giving up on the person you love. Callie had given a lot of thought to that since her awful conversation with Hunter, and before that night, she would have believed it.

"He did let me down," she said quietly.

"How so?"

"He didn't fight for me." He'd let her go just as easily as she'd seemingly let him go. It had been the hardest thing she'd ever done.

Birdy let out a deep breath. "In this case, I think you need to meet in the middle."

The furnace rattled as the heat in the cottage kicked on. Callie glanced back outside. The stillness from earlier had vanished to give way to swaying trees. Dark clouds floated across the sky. She brought her legs up and crossed them in her lap. The gloom outside matched her insides.

Stubborn and scared, she said, "I'm not sure there is a middle."

CHAPTER THIRTY-NINE

Callie's last appointment took longer than expected. She didn't mind spending extra time with clients. In fact, she loved it. She prided herself on developing relationships, not just taking measurements and deposits. Good service mattered, especially with word of mouth.

She'd benefitted from the Marry Matchmaker moniker, but not enough to alleviate her worries. She had her fingers crossed that if Vivian's feature released with *Bride* magazine, she'd be so busy she'd need to hire help.

A glance at the wall clock told her she might make it in time for dinner at the inn if she hurried. She'd taken all of two steps when someone knocked at the front door. She literally stopped breathing when she saw her sister's face through the cut-out glass. Brooke hadn't said a word about visiting. She hadn't been in touch at all since Thanksgiving.

"Hey, Cal." Brooke added a wave to her greeting.

Callie unlocked the door, stunned at her sister's sudden appearance. "Hi. What are you doing here? Is everything okay?"

Brooke strode inside, dropping her duffel bag on the hardwood floor. "Everything is fine." She looked around the cottage. "Wow, this place is great." Her eyes connected with Callie's. "You did good."

Callie stood there, taken aback from having her sister in the same room, and shocked at the compliment. Her sister didn't give congratulatory praise. "Thank you. That means a lot coming from you."

"*Really?*"

Callie needed a minute—or a thousand—so she walked back to the kitchen. Brooke showing up out of the blue threw her for a giant, carousel-size loop. Callie had resumed her therapy appointments to work through her issues (one of which was sketching Hunter instead of dresses) and now she had one of her biggest stumbling blocks in her home.

"Are you thirsty?" Callie asked.

"Water would be great, thanks." Brooke sat at the small kitchen table. "I love this setup. Did you put in the French doors separating the store from your living quarters?"

"No, it was already there." Callie poured them each a glass of water, then took a seat, too. "Where are mom and dad?"

"Still in Florida."

"How long are you staying?"

"Just the weekend. I didn't want you to be alone on Christmas."

"Okay, who are you and what have you done with my sister?"

Brooke's face fell. She took a minute to read all the emotions crossing Callie's face. "I've been that bad, huh?"

Callie shrugged. "I've tried telling you."

"And I've always ignored it and taken you for granted. Sorry about that."

"I'm not sure what's happening right now." Brooke never apologized. Had her sister changed in the months they'd been apart and was it a change Callie could count on?

"I'm sincerely sorry is what's happening."

"Is that why you're here?"

"Yes. It finally clicked for me when I met a woman around our age who had lost her sister because of a natural disaster, and I thought, *I'm losing mine because I'm selfish and unavailable.* I knew I'd regret it if I didn't do something about it before it was too late."

"So here you are." Callie felt happy tears sting her eyes. She blinked over and over to keep them away.

"Christmas was always your favorite holiday. Is it still?"

"Yes." She squeezed her sister's arm. "And I'm really glad you're here."

"I hope I'm not ruining your plans," Brooke said in that no-nonsense way of hers. Only this time hopefulness laced her words, too.

"I do have a wedding to go to tomorrow, but Christmas is all yours."

"I'd like that. I thought about giving you a heads-up, but I was afraid you'd tell me not to come."

"I'd never do that." Callie always wanted more time with her sister, even when she felt like Brooke didn't prioritize their relationship.

"Deep down I know that, but sometimes I think, *Today is the day my sister outgrows me*, and insecurity sets in."

Callie stared at her older sister, surprised to hear she had insecurities, too. On the outside, nothing looked different. Same pretty brown eyes and straight brown hair. On the inside, though, there'd been a shift. A realization.

"We have a lot to talk about," Callie said, gathering the courage to have a meaningful conversation. "I just need to quickly send a text. She grabbed her phone and sent a group text to Mary Rose, Kennedy, and Nova, letting them know Brooke had shown up so she wouldn't be making it to dinner tonight.

"You're looking at me weird," Brooke said.

"I haven't seen you in person in almost nine months. When I came home from Africa and you guys weren't home, it hurt. A lot. And then you kept extending your trip like being apart was no big deal. Having you here now is taking me a minute."

"I get it. But, Cal, we were needed. And you've always been so independent and focused on what you love doing that we didn't stop to think about it. I've always been jealous of your independence."

"*What?*"

"You're fine on your own. You stand on your own two feet, free to do whatever you want and confident in your choices. I envy you that."

Callie rubbed her ear. She couldn't be hearing her sister right. "And you're not?"

"I work with Mom and Dad," she answered as if that explained everything. When Callie waited for more, she added, "I do like it, but I didn't have a choice. Dad made the decision for me."

"You could have said no."

Brooke fidgeted in her chair. "I could have, but I didn't because I wasn't strong enough to go out on my own. You've always been able to handle anything that came your way. You fought to get back to normal after your accident a thousand times harder than I would have. And ever since then, I've selfishly coasted through life."

Callie sat there with so many questions and emotions swirling through her veins, she didn't know where to start. "You guys have forgotten about me over and over again like it's no big deal. Like I'm an afterthought."

"I'm sorry if you've felt that way." Sincerity ran deep in her apology. "It's not true. If we've treated you that way, it's because we know you can handle it. Honestly, when it comes to our constant trips and last-minute plans, we go on autopilot. And knowing we don't have to worry about you because you can take care of yourself is a comfort. It sounds like we got it wrong, though." Regret creased her forehead.

"I might be independent, but that doesn't mean I don't need you guys. You haven't made me feel like a priority in a long time. More like I'm mediocre and easily forgotten." *Phew*. It felt good to say that and know her sister was really listening this time.

"That's not on you, but them. Trust me. I've been there, too."

"You've been there with Mom and Dad?" Talk about having a conversation ten years too late. Callie wished they'd teamed up like this before, but they couldn't change the past.

"Yes, but I'm much more like them than you are, so my feelings aren't hurt as easily. And I don't mind their ups and downs like you always have."

"You're talking about their marriages?"

"And divorces. They're not exactly the picture of a stable, loving relationship."

No shit. "How does that not affect you?"

Brooke shrugged. "They do the best they can." She reached over to squeeze Callie's hand. "We're not our parents, Cal. Especially you. You have more love in your heart than anyone I know."

Callie sniffled, emotions overwhelming her again. "Promise me we'll keep talking like this. Tonight. Tomorrow. Next year."

"I promise."

"Are you hungry? Want to order a pizza?" For the first time in a week, Callie wanted to eat because she was happy.

"It's on me." Brooke ordered online, and thirty minutes later, they had a steaming hot mushroom-and-olive pizza.

"So tell me what's been going on here." Brooke pulled a string of cheese off her pizza slice. "I want to know everything. Whose wedding are you going to?"

Callie told her about the wedding and the ambassador competition.

"I'm sorry you didn't win."

"Thanks, but I'm happy for Hunter. He deserved the position. His articles were… They flowed with an ease and way of thinking that was relatable and meaningful." She was so proud of him. So moved by his words.

"And I do have some good news." She filled Brooke in on the article Vivian was writing and the Marry Matchmaker nickname. Lastly, she shared what had happened with Hunter.

"Oh my God. You and Hunter Owens. Cal, he has had a crush on you forever."

"How do you know that?"

"Because when I once tried to kiss him—with total attitude by the way—he told me no and that the only Carmichael he'd ever kiss would be you."

Callie rolled her lips together as yet another wave of emotion pressed against her chest. When they'd talked about first kisses, he hadn't said anything. Probably because he didn't want to portray her sister in a negative light. Which was just like him—to safeguard Callie's feelings about herself and her family. "I really miss him."

"Then what's stopping you from going after him?"

"Fear." She'd kept her heart closed off, afraid of the ups and downs of true love and worried if she gave away her whole heart and trusted someone else with it, she'd no longer be in control and they'd have the power to hurt her.

"Pfft." Brooke flicked her hand like, *That is not a good reason*. "Do you know what the opposite of fear is? Confidence. And you have that. Who's the girl who came back from a life-threatening accident completely whole?"

"Me."

"And who's the girl who started her own design business with no help from anyone else?"

"Me," she said, grateful her sister recognized that.

"And what has keeping your distance from Hunter gotten you?"

"A broken heart."

"So, if it's already broken, what more do you have to lose?"

Hunter. She had Hunter to lose.

And tomorrow she'd watch him walk down the aisle in his best man suit and then watch him fall in love with someone else.

Unless she did something about it.

CHAPTER FORTY

Hunter was sick and tired of feeling miserable, so it ended tonight. With two large Christmas trees in the room, flowers arranged by Nova, cocktails flowing, and everyone he cared about assembled at the inn for Maverick and Kennedy's wedding weekend, it should be a piece of cake.

"Can I have everyone's attention?" Hunter's mom asked, his dad standing beside her at the parlor's entrance. Family and friends quickly quieted, even those outside on the inn's veranda. "John and I are so happy you're here to celebrate Maverick and Kennedy's wedding with us. It's been wonderful spending the past few days getting to know those of you staying at the inn with us, and of course, being with family we love and hold dear."

"Right back at you, Auntie Rose!" Derrick shouted in return.

His mom smiled, "As many of you know, it's a tradition here on the ranch that the night before a wedding, the bride and groom add their thumbprints to our book of celebratory trees."

His mom opened the special leatherbound guestbook and showed everyone a white page with a tree drawn on it. In place of tree leaves were different-colored thumbprints. She placed the book on a table and opened three different-colored ink pads.

"Mav and Kennedy, please come leave your thumbprints, then write your name or initials inside or beside them."

Hunter watched his brother take his bride-to-be's hand and kiss her knuckles, the gesture tender and loving. All night, Maverick had doted on Kennedy. Through the wedding rehearsal, through picture-taking—Andrew had appointed himself the unofficial photographer for the evening—and now during cocktail hour before everyone headed downstairs for dinner.

Kennedy wiped the corner of her eye. She'd been doing that a lot, brushing away the happy tears. Before leaving her thumbprint, she wrapped his parents in a hug. After she and Mav left their mark, Mav swept her into a Hollywood movie kiss. Everyone cheered.

Andrew called out, "Take two! I missed it. A guy needs some warning."

Nova sniffled from beside him. "I'm so happy for them."

"Me, too." Maverick had lost his first love to a terrible disease, and to find an even greater love with Kennedy gave Hunter hope he'd find another unicorn, too.

He hadn't seen or talked to Callie since apologizing to her last weekend. The apology had helped ease his conscience. It didn't help how much he missed her. Longed for her. He felt like a quarterback who fumbled the game-winning pass in the last few seconds of the Super Bowl. His confession had cost him the greatest match of his life. And yet, he couldn't regret it entirely. Those three little words had been begging him to set them free.

Thankfully, he'd been busy around the ranch

preparing for the wedding tomorrow. First to rise, last to bed, his motto. Then while waiting for sleep to claim him, he'd worked on final plans for expanding the boot camp to include free opportunities for kids in need. He had meetings scheduled after the first of the year to help with community outreach and to set up a section of the business as a non-profit. He also had work to do as ambassador come January, and he couldn't wait to get started. More than one resident and business owner had expressed their confidence in him, their support and respect.

His professional life was soaring while his personal life was complicated. The local bets on an engagement date for him. Talk of who would claim his heart. A lighthearted write-up in the *Gazette* pitting his bio against the Marry Matchmaker's. A picture of him beside a picture of her, the woman he couldn't get out of his head no matter how hard he tried. What would happen if he told everyone he was in love with the Marry Matchmaker?

Not that he ever would. Callie's business dreams came true if he found lasting love after the wedding tomorrow. He planned to do his best to keep her streak going, even if it hurt.

He glanced around the parlor. He expected to see her here tonight and bit his tongue every time he opened his mouth to ask Nova about her.

"Uncle Hunt, I need you," Jenna said, steepling her hands underneath her chin and looking up at him.

"What is it, pipsqueak?"

She glanced around the room, presumably for her mom or dad. Bethany stood far away chatting with Kennedy and Ava, and Cole had Gia in his arms while he talked to Uncle Tim. "Can you please get me a hot chocolate?"

"I'm guessing you've reached the parental max?"

"Exactly." She dropped her arms. "And they told Brenda to cut me off. How rude is that?"

Brenda, cocktail maker and hot chocolate dealer, stood behind the bar.

"How many have you had?" Nova asked.

"Only two."

"*Only two?*" Nova said, aghast. Jenna had her wrapped around her finger, too.

Hunter, though, remained her favorite. And he'd keep that top spot by giving her exactly what she wanted. That's what uncles were for. Besides, he hadn't gotten to spend much time with her lately, and this would be a great opportunity to change that. "Meet me on the veranda behind the Christmas tree in five."

"I'll be there." She spied their surroundings once more before tiptoeing away.

"That kid," Nova said.

"I know. I better get to work aiding and abetting the hot chocolate fanatic." He ordered two of the delicious warm beverages from Brenda, one with extra whip for his pint-size partner. He found her pretending to admire the ornaments on the tree.

"Thanks, Uncle Hunt." She sighed as she wrapped her hands around the glass mug. "Catch you later."

"Wait. Where are you…?"

Too late. She had no intention of turning around or telling him where she was headed. Probably to hit up her grandmother for a cookie before dinner. Or to regale family members with stories. So much for all that quality uncle-niece time.

"Cheers," Kennedy said, holding up her drink as she walked toward him.

"Hey there." He clinked his mug with her glass. "Needed a break from being the center of attention?"

"I did. It's a little overwhelming."

"In a good way, I hope."

"The best way. I'm so incredibly happy it feels like my heart is about to burst out of my chest."

"Pretty sure I won't be able to save you if that happens."

She chuckled. "What are you doing out here?"

"Sneaking Jenna more hot chocolate before she left me high and dry." He took a sip of his cocoa. Warmth spread through his whole body.

"I noticed you haven't looked your usual self lately. Anything you want to talk about?" Kennedy always knew how to read him. "Or maybe I should say 'anyone'?"

"Nova's been talking your ear off again?"

"That and a certain neighbor across the street from the office could be your twin with the mopey look."

He liked the sound of that. Then hated himself for liking it. He didn't want Callie miserable. "I'm in love with her," he said.

Kennedy put her hand on his arm. "We know."

Of course she did. Everyone did. He hadn't exactly tried to hide it. "She doesn't feel the same."

"How do you know? Telling someone how you truly feel is one of the hardest things anyone can do."

"She made it pretty clear when she didn't respond in kind. She also told me she never wants to get married, and I want to respect that."

"Want to start at the beginning? I'm pretty good at understanding underlying conditions," she half teased. Being a doctor, she did have good instincts with human behavior, too.

He started the story sixteen years ago on the day he first laid eyes on her and several minutes later ended with walking out of her cottage last weekend. Kennedy listened attentively, as she always did. And as always, he found it easy to talk to her. No wonder the entire town loved her and kept her so busy she needed to bring another doctor on, not just to cover her absences.

"I don't think I'm sharing anything Callie wouldn't," Kennedy said. "But one night before she left for Africa, she, Nova, your mom, and I went out for a little goodbye dinner. Her family was supposed to join us, too, but when they didn't show, we started without them. Her parents never texted or called. Halfway through dinner, Brooke texted she'd met some guy on a job site and had gone to dinner with him instead. I think she even texted 'oops,' like that made it okay. But to Callie, it clearly wasn't. Nova called her a terrible sister, and when Callie tried to defend her, she broke down, saying Nova was right."

"I know Callie's family has disappointed her."

"I think it's more than that. I think she feels abandoned and lost. Even though she's an adult and independent and stronger than she gives herself credit for, when your family repeatedly treats you like that, you're always waiting for the other shoe to drop. And so, you put up walls."

"To protect yourself," he said.

"Yes. And when your parents don't set the best example of how love works, that doesn't help, either. I know that from firsthand experience."

"Twice I let her go. The first time after she jumped out of my car, and the second time after I apologized." He ran a hand over his hand and his shorter hair. "She probably thinks she's not worth fighting for." His stomach dropped at the thought.

"I think that could be true. She pushed you away because that's her way of coping. But I also think a big part of her wanted to stay. It was just easier for her not to."

His shoulders slumped. "It's the complete opposite, Ned. I'd go to the ends of the Earth for her. I thought me letting her go would make her happy. I don't want to push her into marriage if that's not what she wants. I guess what I'm trying to say is I want her no matter what. I don't need a piece of paper to tell me what's in my heart."

Kennedy grinned at him.

"What?"

"She's lucky to have you. Now what's your plan?"

A little bell went off in his head. He knew exactly how to tell her how much she meant to him and hopefully still help her business thrive. "I have an important question to ask you," he said, crossing his fingers she'd go along with his plan.

CHAPTER FORTY-ONE

Callie sat next to Birdy inside the wedding tent. Twinkle lights hung above them. Ivy and gorgeous pink-and-white flowers inside giant urns adorned the ends of each row of folding white chairs. Pastor Alvarez stood at the front with a warm smile on his face as a few remaining guests took their seats. Two large, breathtaking flower arrangements flanked the pastor from behind.

Music started. Conversation stopped.

Everyone turned to the back of the tent.

Outside the open flaps, the sun cast its final glow. The first people to walk down the aisle were Maverick, Mary Rose, and John. Callie had never seen Maverick look happier or more handsome. Mary Rose and John looked positively delighted. Next came Nova and a good friend of Maverick's. The bridesmaid dress fit the setting and the mood and her best friend perfectly. Cole and Bethany were next, Gia in Bethany's arms. A wave of sighs fanned out among the small crowd at how cute they were.

Callie barely registered them, though, because right behind the adorable family stood Hunter, Ava, and Andrew.

She'd been afraid to admit Hunter had stolen her heart, and now he stole her breath, too. His trimmed hair was *GQ* styled. Clean shaven, he flashed his dimples and white teeth, and her heart fluttered.

When his bright blue eyes caught her stare and his smile widened, relief flooded her. She smiled back, a wordless promise she'd missed him and had something up her sleeve for him later.

"If I were fifty years younger, I'd give you a run for your money," Birdy whispered from beside her. "I think several panties just melted."

"*Birdy*. Shh." Callie wouldn't admit aloud she was one of those panty-melting people. But then she glanced down Hunter's body, starting at his broad shoulders, sliding over his chest and abs, then down his legs, and to hell with it… "You're totally right, though."

But wait a minute. He wasn't wearing the suit she'd designed for him.

She blinked to refocus and make sure she was seeing him clearly. Nope. Not her suit. Had something happened to it? Or worse, was he still upset with her so he'd decided not to give her the publicity she hoped for? Her gaze slid sideways to Ava, who looked beautiful in her MOH dress and then to Andrew who…was wearing Hunter's suit.

She knew it as sure as she knew her own name. Why wasn't Hunter wearing it?

The threesome walked by and took their places on either side of Pastor Alvarez.

Jenna came down the aisle next, confident and cheerful and absolutely adorable in her dress. She dropped rose petals down the aisle with flourish, her attention touching on guests until she reached the front row where she sat down next to her grandma and grandpa.

Maverick's dog Barley took center stage after

that, drawing oohs and ahhs from everyone. A white satin pillow tied to her back designated her the official ring bearer. She reached Maverick and waited for him to untie the gold bands before sitting beside the groomsmen.

As the music transitioned to the traditional wedding march, guests stood to watch Kennedy glide down the aisle on her father's arm. Callie had never seen a more gorgeous bride. Love and joy radiated from her. She took her spot beside a beaming Maverick.

The simple ceremony had people laughing and crying. When Pastor Alvarez declared them husband and wife, Maverick gave her one hell of a kiss. They strode down the aisle hand-in-hand, the wedding party filing in behind them.

Callie only had eyes for Hunter's suit, double-checking to make sure she hadn't been mistaken. "Hunter isn't wearing the suit I made him," she said to Birdy.

"That's interesting."

Very, but she didn't have time to find out why now.

Birdy wrapped her arm around Callie's as they walked to the other side of the ginormous tent where appetizers and cocktails were being served. They mingled with other guests, many of whom chatted about Callie's business and wanted to know all about how she made her dresses and would she be making more suits like Hunter's. She appreciated their interest. She shared she hadn't decided on men's suits yet and then excused herself when she noticed Vivian step outside.

Christmas Eve all by itself was magical, but stepping outside the tent to find stars twinkling in the sky and then decorative stars hanging from the trees, the smell of a fire blazing inside the inn a few hundred feet away, and lighted displays of reindeer, lampposts, and cone trees, made Callie believe wishes could come true. She was sure if she stood there long enough, she'd hear Santa ho-ho-ho-ing in the distance, delivering on wishes to kids across the globe.

She had a wish to make come true tonight.

"Hi, Vivian. You look lovely tonight."

"Hi, Callie. Thank you. You do, too."

They awkwardly stared at each other before both speaking at the same time. "You first," Callie said.

"The maid of honor dress was gorgeous. And the best man suit…"

"Was worn by Andrew," she finished.

"How did you…of course, you knew. You could probably tell the second they walked down the aisle. Hunter tried to find a suit as similar to your design as possible."

Callie's brows knit in confusion. "How, why—"

"I've said too much already. I'm sure Hunter will explain." She waved away the statement like it wasn't a big deal. "What did you want to tell me?"

"Just that I'd noticed Hunter wasn't wearing the suit but I hope you'll stick around a little longer."

Vivian narrowed her eyes. "For reasons that have to do with my article?"

"Yes."

"Shall I wait for your signal that it's okay for me to leave, then?"

"I'm confident you'll know when." She smiled in goodbye and strode back into the tent. In her periphery, she'd noticed the bridal party had finished with photos and was trickling back into the tent. She made a quick stop to remind the bandleader of the plan before taking residence along the perimeter of the tent so as not to be noticed.

The only glitch to her plan was only she knew about it and she hoped Kennedy and Maverick wouldn't be upset with her.

She thrummed her fingers on her leg. The wait was killing her.

The bride and groom took to the dance floor for their first dance. "All of Me" by John Legend. The bridal party joined afterward, Hunter twirling Jenna while Andrew danced with Ava. Andrew did look exceptionally handsome in her designer suit. She hoped it made him lucky in love.

Before she could ponder why Hunter hadn't worn it, she stepped closer to the dance floor. The band had transitioned to a pop song and invited everyone to dance. Callie nodded to the band leader, who nodded back. The next song was hers.

She'd kept an eye on Hunter and noticed him looking around. Finally spotting someone or something, he made a beeline and ended up in front of Birdy. Birdy shook her head. Uh-oh. Hunt spun around, searched again, and this time his eyes found hers.

"Ladies and gentlemen, if you could please clear the dancefloor, we have something special for you," the bandleader said.

Hunter wasted no time marching toward her. He

reached her just before the bandleader said, "Hunter, this one's for you."

He turned toward the band with adorable confusion. "Be right back, cowboy," she whispered to him.

You've got this, Callie Carmichael. She accepted a microphone from the bandleader. "Good evening, everyone," she said, testing the mic and tapping it with her hand.

"We can hear you!" Nova called out, clearly excited about whatever Callie was about to do.

"First off, congratulations, Kennedy and Maverick!"

The guests cheered and offered more congrats.

"Secondly, I'm sorry I didn't clear this with you in advance, but I wanted the first person to know about it to be standing right there." She pointed to Hunter. Then heart hammering, she gave a nod to the bandleader, and the band started to play "Marry You" by Bruno Mars.

With help from the band—thank God, because she couldn't carry a tune at all—Callie sang the song to Hunter.

She never once took her eyes off him.

He never once took his eyes off her.

She slowly walked toward him, taking baby steps.

He stayed rooted to his spot until someone gave him a little push that knocked him off-balance. He took baby steps toward her.

Everyone in the ballroom disappeared. It was just the two of them. It wasn't the most original idea. It might even be cliché. But Callie couldn't think of a better song to tell Hunter she loved him.

She loved him so much.

As the song came to a close, whistles, cheers,

sighs, and applause surrounded them. Callie was pretty sure there wasn't a person who remained in their seat.

When the song ended, Hunter picked her up and swung her around. "That was awesome," he said, placing her back on the floor. She'd never seen him smile wider.

"So, what do you say?" Callie said into the microphone. "Hunter Owens, will you marry me?" She didn't get down on one knee. She thought he might like to do that sometime.

He took the microphone from her. "Callie Carmichael, you bet your sweet ass I'll marry you, but how about we slow down a little and date for a while first?"

How had she ever doubted him the perfect man for her? He inherently knew going slow would make her happy. "You've got yourself a deal."

They stuck around for congratulations before stumbling outside, high on happiness—and craving some quiet, alone time.

"Penny for your thoughts." Hunter's soft, sexy voice in her ear sent quivers up and down her arms. His arms were wrapped around her from behind, keeping her safe. Protected.

That dizzy feeling that filled her head and belly and had been absent for the past two weeks they'd been apart came flooding back. "I was thinking about how magical it is this time of year," she said softly.

"I believed in Santa until I was nine. Maverick and Cole kept him alive for me even when kids at school told me he wasn't real."

"Were you devastated when you found out the truth?"

"Of course. Weren't you?"

She nodded and shivered, the cold penetrating their embrace. He quickly took off his suit coat and wrapped it around her shoulders, and she *knew*. She knew without a doubt he'd keep her heart safe and warm and forever be there when she needed him. Without complaint. Without a second thought. The little things would never go unnoticed.

They stayed like that for a few quiet moments, enjoying the stars and Christmas lights. The sounds of joy behind them in the tent. The comfort of home glowing in the windows of the inn in front of them. He clasped their fingers and led her inside, to the library where a blazing fire warmed the room and books lined every shelf.

Hunter sat them down on the couch, never letting go of her hand. "You are the most gorgeous thing I've ever laid eyes on, and that performance was one I will never ever forget. Thank you." His gaze raked over her, slowly, appreciatively. Her body quivered yet again.

"Thank you for saying yes."

"Was there ever any doubt?"

"A little."

"Callie, Callie, Callie. There is no one for me but you."

She loved the sound of that. "Is that why you aren't wearing the suit I made?"

"Yes. I asked Kennedy if I could wear something else, and she was fine with it. As luck would have it, Andrew and I are close enough in size that we just switched. I let Vivian know so she could follow up with Andrew now."

"But no one else knows," she said. "I noticed, of course, but to everyone else, you were in my suit."

The corners of his mouth lifted. "True. But I think after the show you just gave, that story is going to take a backseat." He turned his body so he faced her fully. "We both wanted to show each other how much we meant to one another. I didn't wear the suit because I've already found the love of my life." He made a fist with his free hand and placed it over his heart. "She's been right here for a very long time, but it wasn't until we became adults that we connected on the level I've been wishing for. And I don't mean just in bed. I want to be with her all the time, hear everything she has to say, and learn all her secrets and hopes and plans for the future."

Callie's own heart doubled in size, reaching for his.

"I love you, Triple C, more than you'll ever know. I shouldn't have let you walk out of my car that night. I should have stayed and fought. With you. For you. I won't make the same mistake again. And I meant what I said about us going slow. We can be engaged forever if you want. I don't know how to not love you. You're the person I want to keep. You've always been that person."

Were her feet touching the ground? She didn't think so. "I love you, too. And I'm ready. To never let go and to trust you won't let me down. I'm ready to give you my heart and be open to love and any mistakes and messy situations we find ourselves in. I promise to never give up on you. On us. I know there are no guarantees in life, but you're the person I want to keep, too, and I'm so sorry for pushing you away."

"I'm a guarantee, Cal." He touched his forehead to hers, looked deep into her eyes. "I love you so much."

"I love you more."

He kissed her. The kind of kiss she'd never ever forget. Full of admiration. Passion. Affection. Desire and love. She kissed him back, wrapped her arms around his neck, melted against him. Open-mouthed kisses. Close-mouthed kisses. Every swipe of his tongue and press of his lips sealed the commitment they made to each other.

"I think I might be addicted to you," she teased when he pulled back.

"Thank God, because I'm definitely addicted to you." He leaned forward, put his mouth to her ear. "I want to lift your dress and lick between your legs so bad right now." The husky, erotic whisper had her pulling in a sharp breath.

"But." He scooted back. "My brother is only getting married once, and I don't want to miss out on the fun and celebration, so what do you say we save that for later and go party with our family and friends?"

He said "our." Not "my." She wanted to kiss him until tomorrow. Thank him for making her feel like she truly belonged. She also understood how much he needed to be back inside the tent.

She jumped to her feet. "Let's go."

They joined the reception. They ate, drank, and danced. Word spread about the suit switch, and when Hunter spun her to the middle of the dance floor, dipped her, and then kissed her senseless in front of everyone, she didn't fight it. Or doubt it.

She'd already asked him to marry her in front of everyone.

"Every kiss has led to this," he told her on the upswing.

And they were just getting started.

EPILOGUE

WINDSONG GAZETTE
February 14th

Happy Valentine's Day, Windsongers! And what a happy day it is. Our Marry Matchmaker has struck matrimonial gold once again. Dr. Kennedy Owens' best friend, Andrew Walker, is engaged! As you might remember, Andrew and Hunter Owens switched best man suits at Kennedy's wedding in December. Two days later, on his drive back to Los Angeles, Andrew pulled over with a flat tire and who should stop to help? Mr. Aiden Cane. Yes, that Aiden Cane. Star of the wildly popular HGTV show This Is How We Build It. *According to Andrew, it was love at first sight, and last weekend Aiden proposed! Congratulations to the happy couple!*

In other romantic news, Hunter Owens got down on one knee yesterday to do his own proposing, asking his fiancée to marry him! Callie Carmichael's "Marry Me" proposal took everyone by surprise—especially Hunter—and he had something special up his sleeve to return the favor. Something sparkly and worn on the ring finger of the left hand accompanied this proposal, and word through the grapevine is the two are holed up in some sort of love nest near Big Sur. This means that Birdy Friedel wins the coveted prize for picking Friday the 13th for Hunter to pop the question. To any naysayers out there, we're putting this one in the win column now that Hunter has put a ring on it.

Valentine's Day wouldn't be complete without mention of local business, Callie Designs' lucrative mentorship with Vera Wang. It seems Ms. Wang believes in magic and our very own dressmaker Callie Carmichael's talent to go along with it. I see a Vera wedding gown in Callie's future. And a charmed maid of honor dress for Nova Owens.

Finally, the rumor mill is abuzz with horseback-riding lessons taking place at The Owens Inn and Guest Ranch. It's been reported that a red-haired woman has been seen joining in on Hunter Owens' private lessons and sharing the history of the ranch, including talk of buried treasure. "Who doesn't love a treasure hunt?" Ambassador Owens asked, and an influx of visitors to our small town are here to prove they do.

Until next time,
Vivian Fisher

ACKNOWLEDGMENTS

Thank you to my wonderful editor Stacy Abrams. As always, your patience, wisdom, and guidance are appreciated more than I can say.

Thank you to the Entangled team for everything you do. I'm so grateful to be part of the EP family.

To the best writer friends a girl could ask for: Samanthe Beck, Maggie Kelly, Roxanne Snopek, Paula Altenburg, Marilyn Brant, Julie Gardner, Jennifer Shirk, Charlene Sands, and Hayson Manning, hugs and huge thanks for your support, friendship, and always being there for me over the years.

Readers are so incredibly special, and I'm beyond grateful to everyone who has read one of my books. Thank you so much for your support, time, and kind words. Extra special hugs and thanks to Elena, Nicola, Rachel, and Shari for being with me from the very beginning. Love you!

And to my family, I love you so much! Thank you for everything.

A shy woman. Her outdoorsy crush. And the bet that could bring them together…or implode spectacularly.

first
Bride
to fall

NEW YORK TIMES BESTSELLING AUTHOR
GINNY BAIRD

Nell Delaney will do almost anything for her parents and her two sisters. But enter a marriage of convenience to save the family's coffee shop? Too far. So Nell and her sisters strike a deal: whoever hasn't found love in thirty days has to step up to take one for the team. The good news? Nell knows the perfect guy to fall in love with. The bad news? She's going to have to pretend she likes the outdoors…a lot.

Adventure guide Grant Williams knows immediately that Nell is not exactly Little Miss Outdoorsy. She's a walking natural disaster—an amazingly adorable disaster. And whoa, their chemistry is unbelievable. Everything between them is so perfect, he's not even a little bit shocked when he starts thinking of forever…

Right up until he catches the town gossiping about the Delaney sisters' bargain and realizes she's just using him to win a bet. Unfortunately, his family's unreliable reputation means he can't just dump one of the town's sweethearts. No, she needs to dump him. If she's going to pretend to be the perfect doting bride, well, he'll just pretend to be the worst bachelor on the market.

Let the games begin…

The chance of a lifetime requires a leap of faith...and only one dollar in this new contemporary romance.

it takes a
VILLA

USA TODAY BESTSELLING AUTHOR
KILBY BLADES

For the reasonable price of $1, Natalie Malone just bought herself an abandoned villa on the Amalfi Coast. With a detailed spreadsheet and an ancient key, she's arrived in Italy ready to renovate—and only six months to do it. Which seemed reasonable until architect Pietro Indelicato began critically watching her every move...

From the sweeping ocean views to the scent of the lemon trees, there's nothing Pietro loves more than his hometown. And after seeing too many botched jobs and garish design choices, he's done watching from the sidelines. As far as he's concerned, Natalie should quit before the project drains her entire bank account and her ridiculously sunny optimism.

With Natalie determined to move forward, the gorgeous architect reluctantly agrees to pitch in, giving her a real chance to succeed. But when the fine print on Natalie's contract is brought to light, she might have no choice but to leave her dream, and Pietro, behind.

AMARA
an imprint of Entangled Publishing LLC